MY SOLDIER TOO

BLUE FEATHER BOOKS, LTD.

For K.C. It's because of you that I know true love. And for all of the gay and lesbian members of the military who serve our country so valiantly.

MY SOLDIER TOO

A BLUE FEATHER BOOK

BY

BEV PRESCOTT

This is a work of fiction. All characters, locales and events are either products of the author's imagination or are used fictitiously.

MY SOLDIER TOO

Cover design by Ann Phillips

A Blue Feather Book
Published by Blue Feather Books, Ltd.

www.bluefeatherbooks.com

ISBN: 978-1-935627-81-4

First edition: May, 2011

Printed in the United States of America and in the United Kingdom.

Acknowledgements

On rare moments, a particular individual crosses our path and we know instantly that person will be a friend forever. My buddy, Lee, you are certainly one of those special people. Thank you for sharing this journey with me. I'll always treasure your friendship.

I owe big thanks to Liane, Linda, and Tracy for being patient readers of the very rough first draft of *My Soldier Too*. Your encouragement and friendship helped propel me forward. Thanks also to Martha and Amy for your advice on all things Army.

To Jane Vollbrecht, my editor, you are one awesome lady. Thank you so much for teaching me that creating a book is like building a house. One has to have more than a good foundation because the fine details of the trim work are what readers will notice first. You are the best, and I'll forever be grateful to you for having faith in me. I'm privileged to have you as my editor as well as a friend.

To Emily Reed, thank you for giving me the opportunity to join the Blue Feather Books family. I hope this book is just the beginning of a long, productive partnership of creating stories we can be proud of. Thanks for seeing the potential in me.

Finally, to my beloved, K.C., thank you for always loving and supporting me in all of my endeavors. You are truly my best friend, and my heart will always belong to you.

Chapter 1

Isabella Parisi hesitated outside the William J. Pepine Veterans' Shelter. It wasn't out of the ordinary to see a ragged man slumped on the bench by the entryway of the stark concrete building. But something about this guy was different. He lifted his shaggy gray head. She looked into his eyes and saw nothing there but blackness. The tiny hairs on the back of her neck prickled. Her instinct was to run, but Isabella had a job to do and wouldn't let this despondent stranger intimidate her.

She took a step toward him. "I don't think we've ever met. Why don't you come inside where you can get warm? It's awfully cold to be sitting out here."

"My heart burns in the fires of war." His expression was blank and his tone flat. "The cold can't touch me." He inhaled deeply and let out a breath that appeared more like smoke in the frigid February air.

Isabella shuddered. She hoped he hadn't noticed. His stare was so frightening that she glanced away, fixing her eyes instead on the plain block letters above the entryway of the Boston shelter. She looked at him again. "All right then. But if you're still here after my appointment this morning, maybe we could talk for a while."

He sighed, turned his eyes back toward the ground, and didn't say another word.

Isabella gathered her courage and calmly finished making her way up the steps past him, a little faster than she normally would have. When she reached for the glass door, it was opened wide from inside by Ben Jackson, an attorney from the law firm of Galliano, Lawton, and Simpson. Ben and the other lawyers in his firm were required to do a certain amount of pro bono work each month. Isabella suspected he did his at the shelter, not because of any particular interest he had in helping its residents, but because it was an opportunity to win favor with her.

"Good morning, sweetheart. You surprised to see me? Didn't you get my text?" Ben asked.

The handsome, well-groomed young lawyer was the last person she'd expected to see at the shelter. After her interaction with the man outside, she was relieved to see his friendly face.

"No, I haven't had a chance to check messages yet. It's been a crazy morning. Did one of the guys get into trouble again?" Isabella stepped across the threshold.

"No, none of your fellows did anything to require my assistance this time. Court got cancelled this morning. Since I was nearby, I thought maybe we could go for a quick cup of coffee." Ben gestured toward the door he was still holding open. When she didn't answer, he followed with, "Come on, what do you say? What could be more important than us starting our day together?"

"I can't, Ben. David Cutter has a doctor's appointment this morning."

"I'll go with you. I need to talk with him anyway about his being a witness at Carl Woods's upcoming sentencing hearing."

She tried to hide the frustration in her voice. "This isn't a good time. I've got lots of other commitments today already."

"I thought getting Carl into a drug treatment program instead of jail is what you wanted."

"Of course it is, but—" Before Isabella could finish her statement, the hulking man who'd been on the bench outside lunged through the still open door. He grabbed her from behind into a tight bear hug and lifted her off of her feet like a rag doll.

A rush of fear shot through her. She hadn't noticed the man's size until she was helpless in his grip. Now, she was acutely aware of his powerful arms that threatened to squeeze the life out of her.

He put his lips next to her ear and whispered, "They broke me, and now I'm going to break you, my little bluebird."

His unkempt, filthy beard brushed the back of her neck. Ignoring his foul breath, she fought the impulse to panic. She needed to stay calm and rely on her training to resolve the situation. She concentrated on keeping her breathing even. "I know you're upset, but all I want to do is help you. If you let go of me, we can talk."

Ben squared his shoulders and glared at the man. He bristled with anger. Before she could tell him to stay out of the situation, he gritted his teeth and ordered, "Put her down. Now."

The command fanned the man's rage. He took a step away from Ben, dragging Isabella with him, and roared, "You bastard, do

you know what I do with my little birds? I crush them, and then..."
He slowly licked Isabella's cheek. "I eat them."

Isabella was terrified. What awful demons clawed at the fringes
of his mind? What were those demons capable of? To get away, she
needed to nudge him toward a moment of clarity. She had to get
him talking.

Ben's jaw clenched and his body tightened. Just before he
lunged for the man, Isabella spoke forcefully. "Back off, Ben, and
give us some space. I can handle this."

The man jeered in Ben's direction. "See? My little prize
doesn't need her white knight in shining armor."

Ben pointed a finger at him. "If you so much as harm a hair on
her head, I'll make sure you're locked up for the rest of your life."

"You think I give a damn?" The man laughed. "I'm already in
hell."

A large gathering of shelter residents had formed around them.
To Isabella's relief, one of the men grabbed Ben by the elbow and
said, "Leave it alone. The General is here. He and Isabella will take
care of this."

An old man with a pronounced limp in his left leg approached,
and the crowd parted like the Red Sea, as if Moses himself had
come down and beckoned them to break ranks.

The man wore a tattered green fatigue jacket and pants. Even
though his clothes were frayed and old, they were clean and his
shirttails were tucked neatly into his trousers. His pure white hair
was cut in military style. He carried himself with pride as he drew
nearer to Isabella and the man.

With a piercing stare and slow southern drawl, the old veteran,
formerly Sergeant David Cutter but now known as the General,
eyed the man and asked, "Son, what the hell do you think you're
doing manhandling Isabella? I suggest you put her down now, ever
so gently. If you don't, I will personally see to it that you never lay a
hand on another woman for the rest of your days."

The General waited for his words to register. "I am the
commanding officer here. That was a direct order." He took another
step toward Isabella's captor. "You listen to me. Back during the
war, I ate men meaner and bigger than you for breakfast. Not that I
wouldn't like to, but don't think for a second I have to deal with you
on my own." The General cocked his head toward the onlookers.
"You see those boys over there? All I have to do is give them the
word, and they'll be on you like a pack of wolves. You hear me,
boy?"

A long moment passed. The man loosened his hold on Isabella. "I wish it all would go away... I want to forget, but I can't."

The General's voice softened. "Son, I know what you're going through. But this isn't the way. You need to let Isabella go. She's not the enemy. Let her be, so she can help you. I promise she'll try as best she can. You won't find a better ally than her."

The man lowered Isabella and dropped his arms from around her. Her feet no more than touched the floor when four police officers rushed in and tackled him. Instead of putting up a fight, he curled into the fetal position and sobbed. The officers slapped handcuffs on his wrists.

Instantly, deep sadness replaced Isabella's fear. The sight of a devastated, homeless veteran being handcuffed and hauled away was all too familiar to her. He probably wasn't a bad man, but rather one trapped in memories of war too powerful to overcome. Isabella said, "I hope you'll consider taking him to a hospital instead of jail. He needs psychiatric care before he hurts himself or someone else."

The officer in charge said, "Of course, but first we have to take him to the station for booking. You know the routine. Once that's done, we'll take him over to Boston Central for a medical evaluation." He motioned for the other officers to escort the man from the building.

After the officers had left the shelter, Isabella spoke to the General. "Thank you." Not only had he possibly saved her life, he'd reminded her again how important her job was. Even though her work was a constant uphill battle, she was fortunate to know people like him and his men and to be in a position to try to help them.

The General took a black baseball cap out of his jacket pocket and put it on his head. The hat was embroidered with the words "Vietnam Veteran" in gold below a gold wreath surrounding a military ribbon that signified the war. He tipped his hat to Isabella. To the crowd of residents surrounding them he said, "All right, boys. The excitement's over. Give Isabella some room to breathe. Go on your way now."

Ben hurried to her as the men dispersed. "That son of a bitch. Are you all right? I was so afraid he was going to hurt you." He put his hands on her shoulders. "Your coming here alone is completely unacceptable. Quite frankly, I think it borders on negligence for Social Services to send you here by yourself."

Isabella moved away from him and crossed her arms. As much as she valued his friendship, his touch suddenly made her feel claustrophobic. "Ben, I'm fine. This is part of my job, and I'm really in no mood for a lecture."

"I don't want anything to happen to you. That's all. I really think you should be accompanied by a guard or another social worker when you come here." He lowered his voice. "I'd be lost without you."

"Why do you always have to make things be about you? I don't need a security guard, another social worker, or you when I come here. All I need is to be more careful and have the space to do my work. You certainly didn't give me that by interfering."

"I'm sorry. Of course this isn't about me. It's about making sure you stay safe. These people can be dangerous. What if he had injured you, or worse?" Ben caressed her arm. "Why don't you let me take you home? You deserve the morning off after being attacked by a madman."

Isabella tried to stifle her growing impatience. "I'm not going home. The General has an appointment at the Veterans Affairs clinic, and I intend to take him. I'd also like to point out that he's one of 'these people,' as you called them. Yet, he's the one who managed to talk that guy out of doing anything drastic."

"You're right. I shouldn't have said it that way. You can't blame me for being worried about you though."

Isabella tried to lighten the mood. "I appreciate your concern, really I do. But I've got work to do. Besides, it's not the end of the world to be squeezed and licked on the cheek by a guy who's down on his luck. Granted, it would've been nice if he'd asked first, but there was no harm done. Now, if you don't mind, I'd like to go wash up a little. You really should get back to work. I'll call you later, I promise." She kissed his cheek.

"I don't know why you always stick up for these guys. I hope you know what's best." Ben shook his head. "Someday, you're going to realize you can't save them all."

"I'm not that naïve, Ben. I wish you'd give me credit for knowing how to do my job."

"It's not that I don't think you can. It's that your work is dangerous no matter how good you are."

Isabella sighed. "You're blowing this way out of proportion."

"Am I?" Ben asked as he opened the door to leave. Beth Adams, in a rush, crashed into him on his way out.

"Hi, Ben. Excuse me." Beth tried to push past him. "I got here as soon as I could. We got a call that Isabella was in an altercation with a resident. Is she okay?"

"So that's what you call it over there at Social Services, an altercation? Isabella could've been killed. After all the time you've worked there, you should know better than to send a woman alone into harm's way. You're supposed to be looking out for her."

"Isabella is a professional. She's perfectly capable of making a determination herself whether a situation warrants having someone with her. I trust her judgment, and so should you."

"That's not the point." He brushed her aside and stormed out.

Beth stared at him as he stomped away. Under her breath she mumbled, "Pompous, patronizing ass."

"I heard that," Isabella said, hiding a smirk.

Beth went to her. "Sorry about that. I didn't see you standing there." She set her briefcase on the floor and hugged Isabella. "What happened? Are you all right?"

Isabella felt the eyes of the remaining men in the lobby on her. "I'm fine. Do you mind if we talk in the ladies' room? I'd like to wash up."

"No, not at all." Beth followed Isabella into the privacy of the restroom. "Do you know the guy who attacked you?" she asked, once they were behind the closed door.

Isabella turned on the faucet and put her hands under the water. "I don't think he's a resident here. I've never seen him before. He grabbed me when I turned my back to him to come inside. He came a lot closer to hurting me than I'd like to admit. He rattled me at first, but I'm okay." She wet a paper towel and washed her cheek. She dried her face and her hands with another paper towel. "I'll follow up with the police later. They said they'd take him to the hospital. Given his age, he's probably a Gulf War veteran suffering from post-traumatic stress disorder, the old PTSD. I should've listened to my instincts when I first saw him. Something about him didn't feel right."

"Desperate men do desperate things. Don't beat yourself up over it. You can't always predict what might happen. That comes with the territory. Be careful, and rely on your instincts and training. That's all you can do. If you'd like to take the rest of the day off, I can find someone to cover."

"I appreciate the offer, and I might have taken you up on it if the General didn't have a doctor's appointment this morning. He's the one who talked the guy into letting me go. He kept the situation from getting out of hand, so I don't want to break my commitment to him about going with him to the doctor. Besides, he hasn't been feeling well lately. I'm worried about him. You know he won't go unless I walk with him."

"That man will be walking wherever he goes until his last days. PTSD sure does have a funny way of manifesting itself sometimes," Beth said.

"Yeah, forty-three years after the ambush of his squad in Vietnam, and he still refuses to ever ride in any kind of vehicle. I wish I could find a way to convince him to let go of the ghosts of the soldiers who died that day."

"We can't know how awful that must have been for him to see his friends die. At least he has you to accommodate his phobias and look out for him. Any luck getting him to agree to being placed in the veterans' home yet?" Beth asked.

"No. He still refuses to leave the other guys. Too bad we can't figure out how to get them all off the street and into proper care. As for being lucky, I feel pretty lucky to have him as a friend." Isabella gathered her belongings. "Hey, shouldn't you be home packing for your trip this weekend with Marcy?"

"Yeah, but I needed to stop and pick up a few files to take with me. While I was at the office, I got a call that you were in trouble. So I came right over."

"Thanks for checking on me. You better get going, though. Marcy may be your devoted and forgiving partner, but I bet she wouldn't be too happy if you miss your flight. Or that you're taking work along."

"The good news is that, after twenty years together, she won't be surprised at all if I bring work with me or if we have to race through the airport to get to our gate. When you've been together as long as we have, you learn some things never change. By the way, what was Ben's problem? I know he must have been worried, but he seemed awfully cranky. Is everything all right between you two?"

Isabella took a hair clip out of her shoulder bag. "I was kind of tough on him. I might have taken my frustration over what happened with the homeless guy out on him. His persistence about our relationship is starting to wear on me." She fastened her thick auburn curls into a ponytail. "I don't know what's wrong. He's a great guy, and I really do care about him. But I want what you and Marcy have. I want my heart to skip a beat every time he looks at me. The way he acted this morning reminded me that, most of the time, he carries on as if he's the only person who matters. He definitely doesn't respect my work, either. None of the feelings I want to have for a boyfriend are there."

8

"Maybe you need to consider he might not be the one for you. Have you thought about dating other guys?"

"No, I haven't. Ben doesn't take no for an answer. I guess I've been content enough with how things are. But he's really starting to pressure me for more of a commitment, and I'm not feeling so content. I'm not sure what would be worse though, breaking up with him or having to tell my family about it."

"Isabella, you can't choose a husband based on what your family wants. You've got to decide that for yourself, even if it means breaking up with Ben. As the old cliché says, there are lots of other fish in the sea. You have to be responsible for your own happiness."

Isabella didn't want to spend another second talking about Ben. "I know. You're right. I guess I've been taking the path of least resistance lately where he's concerned. Listen, you really better get going. Besides, I need to get the General to his appointment. Thanks again for coming over to check on me. I'll figure things out with Ben, eventually. Have a safe trip. I'll see you when you get back. Say hi to Marcy for me."

"I will, honey. You take care." Beth picked up her briefcase and left the ladies' room.

Isabella finished tidying herself up and went in search of the General. She found him waiting for her in a chair propped against the wall in the lobby. "Are you ready to go to your appointment, David?"

Even though everyone else referred to him as the General, Isabella always addressed him by his given name.

He stood and, like a gentleman, bent his right elbow away from his body so she could take his arm as they walked. "Thank you for indulging me with a walk," he said.

"I'm happy to do it. Especially after you got me out of that jam this morning."

"I'll always look after your safety, my dear. It feels good to have earned my stroll with you this morning, though."

"I know you prefer to walk. It's the least I can do for a friend."

With his free hand, David reached over and squeezed Isabella's. "Friend, indeed."

As they had done once a month for the past several years, Isabella and the old man walked to the small VA clinic housed within Boston Central Hospital.

Chapter 2

Army Reserve Captain Madison Brown stepped out of the subway into the cold morning and turned left toward Boston Central Hospital. As a trauma nurse, she usually worked in the emergency room, but occasionally she worked in the VA clinic as part of her reserve duties. This was one such morning.

Dressed in a finely pressed Class A uniform with dress jacket, skirt, and wool overcoat, she wrapped her arms tightly around her body and shivered in the cold. What was she thinking when she chose to wear a skirt this morning?

Hurrying along, she took care not to slip on the icy sidewalks. The slushy snow from the day before had frozen solid in the morning's frigid temperature. Despite the cold, she didn't mind the walk. She enjoyed taking in the city's varied architecture, old buildings, and seemingly endless changes brought on by continual construction efforts, which would allegedly relieve traffic congestion. Unfortunately, no matter what changes were made, the snarl of vehicles always seemed the same: awful.

Once she'd begun living along the shore in the town of Ipswich, she vowed she'd never live in the city again, but nonetheless, she enjoyed working in Boston. The tour she'd served in Iraq made her especially appreciative of the sights and sounds of this historic American city. Iraq had opened her eyes to the beauty in the simple things that she'd previously taken for granted—things like the hustle and bustle of rush hour as the sun rises over the tall buildings. Or the wild, resourceful birds that made urban homes alongside the city's human inhabitants. Not to mention the genius of the Zakim Bridge over the Charles River.

Unfortunately this morning, thanks to the treacherous sidewalks, she had to peer down at her feet instead of at the wonders around her. When she did glance up to check her progress, she saw a young woman ahead of her, carefully helping an old man. They were walking the same direction as she was, toward the hospital.

The woman was of average height with a slight figure and alluring backside. She was wearing a charcoal-colored skirt that fell slightly above her knees, knee-high black boots, and a waist-length wool coat. They were making good progress, except that the woman was struggling to juggle her shoulder bag and to keep her companion from falling on the ice.

Sensing she could use some help, Madison quickened her pace. She was only an arm's length away when the young woman lost her footing on a slippery patch. To Madison's amazement, she managed not to take the old man down with her.

Madison hurried around in front of her and saw the most stunning woman she'd ever laid eyes on. She was adorably cute and alluringly sexy all at the same time. Her silky auburn curls were pulled back into a ponytail. Absolutely gorgeous, she had flawless olive skin and emerald green eyes that Madison found impossible to look away from. Something about the woman made her want to laugh out loud, not at her, but with her. She extended a hand. "Here, let me help you."

The woman put her hand out.

Madison grasped it and pulled her up so quickly that they both lost their balance and started to slip. Madison grabbed her, steadied herself, and kept them from falling. She was instantly even more attracted to the woman she held in her arms. A flutter of something she hadn't felt in a long time passed through her. She wasn't sure she wanted to feel it now and pushed it away as quickly as it had come. The woman stared at her speechless, as if the wind had been knocked out of her. "Are you all right?" Madison asked.

"Yes, I'm okay, thanks to you." She brushed a strand of hair out of her eyes. "I must have been quite the sight splattered all over the sidewalk."

"You could say that. It might not have been the most graceful fall I've ever seen. But on a scale of one to ten, I'd still give you a nine for style."

"That's something to be proud of, I suppose."

The woman laughed, and her grip on Madison's forearm tightened. Her infectious mirth caused Madison to laugh easily with her.

The old man spoke. "If you two are done giggling like a couple of schoolgirls, I'd like to get moving before I freeze to death, right here in my tracks." He winked at them. "If I didn't know any better, I'd guess you were a couple of long-lost friends seeing each other for the first time in ages."

The woman's gaze lingered on Madison's face. "I'm sorry. I don't usually hang onto strangers as if my life depended on it."

"It's okay. I don't either." Madison let go of her and extended her hand. "I'm Madison Brown."

The woman clasped Madison's outstretched hand. "I'm Isabella Parisi. It's really nice to meet you, and thanks for stopping to help us." She gestured toward the General and said, "This is my friend, David. We're on our way to the VA clinic at Boston Central."

"It's nice to meet you both. I'm on my way to the clinic, too. I'd be happy to walk the rest of the way with you, if you'd like."

The General tipped his hat to Madison. "This is one fine morning. We'd be happy to have your assistance, Captain. It's some good luck for an old man to be flanked by two beautiful women on a walk through the city."

Madison put one hand on the General's shoulder while shaking his hand with the other. "I'm happy to help. It's nice to meet you, sir." She turned her attention to Isabella. "Here, let me carry your bag."

"Thank you. We really do appreciate the help." Isabella took the General's arm as they resumed their journey. "I've never seen you at the clinic. Do you work there?"

"Not usually. I normally work in the emergency room of the hospital, but the Army assigned me to work at the clinic for about a month as part of my reserve duties. How about you? What line of work are you in?" Madison asked.

"I'm a social worker. I mostly work with veterans."

The General chimed in. "Isabella takes me to my appointments. We go the third Wednesday of every month. She's the best social worker in the city and an even better friend. I don't know how I'd manage the guys at the shelter without her."

"You mean the Pepine?" Madison asked.

"Yes. I stay there to watch over my brothers. Isabella would prefer it if I lived in the veterans' home instead. But I'm sure you can understand that the call of duty to our brothers and sisters in arms can be stronger than a man's need for his own comfort. I see from the service medal on your chest that you've been to Iraq."

"I have, and I do understand, all too well." The sense of connection to the old man because of their shared war experiences didn't surprise Madison. What did surprise her was the connection she felt to Isabella.

"No veteran," Isabella said, "should ever live on the streets. I only wish we spent half as much money caring for them when they come home as we do on the wars we send them to. Then maybe my friend here would let me help him find a warm, safe place to live."

"That would be awfully nice," David said. "But until that happens, I'll keep doing my part to take care of those boys. I'd be bored out of my skull otherwise. You're no different, my dear Isabella. You work just as hard as I do to look out for them."

David addressed Madison. "She's a special lady. Karma blessed you today because you got to cross paths with her."

"I guess I was lucky enough to be in the right place at the right time this morning," Madison said.

When they reached the clinic, Madison shook hands with David. "It was a pleasure to walk with you. Take care of yourself." She handed Isabella her bag and extended a hand. "I'm glad to have met you, too."

Isabella took Madison's hand. "Me, too, and I really do appreciate your help. Could I buy you a coffee sometime to say thank you?"

"I'd like that. Please stop by the clinic anytime. Like I said, I'll be here for the next month or so." Madison motioned over her shoulder to the entry of the building. "I better get going or I'll be late for my morning appointments. I'll see you around."

Chapter 3

The clock on the wall read almost eleven. Madison glanced at the day's list of patients on the clipboard that she carried. David Cutter was on the schedule for early afternoon. A month had gone by since she met him and Isabella out on the street. She hated to admit it, but she hadn't been able to stop thinking about her. He'd said that Isabella always accompanied him to his appointments. The prospect of seeing her again made butterflies dance in her stomach.

Only one person sat in the waiting room. Madison watched the lanky man fidget on the stiff aluminum chair. His face was lined with the wrinkles of time. The name Ernie Gilmore was the next one on the schedule. She assumed the fellow in the waiting room was Ernie. When he shifted his body, dried corn kernels dropped from the hole in the left pocket of his worn jacket. He leaned down and, with shaky hands, picked them up one by one. Madison guessed that the city's pigeons wouldn't go hungry if Ernie Gilmore had anything to say about it.

She called out to him. "Mr. Gilmore?"

Ernie looked up from his task. "I don't like this place. It's full of sick people and needles."

Madison walked to him and put a hand on his shoulder. "I know, sir. But I promise, no needles for you today."

"I been called all kinds of things on the street, but no one ain't never called me 'sir' before." Ernie stood. When he did, several kernels fell again from the pesky hole in his pocket to the floor. "Especially by an officer like yourself."

Madison bent over and picked up the kernels for the old man. She put them into the pocket of the dark green Army sweater she wore over her scrubs. "Maybe they should. You served your country. You deserve that much, even from an officer like me. Your service was as valuable as mine."

Ernie beamed. "Thank you, ma'am."

"You're welcome. Feel free to call me Madison if you'd like. Please, come with me."

He followed her into the examination room. She pulled open a stainless steel drawer and removed a roll of white medical tape. She cut off a piece big enough to cover the hole in Ernie's pocket and gently smoothed the tape over it. "I see that you carry food for the birds. I live in Ipswich. I know the birds out there pretty well, but I'm not sure about the ones in the city." She handed him the kernels from her own pocket and asked, "What kinds of birds do you feed around here?"

He seemed to relax with the conversation. "Pigeons, mostly, but sometimes starlings. What kinds of birds do you got where you live?"

Madison reached for the blood pressure monitor. "In winter, mostly cardinals and chickadees. Would you mind taking off your jacket so I can take your blood pressure?"

Ernie eyed the monitor with suspicion as he reluctantly removed his coat. Unease crept into his expression when Madison wrapped the cuff around the upper part of his right arm. She kept him talking in hopes of making him feel less nervous. "Where do you feed the pigeons?" she asked.

"On the sidewalk out in front of the veterans' shelter where I stay sometimes." His focus turned to the cuff. "Is that thing going to hurt?"

"No, it won't hurt." She squeezed the bulb attached to the monitor several times. "I met a man named David Cutter who stays at the shelter, too. Do you know him?"

"Oh yeah." Ernie perked up. "Everybody knows him. We call him the General, though. He might be the oldest guy in the city, but for sure, he's damn near the toughest. A few weeks back, he scared some angry bastard half out of his mind for grabbing our girl Isabella."

"Isabella Parisi?" Madison asked.

"That's her."

Concern for Isabella tugged at Madison. "Did she get hurt?"

"No, but we thought he'd squeeze the life out of the poor girl until the General stepped in." Ernie shook his head. "*Nobody* messes with him. We would have had his back if he gave us the word, though. Besides, we love Isabella, too. We'd never let anything bad happen to her."

Isabella must make everyone who knows her crazy about her. Madison felt justified in her preoccupation with Isabella. "She's lucky to have you guys." Madison removed the cuff from his arm. "Okay, Ernie, your blood pressure's fine. I'll let the doctor know you're ready to see him. Don't be nervous. He's only going to ask you a few questions and give you a quick exam." She patted his arm. "You'll be all right. You take care of yourself and the pigeons."

A familiar voice called her name as she headed back down the hallway toward the patient waiting area. She turned to see the source. "Hey, Dr. Barns, great to see you. I'm so glad you're home safe and sound. Have you been assigned a rotation here?"

"It's Jim, remember? Yes, I'm here for the next month or so. You, too?"

"The same. When did you get back from Iraq?"

"A few weeks ago. I sure did miss having you there those last days of my tour."

"I can't say that I missed being there, but I'm glad to see you now. It'll be nice to work together under less harsh circumstances."

"Funny you should say that. I just got a call from the veterans' shelter. Apparently there's been a skirmish, and they've managed to draw blood. The two guys involved refuse to go to a hospital. Plus, the social worker who got caught up in the middle is being just as stubborn."

"Did you catch the social worker's name?"

"Isabella Parisi. Do you know her?"

"Yes, I do. We should send someone over to check on them."

"That's what I thought. The schedule's light today. Dr. Evans suggested I go over there now. You interested in coming along to give me a hand?"

"Absolutely." The word left her lips before her brain had a chance to form a less urgent-sounding response. "I'll grab my coat and a medical bag."

Jim pulled on his suit jacket, "Okay. Meet me out front. We'll take the clinic van. On your way out, stop and let Dr. Evans know we're both going." He went out the door.

* * *

The shelter was only five blocks away, but to Madison, the drive seemed like miles. When they arrived, she followed Jim up the steps through the entrance. Her stomach was in knots—both with worry over Isabella's welfare and in anticipation of seeing her again.

A balding, middle-aged security guard came out of the dormitory and ambled toward them. He pulled his wrinkled uniform trousers up over his belly. The unpolished name tag over his left breast pocket read "Billy Dean." Madison suspected his wide girth suggested a fondness for sitting in front of the television while drinking beer and eating potato chips.

"Hey, Doc, thanks for coming over. Buxton and Louis got into a fistfight over a card game. They shoved each other around pretty good. Louis got the better of Buxton this time," Billy said with a sneer. "Buxton's busted lip bled all over the place, and I had to get the mop out to clean up the damn floor. They're lucky I didn't knock some heads together to get them to behave themselves."

"We got a report that one of the social workers may have been involved. Is that true?" Jim asked.

Billy looped his thumbs over his black leather belt. Rocking back on his heels, he pushed his chest out like a peacock staking its claim on a patch of grass. "It was that damn headstrong Isabella Parisi. She tried to break up the fight while fists were flying. I told her to stay the hell out of it and that I'd take care of the situation. But she's as stubborn as a mule. One of these days, she'll get herself seriously hurt for all her cockiness around these guys." He shook his head. "It serves her right."

What a jackass. "Where is she?" Madison asked.

Billy gave her a patronizing stare. He nodded toward a small conference room off to the left of the dormitory. "She's in there."

Jim spoke to Madison. "Why don't you go check on Isabella? I'll see to Buxton and Louis."

Madison was on her way to the conference room as she replied. "Sure."

She opened the door. Isabella was sitting at a small table resting her head on the palm of her right hand. With the other hand, she held an ice pack over her left eye.

Without moving, Isabella said, "I'm fine. Just give me some time alone."

Madison stepped into the room. "I'm sorry for interrupting. I came to make sure you're okay. Do you mind?"

Isabella put the ice pack down and raised her head. "It appears you've come to my rescue again, Capt. Brown." Her expression softened. "I hoped I'd see you again, but this was hardly the way I pictured it."

Madison sat down in the chair next to her. She reached out and brushed a strand of hair away from Isabella's face. When she did, she saw that one of those "flying fists" the guard had referred to had made contact with Isabella. There was considerable swelling and a small cut above her left eye. "Is it all right if I examine your injury?"

"Thank you. I'd appreciate it."

Madison gently tilted Isabella's head back and examined the bone around the eye for any sign that it might be broken. "Why are you smiling?"

"I was just thinking that you're very good at making a person feel cared for. I hardly know you, but you make me feel safe."

"I'm a nurse. That's my job," Madison responded. *And you're quite the flirt.*

"So, what's your diagnosis?" Isabella asked.

"Do you want the good news or the bad news first?"

"That's not really the kind of question one wants to be asked by a medical professional, but I guess I'll take the bad first."

Madison retrieved the ice pack from the table and handed it to Isabella. "You're going to have one hell of a black eye tomorrow. The good news is that I don't think anything is broken, and you won't need stitches." Madison reached into her medical bag. She took out an antiseptic wipe and a small butterfly bandage. Holding Isabella's chin, she gently wiped the cut with the antiseptic.

Isabella flinched.

"I'm sorry. I guess I should've warned you it might sting." Madison started to open the bandage.

Isabella laid a hand on her wrist. "It's okay. Thank you for taking care of me."

Madison looked away. Flirt or not, Isabella's touch went deeper than the surface of her skin.

Isabella removed her hand. "I didn't mean to make you uncomfortable."

Madison resumed opening the bandage. "It's all right. You didn't." She placed the Band-Aid over the small cut. "What happened, anyway?" The air in the room felt heavy.

Isabella placed the ice pack back over her eye. "I thought I could get them to stop fighting before they got kicked out of the shelter. They don't have anyplace else to go, and it's too cold for them to sleep out on the streets. I should've known better than to get in between them. Blissfully naïve, that's what my father says about me. Sometimes I wonder if he's right. Maybe my efforts are wasted on some of these guys."

Almost in a whisper Madison said, "I think you're beautiful." She couldn't believe she had let her words tumble out unrestrained. "I mean… I think you're a beautiful person to do the work that you do. I've seen what war does to soldiers. You might not be able to fix everything that's broken, but believe me, having someone like you to care about them matters."

"Thank you. That means a lot coming from a veteran who understands war." Isabella glanced at her watch and pushed her chair back from the table. "I should be going. The General—the fellow you met that morning after I flubbed my double-Lutz on the ice—has an appointment this afternoon. I'm really glad I got to see you again."

"Wait." Madison put a hand on the back of Isabella's chair to keep her from scooting it out farther. "You really should take it easy today. Dr. Barns is here checking on Louis and Buxton. We can save you a trip by giving the General his checkup here."

"You've already gone to enough trouble. You really don't have to do that for me."

"I want to."

"Not only do you make me feel safe, but it's hard to say no to you."

"Good, because I have another suggestion. I hope you won't think I'm being pushy, but why don't you come with me to my gym sometime? I'd like to teach you how to protect yourself. I box, and I know some really effective self-defense techniques. I'd hate for you to get hurt again." Madison took a business card out of her shoulder bag and wrote the name and address of Bixby's Gym on the back. She included her cell phone number as well. "Boxing is great exercise and good for blowing off steam. Plus, I guarantee that hitting something hard without the worry of hurting yourself is very cathartic."

Isabella looked her up and down. "Boxing? Really?"

"Why does that surprise you?"

"You're so pretty and feminine. I wouldn't have guessed you'd be the type."

"Isabella, you can't be serious. This from a very beautiful woman who's holding an ice pack over a black eye she got scuffling with a couple of large, angry men. Trust me. Pretty girls can be tough girls, too." Madison handed the card to her. "Meet me there on Saturday morning at ten."

"Okay, I'll be there. But remember, I'm smaller than you. I don't want to go home with a second black eye to match the one I've already got."

Madison lightly touched Isabella's arm. "Don't worry. I promise not to let anything bad happen."

"There's something about you that makes that entirely believable. I'd love to."

"Then I'll do my best not to disappoint you."

The comfortable quiet of the room was shattered by a man storming in. "My God, Isabella, what the hell happened this time?"

Madison moved out of his way as he knelt down beside Isabella, gave her a grim glare, and touched the left side of her face. "Sweetheart, we need to get you to a hospital to have that examined right away. Where are your bag and coat? I'm taking you there now."

"Ben," Isabella said, "in case you hadn't noticed, a very capable Army nurse is standing next to you. Capt. Brown already checked my eye and said everything's fine. What are you doing here, anyway?"

Ben stood. "After you were attacked last time at the shelter, I asked to be informed if anything happened again. The receptionist called to let me know you'd been hurt. I came right over." Ben extended his hand to Madison. "I'm Ben Jackson."

She shook it with a firm grip. "Hi, I'm Madison Brown. Other than a black eye by morning, I do think Isabella will be fine. But we can have our doctor, Maj. Barns, step in to have a look if that will make you feel better."

Madison glanced over and saw Jim standing in the doorway to the room.

Ben said, "I don't think we should rely on your diagnosis. I want Isabella to be seen by the major, or better yet, taken to a hospital for a complete examination."

Jim stepped into the room. "I'm Maj. Barns, and with all due respect, sir, I served in Iraq with Capt. Brown. I have as much confidence in her abilities as I have in most doctors." He stepped closer to Ben. "I stood next to her when she massaged the heart of a dying soldier with her own hands while I tried to keep him from bleeding to death after his chest was blown apart. Don't ever question the capabilities of Capt. Brown in my presence. Now, unless Ms. Parisi wishes otherwise, I think we're finished here."

If a pin had dropped in that moment, the sound would have reverberated around the room like a cannon shot.

Ben regained his composure. "I'm sure Capt. Brown is a competent nurse. That doesn't mean there shouldn't be a second opinion to confirm her diagnosis." He struck a defensive posture. "My concern is for Isabella."

Isabella captured Madison's gaze. "Capt. Brown took excellent care of me. I don't want to see anyone else."

Madison hoped Isabella couldn't see past her eyes and into her heart and glimpse the awful memories of war that suddenly seized her. She neither wanted to share nor expose them. They were best kept hidden. She looked away and picked up her medical bag. In the most distant professional voice she could muster, she said, "It was good to see you. Be sure to ice that eye twenty minutes every hour for the rest of the day. You really should consider taking the rest of the day off. Don't worry about the General's appointment. Dr. Barns and I will see him before we leave."

Jim seconded the advice. "I agree with the captain. We can give you a ride back to Social Services, if you'd like."

Ben said, "That won't be necessary. I'll take her home."

He called her sweetheart. Madison found it hard to connect Isabella to such an overbearing man. She regretted having invited her to Bixby's. Her libido had managed to get the better of her good sense. "Isabella, maybe we should cancel our plans for Saturday until you're feeling better."

"No. I'd really like to go. It would be fun. Besides, I'd love to spend time getting to know you better," Isabella said.

"Don't be silly, sweetheart," Ben said. "You really do need to take some time to rest. Cancel your plans as the captain suggests, and I'll take good care of you myself this weekend."

I bet you will, Madison thought. "Why don't you decide when the time comes whether you're up for it? I'll be there regardless. Good to see you." Madison and Jim left Isabella in the conference room with her annoying boyfriend. Perhaps it would be best if she didn't see Isabella again.

Chapter 4

Isabella turned onto a narrow one-way side street in the Boston suburb of Dorchester. She'd heard this part of town could be dangerous, even on a Saturday morning. Her GPS told her she was nearing her destination. "In point two miles, arrive at Bixby's Gym, on left." She was assailed by second thoughts, and not because Bixby's happened to be in a rough neighborhood.

She parked her Toyota Highlander next to a rusty Buick in the small lot behind Bixby's. With fifteen minutes to kill before she was supposed to meet Madison, she surveyed the surroundings.

Bixby's was tucked between two large, decaying brick buildings whose heyday had long passed. Bixby's, on the other hand, was meticulously maintained. It stood like a proud prizefighter among the more imposing buildings that crumbled around it. A single wooden sign with the image of two men engaged in a boxing match adorned the right side of the back door. Besides the Buick, an old, but well-kept Audi and a red pickup were the only other vehicles in the lot.

Isabella shivered now that the engine and heat were off. Although it was the end of March, winter hadn't loosened its grip on Massachusetts. She wore only running pants and a thin sweatshirt over a short-sleeved cotton T-shirt, and the cold claimed her quickly.

Her stomach was in knots. What was she doing in a seedy section of town, meeting a woman she couldn't stop thinking about, who was going to teach her how to hit things? Maybe she'd stepped into some weird alternative dimension. Despite her misgivings about the whole situation, one thing was certain. She had to get to know the enigmatic Capt. Madison Brown better. She glanced toward the rearview mirror and caught sight of the black and blue bruising around her left eye. *At least I'll fit in.*

Isabella hugged herself against the morning chill as she walked toward the door. Butterflies did the rhumba in her stomach.

Inside the building, a tall, redheaded woman flipped through a Vogue magazine as she leaned against a wooden desk. She wore a tight yellow tank top and black spandex capri workout pants that showed off her well-developed muscles. Her forearm and biceps muscles were imposing. Ironically, her hard physique was softened by delicate feminine facial features. Isabella found the contrast surprisingly attractive. "Statuesque" was the best adjective she could come up with for her.

The redhead glanced up from her magazine. "Hi, honey, can I help you?" Her eyes settled on Isabella's. "You need more than a boxing lesson, sweetheart. You ought to be at the police station instead of here if some man did that to you."

Isabella felt intimidated. "I... I'm here to meet someone, and the black eye was an accident."

"If I had a nickel for every woman who came in here hoping to learn how to defend herself against an asshole husband or boyfriend, I'd be a rich woman." She picked up her cell phone. "Let me call the cops for you."

"No, please. I'm telling you the truth. I'm here to meet Madison Brown."

The woman became cheerful. "Oh, that's right. She said a friend might be coming by this morning. You must be Isabella, right?" She put down her cell phone. "I'm Bobbie Bixby. My husband, Jerome, and I own this place. We've known Maddie for years. She's been coming here ever since we opened. She's one of the best women boxers we've seen. It's a shame she doesn't compete." She scrutinized Isabella. "You must be special. I don't think she's ever invited anyone to the gym before."

"I don't know about that. We hardly know each other."

A stocky bald man came from the hallway behind Bobbie and joined them. To Isabella, his arms appeared to be the size of tree trunks. He looked like he'd just successfully wrestled a grizzly.

"Hey, Lucas, Maddie's friend Isabella is here to see her. Is she still in the sparring room with Jerome?" Bobbie asked.

Lucas stared at Isabella for so long that she became uncomfortable. He gave Isabella the distinct impression that she wasn't welcome.

I'm completely out of my mind to be here, she thought.

He grunted and said, "Yes, she's there." Lucas pulled the hood of his heavy gray sweatshirt up over his head and shuffled out the door.

"Kind of a menacing guy, wouldn't you say?" Isabella tried not to sound alarmed.

Bobbie rolled her eyes. "Don't mind him. He's a dopey dinosaur. He's more afraid of you than you should be of him."

"Are you kidding? That guy could squash me like a bug."

"He's harmless. He'd never hurt a woman in a million years. He probably thinks you're new competition for Madison's affections. He has this crazy crush on her. I keep telling him he's barking up the wrong tree. But, for whatever reason, he still believes he can turn a lesbian straight. Funny thing is, he's the kind of guy capable of quite the opposite." Bobbie motioned over her shoulder. "If you follow the hallway and take the first left, you'll end up in the sparring room. That's where you'll find Maddie. Go in and have a seat on the bleachers. She and Jerome should be finished soon."

Madison was gay? No big deal. After all, Beth and Marcy were two of her best friends. They had the kind of relationship she envied. She wished she could think of a graceful way to leave without seeing Madison. The last thing she wanted to do was give Madison the wrong idea about their friendship.

"Thanks, it was nice to meet you," Isabella said.

"Nice to meet you, too."

Isabella took her time walking to the sparring room. The place was sparsely decorated. The only pictures hanging on the off-white walls were of boxers in the ring. A five-gallon water dispenser with paper cups sat outside the sparring room. The floor was done in gray tile. Except for the air freshener she'd noticed on Bobbie's desk, stale sweat and bleach were the dominant odors.

Isabella opened the door to the sparring room. Madison never took her eyes off of Jerome. He loomed over her like a mountain. Madison was tall, but Jerome was significantly taller, with a huge head and angular jaw. His limbs were enormous. Isabella worried for Madison's safety.

But only Madison was throwing punches. Her punches and jabs landed on large pads strapped to Jerome's wrists.

Madison's and Jerome's movements looked like a synchronized, energetic, graceful dance. The motion of Madison's body revealed the muscle definition in her legs, arms, and shoulders. She wore loose-fitting shorts and a sports bra that exposed her flat stomach. Madison's long, sandy-blonde hair was pulled back into a ponytail. A couple of strands hung loose at the base of her neck. Isabella noticed how smooth the back of Madison's neck seemed.

What the hell is the matter with me? A cacophony of warning bells clamored in her head. *I am not attracted to her.*

Isabella forced herself to concentrate on the boxing. Even though she knew next to nothing about the sport, it obviously required skill, concentration, and agility. Madison possessed them all. Her feet moved in harmony with her upper body. She led her punches with her left shoulder. She tucked her elbows close to her sides with her forearms up, mostly jabbing at Jerome. She moved from side to side, blocking, ducking, and landing blows on the pads Jerome held in front of her. Occasionally, when the opportunity arose, she would throw a more significant punch. Watching her gave Isabella a new appreciation for boxing. It seemed a more agile, athletic waltz than the brutal sport she'd envisioned.

The rhythm of Madison's movements and her cat-like nimbleness put Isabella into a daydream until a loud buzzer snapped her out of her reverie. Jerome pulled off his mitts and patted Madison on the back. "Good job today, Maddie. I'll see you here Wednesday night."

"Thanks, Jerome," Madison said as he waved to Isabella and left. Madison grabbed a towel off of the bench and wiped the sweat from her face. "Hi, Isabella. I'm glad you could make it. How's your eye?"

Words were momentarily trapped by Isabella's tongue-tied reaction to the innocent greeting. Then again, Madison was standing right beside her, wearing only a sports bra and shorts. "Good, thank you," Isabella managed to say.

Madison took off her boxing gloves and pulled an Army sweatshirt out of her bag. As she yanked the shirt on, she studied Isabella's eye. "It does appear to be a lot better. The swelling has gone down quite a bit. I hope the things I show you today will help keep you out of trouble next time. The best thing to learn is how to get away from an attacker." She picked up her bag. "Come on, follow me."

They turned left out of the sparring room and entered a smaller room that had four large bags suspended from the ceiling, one in each corner. Mirrors lined the walls. A wooden bench ran along the length of one wall. Madison straddled it and motioned for Isabella to join her.

"Have you ever boxed before?" Madison asked.

Isabella sat down facing her. "You're kidding, right?" She shifted her weight to sit more comfortably. "To be honest, until today, I never thought of it as a sport. You changed my mind about that, though. I enjoyed watching you."

"Most people aren't open-minded enough to give it a chance. If they did, they'd realize there's a lot about boxing that's useful in other parts of life. It doesn't have to be about violent men beating each other to a pulp. After we go through a couple of self-defense techniques, I'll teach you how to hit the heavy bag. There's the speed bag, too. I love to meditate to its rhythm. You should try it."

"Maybe I will. How is boxing useful in other parts of your life?"

Madison took two white Velcro straps out of her bag. "Besides being an excellent workout and stress reliever, it helps me keep my mind and body connected. I've found that the two work best when they function together. I prefer to keep all of my senses sharp. That way, I can protect myself from whatever life, or the people in it, throw at me." She unraveled the Velcro straps. "I hope that didn't come out sounding paranoid."

Isabella recalled that Madison had spent time in Iraq. "No, it didn't. Remember, I work with war veterans. I can't imagine being in a place where every morning you get up could be your last. I would suppose it's hard to let go of that even when you're home. I'd probably feel the need to always be on guard, too." Isabella pointed to her eye. "Obviously, I could use a lesson in learning to pay better attention to what's going on around me. Speaking of which, what are the straps for?"

Madison took Isabella's right hand and turned it palm up. "You're more perceptive than you give yourself credit for. I'll have to keep that in mind. The straps are for protecting your hands when you hit the bags. You've got lots of fragile bones that are easily broken. I want you to avoid that."

A spark of sensation began in Isabella's fingertips and traveled all the way to her heart. She'd never experienced anything like it. Its power startled her. Pay attention, she reminded herself. "You never said anything about the possibility of broken bones."

"That's because I promised not to let anything bad happen to you."

"Are you always so confident?"

"Only when it matters."

Isabella struggled with an abundance of unfamiliar feelings. She wasn't supposed to have these sorts of reactions to a woman. "How long have you been boxing?"

Madison took Isabella's other hand to wrap it. "Since I was a little girl. When my dad was young, he was an amateur boxer in Chicago. I used to hang around the gym with him. He taught me how to box."

"Did you grow up in Illinois?"

"Born and raised."

"Are your parents still there?"

Madison paused momentarily. "My father died in a car crash when I was in high school. Mom still lives in Illinois, though. She's remarried now to the kind of man she thought my dad could never be."

Isabella caught a flicker of sadness in Madison's eyes.

"Another reason I like to box is that it reminds me of him. My mother was wrong. He was a good guy, despite his problems." She gave Isabella's hand a gentle squeeze. "Okay, enough talking about sad things. It's time to teach you how to protect yourself." She stood and pulled Isabella to her feet.

"I'm sorry about your dad."

"It's all right. I wish I hadn't brought it up. My family's a subject I rarely discuss with anyone."

"I'm glad you did. It helps me know you better. Bobbie told me you're one of the best women boxers around. Why don't you compete?"

"I was right about you being perceptive." Madison moved to face her. "I'm not interested in hitting or being hit by anyone else. I box solely to challenge myself. Besides, there are very few people other than Jerome and Bobbie I trust enough to spar with." Madison placed her hands on Isabella's waist. "All right, the first rule of self-defense is to run from trouble before it has a chance to get you first. Try to run away, because fighting should always be the last resort."

Madison moved around behind Isabella without breaking contact. "More often than not, an attacker will come at you from behind. I'm going to put my arms around you and talk you through what to do next." She slid her arms around Isabella and wrapped her into a tight embrace.

The pounding of Isabella's heart made it difficult to hear what Madison was saying. She hoped it wouldn't give her away. What had been butterflies earlier was now a rumbling freight train. *Can this be happening?*

"Focus in the mirror so you can see what you're doing. I want you to take a foot and bring it up right below my knee. A person's shin is a vulnerable spot. If you rake the side of your foot as hard as you can down the length of your attacker's shin, you'll probably cause enough pain for him to momentarily let go. Then, run like hell." Madison squeezed her tighter. "Please remember we're only pretending."

Isabella couldn't breathe, let alone think. If this was just a simulation, why was Madison holding her so close? Enchanting warmth came off of Madison's body, or maybe it was coming off of her own. She wasn't sure. An epiphany as crisp as a cloudless winter sky took shape. It was as unsettling and confusing as it was crystal clear. *Oh my God. I'm physically attracted to her.*

The door to the room opened, and Bobbie popped in. "Hey, Maddie, sorry to interrupt the lesson, but Jerome's next group is due in ten minutes."

Madison let go of Isabella. "No problem, Bobbie. We'll wrap it up now."

Bobbie left, closing the door behind her.

"I guess you're going to have to come back again if you want a chance to hit the heavy bag. I'm sorry we didn't get more done today. I didn't realize the time had gone by so quickly."

To Isabella, the room felt suddenly cold with Madison's arms no longer around her. Even though she was standing right next to her, Madison and her warmth were a million miles away. "I definitely want to come back sometime. Learning to box with you would be fun."

"Here, let me help you with those hand wraps." Madison freed Isabella's hands.

A chorus of voices began singing in Isabella's head—the words she used to hear when she was about to do something that neither her mother nor the nuns at her Catholic school would've approved of. "Don't do it. It's a very bad idea." The naysayers almost always prevailed over her desires. Occasionally, however, desire won, and in a split second, she would move forward with her actions, knowing full well she'd suffer the consequences later. Desire won.

Isabella blurted out, "Would you like to come to my place for dinner tonight?"

Madison put away the wraps. "I'm not sure that's such a good idea."

The disappointment was crushing. "Another time then, when you're not busy, maybe."

"Ignore my bad manners. You just caught me off guard. I'd love to join you for dinner. Sometimes my mouth gets ahead of my brain." Madison seemed uneasy.

"Happens to me all the time. Don't worry about it. I'm glad you can come. I live over in the North End. Is six all right?"

"Sure, that's fine. Can I bring anything?"

"Just you."

"Okay, let's go find Bobbie. She'll have something for you to write your address and phone number on for me."

Isabella followed Madison back into the lobby. Bobbie greeted them warmly. "Hello again, ladies. I hope you enjoyed your workout. I apologize for having to interrupt." She shot Madison a look that Isabella didn't comprehend.

Madison picked up a pad of paper and pen from Bobbie's desk and handed it to Isabella. Isabella scribbled her address and phone number on the top sheet and gave it to Madison.

"I'm going to walk Isabella to her car. I'll be right back," Madison said to Bobbie.

Bobbie grinned. "I'll be waiting. Good to meet you, Isabella. I hope we see you here again soon. Feel free to stop by anytime."

Isabella and Madison walked to Isabella's car. They stood awkwardly by the driver's door, and Isabella impulsively embraced Madison. She whispered in her ear, "I'm really glad to have met you." She sensed every inch of Madison's body next to hers. Holding her close felt right. The chorus of voices picked up their usual refrain: "Don't do it, it's a very bad idea." The softness of Madison's cheek next to hers was like velvet. The contradiction in her emotions made her light-headed. Isabella closed her eyes. *Is she feeling the same things?*

Isabella let go. "I'll see you around six, then."

"Yeah, that sounds good."

Isabella got into her car. As she drove away, she wondered if she really knew herself at all.

* * *

"All right, Maddie, out with it. Don't hold back. I want the whole story. Who is she?" Bobbie propped her elbows on the front desk and stared at Madison.

Madison sat in the chair next to Bobbie's desk. "I met her about a month ago working at the VA clinic. She's a social worker who takes care of veterans. I like her. That's it. We're just getting to know each other."

"And the reason she gave you her address is that you have a date tonight?"

"She's making me dinner. It's not a date."

Bobbie shrugged. "Call it what you want, sweetheart. But I know what I saw. The way that girl was staring at you says otherwise. You and I have known each other for years. I haven't ever seen you that mesmerized by anyone."

"Okay, I admit it. I'm captivated by her innocent charm and stunning good looks. She lights up the room when she walks into it. I don't want anything from her other than friendship, though."

"Why?"

"I'd rather keep my life uncomplicated. If I let my fascination with her get out of hand, it's only going to bring me trouble. I'm still on active duty in the military, and with Iraq looming in the background, my having a crush on a woman—who apparently has a boyfriend, by the way—could only lead to disaster."

Bobbie sighed. "You overthink everything. Besides, don't you ever get lonely?"

"Yeah, but at least loneliness doesn't hurt. I refuse to fall for her."

Bobbie shook her head. "You don't get to choose who to fall in love with or when it happens. Love chooses you when you least expect it, and you certainly don't have any control over it. Love just is."

"That may be, but don't I have control over what I do about it?"

"You think so?"

"I do."

"Whatever you say. At least try to have a little fun while you're kidding yourself. Maybe it's time to let go of your self-imposed isolation. You might be surprised by what happens."

Chapter 5

Isabella parked in the designated space in the garage of her condominium. She grabbed her shoulder bag from the passenger seat, but instead of going to her unit, she decided to go for a walk to clear her head. Fresh air might help. Plus, some shopping was in order if she was going to make dinner for Madison.

Isabella's grandmother taught her to cook. Like her grandmother, Isabella prided herself on making people happy with food. For the Parisi women, cooking was as much a form of artistic expression as it was sustenance. She planned to make her grandmother's North End homemade pasta with white truffle. She could put it together in a couple of hours, but it would taste like it took the whole day.

She stepped out of the dim light of the parking garage into the bright sunshine of the noon sky. The cold morning had transformed into a delightful early spring day. The warmth drew North End residents out of their winter hibernation in droves. She loved this busy part of Boston with its old brick buildings, colonial history, and Italian culture. Hanover Street was bustling with people as she headed toward her Uncle Alfonso's market, the Napolitano. Many considered it one of the best in all of the North End. There, she'd find the freshest imported Italian ingredients, including delectable white truffles, a variety of oil-cured black olives, cheeses, and the finest Parma prosciutto—all necessary ingredients for the dinner she'd make for Madison.

Isabella was so focused on planning dinner that she failed to consider her appearance. She was still wearing the workout clothes she'd worn to Bixby's. Then there was her eye with its purplish black bruising crying out for attention. The bell over the door at Napolitano's chimed as she entered the market. Her uncle, Alfonso Parisi, came out of the back room.

In a thick Italian accent he bellowed, "Isabella, my child, what happened to you?" He came around from behind the counter and

30

tilted her chin gently with his hands to better see her eye. He muttered something in Italian she didn't understand, even though she spoke the language well. With her uncle's accent and his penchant for peppering his outbursts with swear words and slang, she frequently struggled to translate his comments.

Alfonso's daughter, Sophia, rushed in from the storage area. "Papa, what is it? People can hear you two blocks away." She caught sight of her cousin. "Isabella, what the hell happened?"

Damn this eye. "It's fine, really. If you must know, I tried to break up a fight at the veterans' shelter. One of the guys inadvertently hit me. He never would have done it on purpose. It was an accident."

Alfonso eyed her with suspicion. "Well, it doesn't look like it was an accident to me. Perhaps the guy needs to be taught the lesson to keep his paws off of my niece. I can call in some favors with a few people I know. *Gli spezzero' le gambe!* This kind of job is right up Joey the Toad's alley."

Sophia patted Alfonso on the shoulder. "Papa, no one is going to break anyone's legs. Besides, Joey wouldn't hurt a fly. You've been watching those Al Pacino movies again, haven't you?"

Alfonso regarded his daughter. "My child, there are things you will never know about your father. I guess it is best we keep it that way. Why run the risk of falling off of the pedestal you keep me on? Go ahead and hold steadfast to your naïveté, my darling."

In Isabella's opinion, Alfonso was one of the sweetest and best men around. He liked to hide it with a tough-guy persona. Nonetheless, it was entirely possible he could call in a few favors, if he chose to. "Thanks, Uncle, but the favors won't be necessary." She touched her eye as if she might be able to gauge the sight of it with her fingertips. "Is it really that bad?"

Sophia looked at her a sympathetically. "Yeah, I'm afraid so. What did Maria say about it? I can't imagine your sister thinking this is a good thing. Or what about your parents? They can't be happy, either."

"They haven't seen it yet, but they probably know all about it. I'm sure Ben has told Maria by now. He hates that I work at the shelter. I think he hates it even more than my parents do. I'm hoping it fades enough for them not to notice before I see them."

"With your brother John returning from Italy next week, you don't have much time for it to get better," Sophia said. "You'll be at my restaurant this Friday to celebrate his coming home, won't you?"

"You know I will. I wouldn't miss that. We're all thrilled that John's going to be the priest for Michael's wedding."

"Yes," Sophia said. "Michael's fortunate to have a brother in the priesthood."

The bell above the door chimed as a large group of shoppers came in.

Alfonso spoke to Isabella. "Accident or not, you need to be more careful. Such a beautiful girl should not be placed in harm's way, let alone be walking around the city looking like a barroom brawler." Alfonso hugged her and kissed both of her cheeks. "Now, I'm sure you didn't come here to get a lecture from your uncle. Plus, it's getting busy in here. What would you like today?"

"I'm making grandmother's pasta with truffle butter for a friend tonight. I'm hoping you have fresh white tartuffe."

"You are in luck. Luigi brought us some white tartuffe from the Langhe yesterday. How much will you need?"

"One ounce would be plenty. I'd also like enough of the best Parma prosciutto, fontina, and asiago for two."

Sophia put on an apron. "Papa, I'll get the tartuffe."

"Excellent. Isabella will also likely want a nice bottle of Barolo to go with her feast. No?" Alfonso busied himself with gathering her items.

"You read my mind, Uncle," Isabella said. "No one is better than you at pairing the right wine with food. One of your best bottles of Barolo would have been my next request."

"How is Nana, by the way?" Sophia asked as she brought over the tartuffe. "I haven't been able to get to see her in a couple of weeks."

Isabella leaned against the counter and watched him and Sophia amass the ingredients. She breathed in the delicious smells of imported Italian delicacies. "Grandmother is fine. She really seems to have adjusted to living with Mom and Dad. She even cooks for them a couple of nights a week." She thought about her parents and their visit to her place last week. Oddly, something about her new friendship with Madison made them feel distant, almost absent.

Alfonso cut a small wedge of asiago from its wheel. "Your grandmother was one of the best cooks in all of the North End. When I was a boy, the special dishes she always cooked for us were my favorite part of coming home from school each day. I hope she is cooking until her last day. That would surely make her happy. She is a lovely woman, Isabella." He carefully wrapped the cheese.

"The apple did not fall far from the tree with you. You must have potential suitors lining up for miles. Why are you not married yet?"

Sophia looked disapprovingly at her father. "Papa, that's kind of a personal question." She looked to Isabella, "I'm sorry. He never stops asking me that question, either. It gets old after a while. I know."

"I keep asking you even though I already know the answer to the question. You're too independent. Plus, you frighten men away because you're so bossy." Alfonso grinned at Sophia. "And successful, of course. It's hard to find a man who isn't intimidated by such a beautiful and capable woman as you, my daughter. Don't worry, I want you to wait until you find a husband who is worthy of you."

The annoyance on Sophia's face softened at her father's statement about her being bossy and unmarried. She put her arm around him and gave him a squeeze. "I'm waiting for a man to come along who is worthy not only of me, but of being your son-in-law as well."

Listening to Alfonso and Sophia talking about the ideal husband made Isabella think about Ben. He was certainly worthy. Most fathers, including her own, would be thrilled to have him as a son-in-law. Unbidden, thoughts of Madison intruded. "I hope I'll know when the right person for me comes along," Isabella said.

Alfonso stopped putting things in the bag. "You will know, my child. There will be no question in your mind. Your heart will tell you in feelings and emotions that will be unmistakable. When I met Sophia's mother, I knew as soon as our eyes met."

Isabella imagined a young Alfonso meeting the love of his life and the romantic notion of falling in love at first sight. The idea of having an instant, unbreakable bond to another human being was what she longed for. More nagging questions about Madison surfaced. Isabella knew she'd felt a connection to her the instant they met. The trouble was that Madison was a *her*, not a him.

"How is Aunt Rosa, anyway?" Isabella asked.

Before Alfonso answered, the bell over the door rang again, signaling another customer entering the market. He raised his arms in greeting.

Sophia leaned over the counter and said to Isabella, "It's your sister, Maria. Guess you're going to have that conversation about your eye here and now." She gave Isabella a knowing smile. "I'll try to intervene… if can get a word in edgewise."

"With Maria, that could be tough. It's probably best I get it over with before John's dinner next Friday night anyway." Isabella looked back over her shoulder. Her larger-than-life sister was coming toward her. Maria was the picture of a beautiful, charismatic, Italian woman. Her mere presence silenced a room as soon as she stepped into it.

Alfonso hurried from behind the counter to hug and kiss her. "Ah, my brother's two beautiful daughters in my shop at the same time. I'm finishing up with Isabella's order. Then Maria, I will get the manicotti you called about earlier."

"Thank you, Uncle." Maria looked at Isabella. "Ben told me you were attacked again at the shelter, but he didn't tell me how bad it was. You look awful. When are you ever going to grow tired of that terrible place? It's too dangerous. I wish you'd consider letting Ben take you away from it all. Trust me, being a wife and mother is far less hazardous."

Maria hugged Isabella and then took a step back and studied her more closely. "I know you don't like to wear makeup, but you really should consider using a little to cover up that bruising. Why don't you come over this afternoon? We'll go to the spa together. The girls should be able to do something to hide that thing. It'll be my treat." She picked up one of Isabella's hands. "You could use a manicure, too. Your hands are starting to look like Nana's."

"I love my job, Maria, and I wasn't attacked. It was an accident that was actually my fault. Ben is overreacting about the whole thing." She reached for a jar of capers on the shelf next to her and tried to appear nonchalant. "I can't go to the spa with you. I already have plans for later."

Maria examined the white truffle and expensive bottle of Barolo on the counter. "My little sister is doing some special shopping for dinner. Are you having a guest over by any chance?"

"What gives you that idea? Isn't it possible that I'm treating myself to a nice home-cooked meal? I have to eat, too, you know."

"Sure, but I know you're not telling me everything." Maria gave her a probing stare and tapped her own chin. "Let me see, you're buying, among other things, white tartuffe and an expensive bottle of wine. I suspect you aren't planning on dining alone. Is my sister making Nana's white truffle pasta for the handsome Ben Jackson? Remember what Nana always says about seducing men with pasta made with truffles, especially imported white truffles from Italy. Is there a special occasion you want to tell me about?"

Isabella was mortified. How in the world was she going to tell her sister that their Nana's man-seducing pasta recipe wasn't for Ben? It wasn't even for another man, but for a woman whom she hardly knew. Isabella's cheeks flushed. *This is ridiculous. Why should I feel guilty about making dinner for Madison? Besides, my sister doesn't have to know everything that I do.*

"Isabella, are you all right? Why is your face so red all of a sudden?" Maria's eyes opened wide. "Wait a second, are you dating someone other than Ben? Is that why you're acting so weird?" She pulled Isabella away from the counter, out of earshot of Alfonso and Sophia. "You know how much I adore Ben, but if you want to date other guys, that's up to you. Just don't keep him hanging on if you're not serious about him. No matter what, I want you to be happy. Now tell me what's going on."

Isabella didn't want to lie to her sister, but she wasn't about to tell the whole truth, either. "No, Ben isn't coming to dinner, and I'm not dating anyone else." She stepped nearer to the counter and reached for the bag of groceries that Alfonso had packed for her. "I've invited the nurse from the VA clinic who took care of my eye over for dinner. I wanted to do something nice for her to say thank you."

"I think that's a very sweet thing of you to do. I don't understand why you're so nervous about it, though. Are you sure everything's all right?" Maria asked.

Isabella wished she were better at hiding her emotions from her sister. "Everything is fine. I promise. It's been an overwhelming week, that's all." She checked her watch. "I've got to get going. Madison will be over at six. I need to make the pasta. I'm glad I ran into you." She hugged Maria, paid Alfonso, and thanked him and Sophia. "I'll see you all next Friday night." She practically ran out the door.

Chapter 6

The doorbell rang at six o'clock. Like the good soldier she was, Capt. Madison Brown was precisely on time. Isabella smoothed the wrinkles from her skirt and hurried toward the door. As she reached for the deadbolt she slowed her pace. Eager anticipation wasn't necessary. This wasn't a date.

She opened the door and stood transfixed. Whether Madison was wearing a uniform, scrubs, gym clothes, or faded jeans, it didn't matter. The result was the same. "Is there anything you don't look good in?"

Madison smiled. "That's an interesting greeting. Is it your way of saying you think I look nice?"

"I don't make a habit of saying this to women, and I hope you don't mind my saying it to you, but I think you're gorgeous." Isabella stood in the doorway taking in the sight in front of her. The powder blue, button-down shirt that Madison wore brought out the blue of her eyes. The wide leather belt accented her tall body and slender waist.

"Thank you. I'll take that as a compliment. You look nice, too." Madison moved the bouquet of flowers she carried and tucked it under her arm. She rubbed her hands together and then put them into the pockets of her leather jacket. "Do you mind if I come in? It was a chilly walk over from the parking garage."

"I'm sorry to leave you standing out there. My mother would be mortified by my lack of etiquette."

Madison stepped into the condo unit. "Don't worry, I won't tell her." She held out the bouquet. "These are for you."

"They're lovely. Thank you." Isabella took them and breathed in their fragrance. "They smell wonderful, like spring, my favorite season. It was sweet of you to bring them." She laid the flowers on the bureau next to the door. "Can I take your jacket?"

"Sure, thanks." Madison slipped it off and handed it to her.

When she did, their hands brushed and once again, Isabella was overwhelmed with feelings she couldn't categorize. She fumbled with the simple task of hanging Madison's jacket in the closet. "Please, have a seat on the sofa while I put the flowers in water. Can I get you a glass of wine?"

"I'd like that."

Madison surveyed the room from the sofa. She felt a definite sense of peacefulness. The place hummed with Isabella's charm and energy. On her way in, she'd noted that the outside of the building couldn't hide its age, which was probably more than a hundred years. Despite that, the inside was a modern, open floor plan. A small island separated the living room from the kitchen. She could see the cherrywood kitchen cabinets and marble countertop from where she sat. A muted shade of green, the color of leaves in late summer, covered the walls, which were adorned with a number of tasteful paintings of wildflowers.

An Italian opera played softly in the background. Smells from the kitchen reminded her that breakfast was a long time ago, and her growling stomach would be an embarrassment if it continued to rumble the way it was.

Photographs in frames occupied almost every inch of available space atop end tables and other furniture in the room. One was of Isabella in a graduation cap and gown. She was flanked by two beaming people, and from the strong resemblance Isabella bore to both of them, Madison suspected they were her parents. She shared her mother's long auburn hair, loose curls, and facial features. Isabella's emerald green eyes and Mediterranean skin tone came from her father.

The photograph that intrigued her most sat on the end table in a walnut frame. A large group of people stood arm in arm or holding hands like they were the happiest clan in the world. The same family characteristics she'd noted in the graduation picture were evident in every person in the photo. One of the men in the picture was a priest, and even he looked like a Parisi. The vegetation and buildings in the background didn't look like anyplace in New England Madison had ever seen. *A family vacation, I bet.*

Melancholy seeped through her. The unbreakable bonds of family. She wondered whether such a thing truly existed. Her experience with love was that it always came with strings attached. It was never unconditional. She'd learned that being alone was preferable to living in the shadow of a family that contorted her into something she wasn't. She looked at the photo again. Maybe Isabella's family was different.

Isabella came into the room and placed a vase with the flowers on the coffee table. She carried an open bottle of wine and two glasses. She sat next to Madison and poured them each a glass of Barolo. "Thanks again for the flowers. I can hardly wait for spring when they're everywhere. I'm ready for the cold weather to be gone." She handed Madison a glass of wine.

With Isabella so close, Madison got a subtle whiff of her perfume. She wanted to inch closer so she could breathe her in. She took a sip of wine. "Me, too. My wildflower garden is already calling me. Putting my hands in dirt and growing something from a speck of seed is one of my most favorite things." She nodded toward the photograph. "Is that your family?"

Isabella picked up the framed photo. "Yes, this was taken a few years ago in Barbaresco, Italy. My brother John is a priest there. It's one of my favorites. It captures the memory of our time there perfectly. We had so much fun on that trip. My grandfather was still alive then, too."

Isabella scooted nearer to Madison. She pointed as she described each person. "This is John, of course. These are my parents and paternal grandparents, my sister, Maria, and her husband, Anthony, with their two children, Spencer and Amanda. And this is my brother Michael with his girlfriend, Sarah." Isabella put the photograph back. "John will be arriving in town next week. He'll be here most of the summer. Michael and Sarah are getting married, and John will officiate. I can't wait to see him. It's been such a long time."

"You sound like a close family."

"We are. They're my world."

"Other than John, do you all live in Boston?"

Isabella turned so she was facing Madison. She took another sip of wine. "Yes. We've always been here, except for the four years we lived in Colorado when my father was in the Air Force. I was a baby then, so I don't remember it. How about you? Do you have brothers and sisters?"

"No, thank goodness."

Isabella lingered over her next sip of wine. "That was a quick response. I've always thought that having siblings is a lot of fun. I should invite you to my parents' home one day when we're all under the same roof, to prove my point."

"I'm sure brothers and sisters can be a gift. But my parents didn't like each other much." Madison paused. "Let me rephrase that. They despised each other. In the grand scheme of things, it was probably a good thing they only produced one accident during their marriage."

"I take it they didn't exactly plan on having you," Isabella said.

"No. I'm the product of raging teenage hormones and overbearing grandparents. Abortion wasn't an option in either of their families. I was born a month after they got married. Dad gave up boxing to work in the mill, and my mother never went to college like she dreamed of. As best I can remember it, they were never happy."

"Do you see your mother much?"

"No, we don't care for each other's company. She has too many expectations of me that I can't live up to." Again Madison waited a moment before continuing. "My father couldn't live up to her expectations of him, either, so he drank himself to death. I remember the night he left home drunk and never came back. They found his truck overturned in a ditch along the highway."

"When we were at the gym, you told me he died when you were in high school. That's an awful thing to have happen at such a young age." Isabella touched Madison's shoulder.

"I'm probably telling you too much."

"No, you aren't. I'm glad you feel you can be honest with me. Whatever happened to you is truth as you know it, and I want to know your truths."

"Thank you, Isabella."

"It's really none of my business, but I can't help thinking your mother is foolish. What more could she want of you? You're a successful nurse and a captain in the Army. You're kind, smart, and beautiful. I think you're amazing."

"Coming from you, that means a lot, because I think you're amazing, too."

Isabella rose from the sofa. "Okay, now we know where we stand with each other." She took Madison's hands and pulled her to her feet. "I hope you're hungry. Dinner is ready."

Madison feared her feet had turned to lead but managed to follow Isabella. "Can I help with anything?"

Isabella led her to the dining room table. "No, you sit while I bring things in from the kitchen."

Madison stole a glance at her hand. She was sure the feel of Isabella's hand in hers had left scorch marks. "Have you lived in your condo a long time?"

Isabella took two small casserole dishes out of the oven and placed them on the table next to a salad. "Only a year or so. It belonged to my grandparents before that. After my grandfather died, my grandmother went to live with my parents. She wanted one of us kids to keep it so that it would stay in the family. I've always loved the North End. My father helped me with a mortgage so I could buy it on a social worker's salary."

"It's enchanting," Madison said. *Like you.*

"I can't imagine living anywhere else." Isabella sat across from Madison and gestured at the various dishes. "First we have the *insalata di finocchi ed agrumi,* which is a fennel and orange salad, then for the first course, we have baked fennel with prosciutto and asiago, also known in Italian as *finocchi alla asiago con prosciutto.* And then finally, we have my grandmother's famous *tartufo* pasta." She passed Madison the salad bowl.

Madison took a portion of each item as Isabella offered them. After the first couple of bites, she wasn't sure what was more delicious: the food, or the way the Italian words slid off Isabella's lips like a sexy purr. "This is fantastic. You really didn't have to go to this much trouble for me." She savored another bite. "But I do appreciate it."

"You're welcome. I wanted to do something nice for you. I'm glad you like it."

Madison finished another mouthful. "I'm curious about something. How did you get involved with veterans? Were you in the military?"

"No, I'm definitely not the type. I hate to make my bed in the morning. Forget about the business of being able to bounce a quarter on it. That's never going to happen."

Madison stifled inappropriate thoughts conjured by the image of Isabella and her messy bed in the same mental picture. "You're funny. Why your devotion to veterans, then?" She took another bite of the salad.

"I work with veterans because of David Cutter—the fellow you met that morning when I slipped on the ice—and because of the things that happened on September eleventh. I was still in college and doing an internship at the VA clinic. A classmate of mine was flying to California to visit her dying grandmother and had asked me to take notes for her. I'll never forget that morning. I had gone to the student center for a cup of coffee before class. A crowd was gathered around the big screen TV. We all watched, stunned, as the second plane hit the North Tower. My classmate was on that flight."

"Oh God, Isabella, I'm so sorry."

"Good sometimes rises out of the ashes of horrible events. David Cutter was at the VA clinic where I was doing my internship. He became one of my best friends that day. I also found my purpose. My way to serve our country is to work with veterans."

"How did you figure it out?"

"Classes were cancelled, and we were all supposed to go home. I couldn't go. I hated feeling useless. I needed to do something positive. So I went to the shelter. I assumed the guys there would be upset, and maybe I could help. The opposite turned out to be true. They'd already known that kind of trauma. Turns out I needed them. David sat with me for hours, just talking, while we watched our country come apart at the seams. His decency and compassion inspired me more than anyone ever has. I've been working with veterans ever since." Isabella dabbed her mouth with her napkin. "I just wish I could convince him to live someplace other than on the streets."

"He's completely devoted to the homeless vets," Madison said. "I bet that's why he won't leave them."

"That's exactly why. When he was in Vietnam, he lost most of his men in an ambush. He's been carrying the guilt around ever since. This is his way of making amends, I think. It's his life's ambition. He lives to take care of them, especially when they get into trouble." Isabella placed her napkin down and folded her hands together under her chin.

"How's that?" Madison asked.

"For example, one of our vets with a drug and alcohol problem was recently convicted of robbing a convenience store. This coming Friday, David will be right there at the sentencing hearing with me and Ben, who was the attorney on the case, trying to convince the judge to send the man to rehab instead of jail. It's too bad David can't spend half as much time trying to forgive himself as he does looking out for the other guys."

"It may not be about forgiveness. It might be about loyalty. You've probably heard that saying about not ever leaving a fellow soldier behind, whether dead or alive. In his mind, he and the other vets are still fighting the wars of their youth. He can't bring himself to leave them behind."

"You speak from experience, don't you?"

"I suppose."

"What about you? Why did you decide to serve in the military?"

"You'll probably be disappointed when I tell you. My reasons for serving aren't selfless like yours." Madison looked away, then she gazed into Isabella's eyes. "I did it for me. It was the only way to escape the bad situation I was in, living with my mother."

"Do you feel differently now that you've been to Iraq? Everybody always says being there or in Afghanistan is an incredible sacrifice."

Madison carried that subject around like a monkey on her back. "It's a sacrifice. I'm not sure for whom or what, though. But still, I am proud of my service. I wouldn't change that." Unwelcome thoughts crowded into her memory. She tried to push the face of Lt. Scott Stevens out of her mind.

"Are you okay, Madison? Maybe I shouldn't have brought this up."

Madison forced a small smile. "I'm sorry. I'm still working through some of my feelings about Iraq. Do you mind if we talk about something else?"

"Okay. I didn't mean to pry." Isabella stacked two of the serving bowls. "We could discuss how glad I am to have met you."

"I'd like that. I'll start by telling you I feel exactly the same way. And this dinner was beyond description."

Isabella and Madison cleared the dishes from the table. After the dishwasher was loaded and the leftovers stashed in the refrigerator, they took their dessert and coffee into the living room.

"I know I said this before, but that was the best dinner anyone has ever made for me." Madison rubbed her stomach. "I should've stopped at one helping, but it was too good to pass up seconds."

"I haven't made dinner for anyone in a while. I'm glad it was for you."

"What about Ben? You must cook for him."

"Occasionally, but he prefers to go out."

"You've got to be kidding me. If you were my girlfriend, I'd want you to cook for me all the time. Nothing at a restaurant could be half as good."

Isabella looked away.

"Uh-oh. I think I touched a nerve."

"Maybe you did. The tough part is that I don't know why that's the case."

"Could it be that you're here with me on a Saturday night instead of with your boyfriend? How long have you two been together?"

"Too long, probably."

"Why do you say that?"

"I haven't admitted this to anyone but myself." Isabella looked at the picture of her family before finishing her comment. "It's because I don't love him."

"Why do you stay with him, then?"

"I'm terrible at saying no to him. Besides, my family worships Ben. I don't want to cause some huge family drama before Michael's wedding. Ben is devoted to me, but there's something missing between us that I can't quite put my finger on." Isabella moved closer to the line she was terrified to cross. "Plus, I think I may have met someone else. Have you ever been in love? I'm not sure I know what it feels like, and since I hardly know this person, I'm afraid I might be making a giant mistake."

Isabella's question hung between them.

At last, Madison answered. "I was in love once, awhile ago." She swallowed twice. "You'll know it when it happens."

"It's funny you should say that. My uncle said the exact same thing earlier today. Who was she, and why aren't you with her now?"

Madison pondered a moment before replying. "Bobbie outed me to you earlier, didn't she?"

"Your being gay doesn't bother me in the least. I hope you don't mind that I know."

"Not at all. Bobbie has good instincts about people. As for my love life, I was head-over-heels in love with a girl named Jennifer back in high school. I would've walked through hell for her. In a lot of ways, I did. Like most love-struck teenagers, we thought we'd be together forever, and we were—right until she told her parents about us. To make a long story short, they told her never to see me again. My mother kicked me out of the house two months before my high school graduation. That's how I ended up in the Army. My uncle let me stay with him until I graduated. Then I signed up for ROTC and came to school here at Northeastern."

Isabella caught a tear as it slipped out of her eye. "Madison Brown, you're the strongest, most unusual person I've ever met. I mean that in a good way." She looked at Madison intently. "But that still doesn't tell me how you knew you were in love with her."

"I knew it when she kissed me. Are you all right? You look like something's bothering you."

A myriad of emotions banged around inside of Isabella. The riotous beat of her heart reverberated in her head. *When she kissed her.* "Something might be."

"Let me guess. Are you wondering about this new person you've met?"

Isabella nodded.

"Do you want to tell me who it is?" Madison asked.

"You."

Madison put her hand on the back of Isabella's neck and gently pulled her forward. With her other hand, she caressed the side of Isabella's face. Then she leaned in and put her lips on Isabella's.

The kiss was slow and perfect. Isabella closed her eyes and experienced the sensation of kissing a woman. The silky softness of Madison was exquisite. She opened to her demand to kiss her more deeply. Isabella whimpered. Madison's taste, the smell of her skin, and the warmth of her breath made Isabella ache. Madison brushed her thumb down Isabella's neck. Isabella's arousal climbed even higher at the thought of that hand moving lower over her body. She kissed Madison harder.

Madison grabbed a handful of Isabella's hair and gently pulled her head back, breaking their connection. She stared breathless into Isabella's eyes. "I can't do this… I have to go."

A bucket of icy cold water couldn't have been more of a jolt. Confusion enveloped Isabella. "I don't understand."

"I shouldn't have kissed you like that. It was a mistake."

"Why?"

"Because you have a boyfriend, and you're not even gay."

"But I told you I don't love Ben. I've never been kissed like that before. If that's what it's like to kiss a woman, then maybe I should be asking whether I'm a lesbian."

"Right now, you're still with him. And what just happened between us was too intense for me."

"I feel like you've pulled the rug out from underneath me," Isabella said. "I don't have any idea what's happening to me. What should I do?"

"You have to make things right with Ben and figure out what you want."

"What about you and me after that?"

"First, we'll focus on being friends." Madison rose to leave. "I really should get home."

Isabella retrieved Madison's jacket from the closet and helped her slip it on. "Thank you for coming tonight." She reached for Madison.

Madison embraced Isabella and kissed her cheek. "Dinner was wonderful." She paused. "I'm sorry if it feels like I misled you with what happened. I meant what I said a minute ago. You need to figure out what you want to do about Ben and do some soul searching about your feelings."

"When can I see you again?" Isabella asked.

"I… I don't know." Madison turned and left.

Isabella shut the door behind her and leaned against it. *What just happened?* Whatever it was, she'd never be the same again after that one amazing kiss. She went to the window overlooking the street below and opened it wide. She breathed in the salty air that blew in off the Atlantic. It was a smell she'd never grow tired of. While the lights of the city blocked out most of the stars, she still enjoyed the inky, cloudless sky. The lights of the city were no substitute for a starry night, but they were still pretty in their own right. She was glad for the cold evening air. Maybe it would help her to think more clearly by morning.

Chapter 7

Madison threw relentless punches and jabs at the heavy bag. Nearly a week had gone by, yet the kiss with Isabella still played over and over in her mind. So much for her plan not to fall for Isabella. She didn't want to feel this way. She willed herself to think of something—anything—else. The dying image of Lt. Scott Stevens raced to the forefront. She should have been more careful in her wish for another thought. His last words rang in her head. "I wish I could've known love in this life."

Madison squeezed her eyes shut to force his memory aside. When she opened them again, she breathed deeply and hit the bag with all her strength. She hit with such force that a protest of pain from an old injury reared its ugly head. "Fuck."

She grabbed her shoulder and slumped on the bench against the wall. The sound of Bobbie's voice surprised her.

"Maddie, what are you trying to do, kill yourself? Or maybe you've got it in for the heavy bag." Bobbie grabbed the bag to stop it from swinging. She sat down next to Madison. "What's going on?"

"I'm too close to the edge of a place I don't want to be." Madison took off her gloves. The pain in her shoulder intensified.

"What place is that?"

Madison stared at the tiles on the floor. "You were right about my having feelings for Isabella. I can't help that I've fallen for her, but everything's wrong about it. If I don't figure out how to back away from her, I'm afraid she'll pull me under. What's worse is this time, I might drown."

Bobbie stretched her legs, crossed her ankles, and rested her head against the wall. "Did you ever stop to think that you've been drowning all along? Maybe Isabella is the one who can finally pull you out."

Madison was tired of spending her life treading water to stay afloat. The situation with Isabella had too much stacked against it.

Self-preservation was her primary concern. "I'm afraid in the end, she'll only break my heart."

"How can you be so sure that will happen?"

"Let's see. We could start with her very close-knit Catholic family, including a brother who's a priest, and a handsome successful boyfriend with a chip on his shoulder. And besides that, I'm the only woman she's ever kissed."

"So, your instincts about her being straight were right. That certainly poses a problem. Unless of course, she's not really straight and hasn't figured it out yet."

"Or she's looking for a temporary diversion from men. Trying lesbianism is sort of the in-thing these days with straight girls. I'm not interested in being her experiment or her vacation. What happens to me when the vacation ends and it's time to go back to her cushy man-for-a-lover world?" Madison turned to Bobbie. "And what if I have to go back to Iraq?"

"You go, and then you come home. It doesn't have to be more complicated than that. Don't think, by the way, that I didn't catch that you said she kissed you. If you're still thinking about it days after it happened, it must have been quite a kiss."

"Yeah, it was. It was unforgettable. If I let myself dwell on it too much, I'll have to admit that it got completely under my skin."

"Did things go farther than a kiss?"

"No. I apologized and left before things got out of hand. It shouldn't have happened in the first place."

"I don't think you're being fair to her or to you. You're jumping to conclusions without giving her a chance. You may not be the only one who's struggling over what happened between the two of you. Stop sabotaging your life with excuses."

Bullshit had never been Bobbie's style, and Madison appreciated that Bobbie rarely let the people around her get away with immersing themselves in it. Even now. "I guess I did leave rather abruptly that night. I probably should've been a better friend and stayed to talk more about what she was feeling."

"Call her and give both of you a chance. You're never going to know if there's anything between the two of you if you don't. Who knows? Maybe you'll turn out to be the love of each other's lives, and you'll live happily ever after. You can't hide your emotions forever. One way or the other, they'll catch up to you."

"I was a jerk. I've missed her all week. I'll call her today. Even though it's Friday, maybe I'll get lucky and she won't already have plans. I'd love to be able to see her tonight."

Bobbie put her arm around Madison. "Good. Now you're using your heart instead of your head. I've got another idea. Why don't I call Jackie and Karen to see if they want to go out dancing tomorrow night? You know I love to go out with you girls. It's my chance to have a good time without having men clamoring for me. Maybe Isabella would want to join us. You should ask her. We haven't all gotten together in a while. Having a little fun might help you out of this funk you're in. I really prefer the confident, fun Madison to the brooding, insecure one who's been around lately."

"Thanks a lot. I didn't know my mood had been that bad." The idea of going out dancing appealed to Madison. Even though the Army's "don't ask, don't tell" policy had been repealed, she'd been around the military long enough to know that actual treatment didn't always match official policy. She still needed to watch her step. "I hope you intended for us to go to the Camilla Club. If I go dancing, I want to go to a lesbian bar, and it needs to be one where I feel safe."

"Definitely, the Camilla's safe for both of us. You don't think Jerome would want me to go out clubbing anyplace other than a lesbian hangout, do you? He's like most guys. He hopes I'll see something juicy happen between two women and have a great story to tell him. Plus, he knows you'll keep me out of trouble and he doesn't have to worry about me straying. Not to mention, it'll give him a chance to have the house to himself. He can invite his buddies over to smoke smelly cigars, drink beer, talk about women, and play poker."

Madison chuckled. "I get the part about women, beer, and playing poker, but smelly cigars, not so much. Dancing would be fun, a nice change of pace. Thanks for talking some sense into me. I'll let you know how it goes with Isabella."

"You won't get away with not telling me."

"That's because you're relentless."

"No, it's because I love you and want you to finally be happy."

Madison gave Bobbie a quick hug. "I love you, too. Do you want me to be the designated driver tomorrow night, as usual?"

"If you don't mind. That always works for me."

"I like to keep my wits about me. I'm happy to drive. Give me a call later to let me know what time I should pick you up."

She stood and grabbed her gym bag. Yes, she would take this chance, especially since Isabella had said she wasn't happy in her relationship with Ben. Maybe this really was an opportunity to have things go in a direction that would finally make her happy again. If the kiss they shared was a true indication of Isabella's feelings for her, then chances were good.

Chapter 8

Ben rose from the worn oak chair. "Your honor, I'd like to call Mr. David Cutter as a character witness." He fastened the button of his lamb's-wool jacket and approached the witness box confidently.

The General leaned close to Isabella and asked, "Do you think he can pull this off?"

"Yes, I think with him asking you the right questions, it's possible. Good luck." Isabella helped him to his feet. He seemed more fragile with each new day.

The General walked slowly to the front of the courtroom. Despite what Isabella had said to the General, she wasn't entirely convinced Ben could win the motion. Ben had told her Judge Agnes rarely granted requests for a reduced sentence. The man to be sentenced, Carl Woods, wasn't a hardened criminal. He was an Iraq war veteran who was battling a drug and alcohol addiction. If they could get him into a treatment program instead of a two-year prison sentence, he might be able to put his life back together. He had robbed a convenience store, however, with a concealed weapon, and that wasn't going to win him any points with the judge.

Judge Agnes addressed Ben. "Counselor, I'd prefer to cut to the chase here. I've already read your motion, and I know Mr. Cutter well from our previous encounters over the years. He's been a character witness in my courtroom for more wayward veterans than I can count. I understand fully what your arguments are. Instead of you asking the same standard questions and Mr. Cutter giving me the same standard answers, I'd like to ask him a few questions of my own. You can decide after I've finished if you have anything to add."

"I have no problem with that, Your Honor," Ben said.

"Excellent. Mr. Cutter, raise your right hand," Judge Agnes instructed. "Do you swear to tell the truth, the whole truth, and nothing but the truth?"

"I do." The General put his hand down and settled into his seat.

Judge Agnes removed her glasses and laid them on the bench. "Mr. Woods committed a serious offense. I get that you believe he's a decent fellow at heart. Otherwise, you wouldn't be here on his behalf. My role, however, is to ensure the safety of the public. Tell me, in your own words, why I should allow this motion."

"In my opinion," the General said, "there are three kinds of people in this world—those who take care of themselves, those who won't, and those who would if they knew how to."

"And you believe Mr. Woods is in the last category?"

"I do. I've spent my life working to help guys like him find their way. Despite my own bad deeds as a young man, I've made amends because I was given a second chance. All Carl needs is for someone to give him a chance, too. He needs the opportunity to make things right. Sometimes, those of us who've hit rock bottom and manage to survive can contribute to making this world a better place. Survival can make a person stronger and better. I believe Carl has it in him to do good things."

"Are you asking me to wipe the slate clean where Mr. Woods is concerned?"

"No. That's not what he deserves. *Tabula Rasa* would be a mistake. In fact, his record should always be a reminder to him of his bad deeds. But I do think you should give him the opportunity to become the man he was meant to be. In the end, if he doesn't do right, lock him up and throw away the key."

Judge Agnes eyed the General. "Still using your Latin, I see."

"At least I got something out of having gone to Plymouth Latin High School before I was drafted." He folded his hands on top of his cane.

"Tell me why you still live on the streets after all this time, Mr. Cutter."

"The thin line between life and death is my reason."

"I'm not good with riddles. You'll have to explain."

The General laid the cane across his lap. "The other day, when I was walking down Cambridge Street, I saw a young starling trying to learn to fly. He must've wandered away from the nest or he was abandoned by his parents. There weren't any other birds around. Despite his struggle, he didn't relent. I watched him for a long time, trying to say words of encouragement he might understand. Finally, he figured out how his wings worked with the wind. He taught himself to soar. The irony with life is, just when you think you've got it all figured out, you fly headfirst into a window, which is what that young starling did. I walked over to him. He lay there motionless on the concrete. I picked up his body and put it in my pocket. Later that day, I buried him in the Common."

"What does that have to do with your still living among homeless veterans? I'm sure the system has a better place for you," the judge said.

"The men at the shelter are like that starling. They've come home from war often abandoned by the life they had before, and now they need to learn to fly all over again. My mission in life is to provide them encouragement and hope. I'm also there for them when they fall or fly into that window. I may not have a comfortable or stable life, but I'm at peace with my usefulness among them. Other than people like Ms. Parisi here"—he pointed toward Isabella—"they've got no one else to look after them. Like I said, there's a thin line between life and death for these men. I don't necessarily mean life in the literal sense, either."

"Ah, not as in whether the body lives or dies, but rather the soul?"

"Precisely, Your Honor."

"Thank you for sharing your philosophy." Judge Agnes put her glasses on. "It's your lucky day, Counsel. I'm granting your motion for a reduced sentence."

She turned to Carl Woods. "Don't ever let me see you in this courtroom again. I won't be so benevolent next time. Thank you, Mr. Cutter, you may step down now. This hearing is adjourned." She banged her gavel on the bench. To the escorting officer she said, "Take Mr. Woods and have him processed for transfer to the Boston Central Drug Rehabilitation Center this afternoon."

Isabella, Ben, and the General gathered outside the courtroom.

Ben slapped the General on the back. "Thank you for that. I don't know how you did it, but you pulled it off, yet again. I was sure the judge was going to send Carl straight to jail without a second chance. Then you came out with that dead bird story. It was brilliant. You have a flair for courtroom theatrics. You'd make a great lawyer."

The General gave Ben a withering stare. "I don't know about that. Even though I respect the work that some lawyers do, I wouldn't be interested in selling my soul to the devil. Now, if you'll excuse me, I'd like to go check on Carl."

Isabella touched the General's arm. "Would you like me to go with you?"

"No, my dear. It's getting late, and I know your brother's big homecoming dinner is tonight. Call it a day, won't you? Me and the boys will be fine. You go and enjoy yourself." The General kissed Isabella's cheek and nodded at Ben. "Counselor." He turned and went on his way.

"He's never liked me, has he?" Ben said.

"I'm sure he respects your skills, and I know he's grateful for the work you did to help Carl," Isabella said. "So am I."

"Respecting someone and liking them are two different things." Ben put his arms around her. "At least you like me, and I'm crazy about you. I can't wait to see John again tonight. I'll bet your parents are thrilled with the idea of having us all under the same roof."

She smiled at the thought. "They are, especially my grandmother. She had Mom take her out shopping for a new dress just for the occasion. I love seeing how happy they all are. It's going to be so much fun tonight."

Ben squeezed her tighter. "I'm so relieved they've accepted me as one of their own. I already feel like a son-in-law, and we're not even married yet."

Being in Ben's arms didn't make Isabella tremble like being in Madison's had. There was comfort in his embrace, though. He was steady, predictable, and the kind of guy she always imagined she'd marry. "My family does love you."

"Good. Listen, I've got a late appointment at five this afternoon. I'll plan on meeting you over at Sophia's afterward. Is that okay?"

"Sure, that's fine."

"Do you mind if I stay over at your place tonight? You know I can't pass up the fine Italian wine I'm sure will be flowing at dinner. You wouldn't want me to drink and drive would you?" His hand slid a touch lower down her back. "Plus, it'll give us a chance to spend some time alone together for a change."

Isabella's cell phone vibrated inside her shoulder bag. At first she wasn't sure if it was the phone or her nerves. She pulled out of his arms and fumbled for her phone. "I need to get this." She glanced at the number and pushed the mute button.

"You look disappointed," Ben said. "Were you expecting a call from someone?"

She dropped her phone and knelt down to retrieve it. "Sort of, I guess."

"What's that supposed to mean?"

"It means I've had a stressful week, okay?"

"I'm not sure why you're getting so snippy. What's the matter with you?"

She plopped her cell phone back into her bag and tried to shake off her sudden agitation with Ben. "I didn't mean to get snippy. I was just hoping that Madison, I mean Capt. Brown, the nurse you met at the shelter, would call. I need to talk to her about something."

"I remember her. You blew me off last Saturday night to make dinner for her. How did that go?"

"Fine. No big deal. It was just dinner."

"Of course it was just dinner. What else would it be?" Ben squinted at Isabella. "Why are we on the verge of arguing?"

Isabella took a deep breath. "I don't know. Maybe because I'm tired. Let's start over right now. All I want to do is have a nice time with you and my family tonight. Yes, please, I want you to stay over, too."

"Great. I'll see you soon, then."

Isabella watched him go. She noticed other women in the hallway looking at him appreciatively. Lots of women would claim him in a second, yet all she could think about was Madison. Still no word from her all week.

Maybe Isabella should make the first move and call her. But what would she say? Nothing like this had ever happened to her before. Gravity didn't seem to anchor her to the world anymore. Maybe it was best that Madison hadn't called. Her feelings for her were a magnetic attraction that pulled her deeper toward a place she wanted to go, but was afraid to enter. *What if I never kiss her again? What if I do?*

Chapter 9

Ben took Isabella into his arms. "I had a nice time with your family tonight. I really enjoyed seeing John again. He told me he'd love to officiate at our wedding one day. Everyone is so happy about Michael and Sarah." He moved to kiss her lips, but she turned her head so that he had to settle for brushing his lips against her cheek. "Your parents will be as thrilled as I am when you finally say yes."

Isabella pulled away from him. "I'd like to change out of this uncomfortable dress. I'm going to put on something else. Maybe we could watch a movie or a TV program when I get back."

"That's not exactly what I hoped we'd do, but sure. I'll take some wine into the living room and choose something. Anything in particular you'd like to see?"

"No. Pick whatever you want." She hurried from the room.

He should have known better than to bring up the subject of marriage. Isabella's already cold feet had recently become polar icecaps when it came to them tying the knot. He'd never admit it to her, but he enjoyed their game of cat and mouse.

He poured a glass of wine and propped his feet on the coffee table. He reached for the TV remote and caught sight of the flashing red button on Isabella's answering machine just as the side of his hand accidentally made contact with it. He leaned toward the machine when he heard the recorded voice.

"Hi, Isabella, this is Madison. I've been thinking about you a lot and about what happened between us the other night. I'm sorry for the way I left things. We'd probably both feel better if we talked about it. If you're free tonight, I'd like to stop by. Maybe you're already out. If I don't hear from you, I'll come over in the morning after my workout at Bixby's. If that's not okay, give me a call. I really need to see you. Bye."

Tiny beads of sweat formed along Ben's brow. That was why Isabella had been more distant lately. He wouldn't let this happen.

Anger swelled within him. His instincts about Madison had been right. He didn't want to know exactly what had happened between her and Isabella, but he'd make damn sure it didn't happen again.

He reached over and hit the delete button. He contemplated what to do the following morning. Maybe he'd take Isabella to breakfast so she wouldn't be there when Madison showed up. Or better yet, he'd be at the condo with Isabella when Madison arrived. They'd be a happy couple enjoying breakfast after a lovely family evening that culminated in a night of lovemaking. That ought to be enough to send a clear message to her that Isabella belonged to him.

Isabella came back into the living room. "Did someone leave a message on the answering machine? I thought I heard a woman's voice."

"It must have been the television. I couldn't find anything good to watch, so I turned it off. Besides, I'm not really interested in TV or a movie right now." He motioned for her to sit with him. "Do you have any idea how special you are to me?"

Isabella nestled into Ben's arms as they sat together on the sofa. She willed herself to listen to her head, not her heart. She kissed his neck and heard his breathing grow heavy with passion. Unbidden, the words her father had said earlier in the evening during his toast to Michael and Sarah replayed in her memory and made her nauseous with guilt. "When all of my children are finally married and carrying on in the Parisi tradition, I will be ready to die a happy man." He'd raised his glass high. "To my precious sons and daughters."

All evening, she'd been working on convincing herself that she should make love to Ben tonight. She had to know if she could feel the same thing for him that she did for Madison. If she could, everything would be so much easier. She'd marry him and live the life she'd always believed she was meant to have. She caressed the side of his face.

He kissed her.

Maybe Madison's kiss was a fluke. Impetuously, she put a hand on either side of Ben's face and returned his kiss with as much passion as she was capable of. *Nothing.* His lips were soft, but not like Madison's. He smelled nice, but his scent didn't leave her breathless like Madison's did. The kiss ended, and she moved her hands to his waist. Underneath his shirt was a flawless washboard stomach. Strange, but at that moment, all she could think about was what it would be like to touch Madison's stomach. Her tortured emotions were interfering with her desire to give herself to Ben.

"Are you all right?" he asked.

"I'm a little out of sorts from this past week, I guess. Everything's fine." She admitted to herself that she was a liar and coward. And like remembering her father's toast, she again felt sick to her stomach. She wanted to feel something, anything for Ben. The slightest tingle would've been enough, but nothing. *Dammit, he loves you.* She pulled him to her and kissed him hard.

His hands roved over her body. "I've been waiting all night for this." He undid her blouse buttons.

Isabella was filled with apprehension. This wasn't the first time they'd slept together, yet his touch seemed foreign to her now. He slid his palms over her stomach and up near her breasts. Tears welled in her eyes. He pushed her down on the sofa and climbed on top of her. She recoiled at the sensation of his arousal against her. The thought of being with him repulsed her. *I don't want to do this.* Remorse and guilt besieged her, not only for leading Ben on, but for kissing someone other than Madison. She'd told Madison she'd end things with Ben, but she was about to sleep with him.

Ben touched her breasts. "Let's go to the bedroom."

Her tears became a sob. She put her hands against his chest and pushed him off of her. "I'm sorry, Ben. This isn't right anymore." She caught her breath between sobs. "To tell the truth, it never was."

He sat woodenly beside her on the sofa. His nostrils flared. "What the hell is the matter with you, Isabella? Can't you make up your mind about anything? I really don't know how much of this I can take. What is it you want?"

She pulled her feet up onto the sofa and wrapped her arms around her knees. If she could make herself smaller, maybe she'd feel less vulnerable. "I don't know." She put her hands to her face and cried even harder. "I didn't mean for any of this to happen."

"What? What didn't you mean to have happen?"

"Please, don't ask me to talk about it. I don't know what words to use." She brought her sobs under control a bit. "Just know that I care about you."

"I shouldn't have lost my temper." Ben rubbed her back. "You might not know what you want, but I do. I want you. No one will love you like I do. No one can give you what I can. Tell me what's wrong. I want to help."

She wanted to scream, "Don't love me, because I don't love you." She didn't. Instead she said, "You can't help me. No one can until I help myself." She looked into his eyes. "I don't want to hurt you anymore."

He took her into his arms. "Come on. Let me put you to bed. A good night's sleep will help you feel better. We'll talk about this in the morning." He pulled her to her feet and led her to the bedroom. Ben tucked her in, left the room, and closed the bedroom door. A good night's sleep was out of the question. Isabella spent the night hating herself for not telling him that things were over for good between them.

Chapter 10

Madison rang Isabella's doorbell a second time. She probably shouldn't have presumed it was all right to drop by. After all, Isabella hadn't called her back after the message she'd left the previous night.

The door opened. Ben, his hair disheveled and wearing only a pair of boxer shorts, stood there looking smug. Madison was disgusted by the thought of Isabella with him.

"Hello. It's Madison, right?" She heard the condescension in his tone. "Sorry for my appearance. Isabella and I were out late. We're finishing breakfast. What can I do for you?"

I'm not some door-to-door salesman, you ass. Couldn't Isabella at least have called and told her not to come over?

Madison heard Isabella's voice. "Who's at the door, Ben?" A moment later she appeared next to Ben in the doorway. He put his arm around her possessively. "Hey, sweetheart, it's your friend Madison from the clinic."

Seeing Isabella wearing a T-shirt without a bra, silk shorts, and standing next to Ben was like being run over by a speeding train.

"I didn't expect you," Isabella said.

"That's obvious, or maybe I don't matter at all to you." She tried to read the look on Isabella's face. "I've got to go. I'm sorry I disturbed you." Madison turned and took two steps away.

"No!" Isabella shouted.

Madison turned back around.

"No, please don't leave. We have to talk." She stepped out of the doorway into the hall. She looked back at Ben. "I need a minute alone to talk to Madison." Isabella took another step and closed the door.

"Isabella, didn't you get the message I left last night? Why didn't you call me to let me know he was staying over? I never would've stopped by if I'd known he was here. I thought you said you were going to end it with him. In case you didn't know, sleeping with a guy isn't exactly the best way to accomplish that."

"It's not what you think. I didn't sleep with him. We were out late, so he stayed over." Isabella took a step closer to Madison. "What message? I didn't get a message."

Madison moved away. "It's really none of my business who you sleep with. I'm sorry I stopped by." She lowered her voice. "And I'm even sorrier that I kissed you."

"Please talk to me, Madison. You're all I think about." Isabella looked over her shoulder at the closed door behind her. "Can you come back later, after Ben leaves?"

Madison felt as though her feet were begging her to stay rooted where they were until Isabella came into her arms. Her instincts to protect herself prevailed. "No, I'm going out to a club with some friends later, so I won't have time. It was a mistake for me to come here anyway. I'd rather forget about what happened last weekend. Let me give you a piece of advice. If what you said about thinking of me all the time is true, you should stop." She turned and walked away.

"Madison, wait," Isabella called as Madison hastened away. She thought about pursuing her, but she was wearing practically nothing, so chasing a woman down the hallway of her condominium building probably wasn't the best idea. Besides, even if she caught her, with Ben still inside they couldn't have the discussion they needed to have. She'd have to figure out how to find Madison later and convince her to talk about the situation.

Isabella went back inside and checked her answering machine. The steady red light indicated no messages. She picked up the phone and checked the caller ID. Madison's name and cell phone number came up as having called last evening at seven while she and Ben were out. She pressed the answering machine button. The mechanical voice chimed in, "No new messages." The machine was working. How could she have missed the call? She remembered having thought she heard a voice on the machine when she went to change clothes. *Ben lied to me.*

Ben was rinsing their breakfast dishes when she went back into the kitchen.

"How could you?"

"How could I what?"

"You knew Madison was coming here this morning because you erased her message. Why would you do that?"

Ben put the dishes down and dried his hands. "I'm sorry, but I did it you for. It was for your own good. I don't know what's going on between you and her, but whatever it is, it needs to stop."

"Who the hell do you think you are? It's not for you to decide what's good for me. How dare you?" She fought for composure. "It's over between us. I want you to leave, now."

He reached for her. "I'm sorry you're upset. Please, let's talk about this."

"No. Go." She turned her back on him.

"You'll regret this, Isabella." His anger was evident as he left the room.

Not as much as I regret the time we've wasted.

Chapter 11

Beth hung up the phone in the North End home she and Marcy shared, only a couple of blocks from Isabella's. "Marcy, you're never going to believe this in a million years."

Sitting at the breakfast table, drinking coffee, and reading her morning newspaper, Marcy lowered the paper enough to see Beth. "Try me. There isn't much I find surprising these days."

Beth took a sip of Marcy's coffee. "I guarantee this will." She made a pained face. "Way too much cream and sugar in your coffee."

Marcy laid the paper down. "All right then, I give. Who was on the phone, and what earth-shattering news did she have to share?"

"Remember when I told you I thought Isabella was making a mistake with that guy, Ben? That he wasn't right for her?"

"Yes, and remember I told you Isabella needed to figure that one out on her own?" Marcy took a long drink of her coffee. "Mmm, that's good."

Beth rolled her eyes. "Well, I think she finally has... the hard way. She didn't give me any details, but it sounds like he may have caught her with someone else. Things got messy. She just threw him out of her place."

"You're right. I'm blown away. I never would've believed Isabella would be caught in a love triangle. It's always the innocent ones who shock you."

"She's on her way over here now. She said she needed to talk to us about it. She sounded pretty upset."

"That's fine. I'm not sure you and I are the best sources of advice for how to deal with jilted boyfriends, though. It would make more sense if she talked to Maria, instead. Her sister has more experience with hetero-drama."

Beth got up and poured a cup of coffee, black with no sugar. "Maybe she needs to talk to someone more neutral when it comes to Ben. Her family's invested in her relationship with him. Isabella might be afraid Maria would try to talk her out of breaking things off." Beth gave Marcy a peck on the cheek. "We are experts in managing a successful long-term relationship, though."

"That's true. But still, I really don't know how much we'll be able to help. The only advice I can think of is to tell her to follow her heart. That's the key to any long-term relationship." She patted Beth's backside. "I do have to admit I can't wait to meet this mystery guy. Whoever he is, he must be a hot ticket to win Isabella's heart over Mr. Perfect, Ben Jackson."

* * *

"Isabella, you look like hell." Marcy pulled a kitchen chair away from the table. "Sit down and tell us what's going on. Spare no details. We want to hear the whole story from beginning to end."

"You're the most brutally honest person I know, Marcy," Isabella said.

Beth gave Marcy a sharp glare. "Yeah, she is. She's living proof that lawyers aren't known for being warm and fuzzy. I've given up trying to teach her the art of gently telling the truth."

"You and I both know that's part of my charm, dear."

"Isabella, would you like some coffee?" Beth asked.

"Yes, thanks. I didn't get much sleep last night. I could use another cup."

Marcy fixed her gaze on Isabella. "Hmm, a sleepless night to boot. I can hardly wait to hear this story. Out with it. Did you and Ben really break up? Is there another guy?"

Isabella rubbed her temples. "Not exactly. Things are over between Ben and me. There is someone else… but not another guy."

Beth and Marcy seemed oblivious to the direct hint. For crying out loud, Isabella thought. If she was going to find Madison, she'd have to be as blunt as Marcy. "Beth, do you remember meeting Madison Brown, an Army nurse, at the clinic a few weeks ago? She's been filling in there temporarily."

"Sure I do." Beth grinned. "The long legs, blue eyes, sandy-blonde hair, and how she fills out her uniform in all the right places." She smacked her lips. "I definitely remember."

Marcy glared at her partner.

Beth feigned innocence. "I may be happily married, but I still appreciate a nice-looking woman."

"Now I know what you're up to under those dark sunglasses you wear to the beach." Marcy cuffed Beth on the shoulder.

"For the record, I'm only protecting my eyes from sun damage."

"Right. Whatever you say, sweet cheeks," Marcy said.

"Can we get back to Isabella?" Beth asked.

"You bet." Marcy took a sip of coffee.

"I kissed her," Isabella blurted.

Marcy choked on the coffee and spewed it all over the newspaper and table.

Isabella winced, but it felt good to say the words aloud.

Beth patted Marcy on the back to ease her coughing. "That's quite the admission, Isabella. What happened to bring this on?"

"I haven't been able to get her out of my mind since the day we met. When she kissed me, I felt it everywhere." Isabella wiggled her fingers up and down in front of her body.

Beth handed Marcy a napkin. "I'm afraid to ask, but did Ben catch you two in the act and that's why you threw him out of your apartment?"

Marcy added, "Like I said before, don't leave out any of the details. I love a good girl-gets-her-girl-and-throws-out-the-guy story."

"No, he didn't catch us. He must have suspected something was going on, though. Last night, when he was at my place, he erased a voice message from Madison while I was changing clothes in the other room. He knew she was going to stop by this morning, but he didn't tell me. He stayed over last night because we were out late with my family. I think he wanted her to show up and think we slept together, even though we didn't."

"Did she think that?" Marcy asked.

"Yes, I tried to explain, but she didn't believe me. She left and won't answer her cell phone. I need to find her. I don't know where she lives, but she did say she was going out to a club tonight. I'm hoping you two might know where I could look for her."

Marcy took the phone book out of a kitchen drawer. "Well, I do have a couple of lesbian hangouts in mind. If I can't find the addresses here, I'll check the Web. By the way, you're not going alone. Beth and I are going with you."

"Honey, it's been years since we've been to a club. Besides, how can you be sure she's going to a lesbian bar?" Beth asked.

Marcy flipped through the pages of the phone book. "Think back to the days before yours truly came into your life." She pointed to herself. "Now, what would you do if you were feeling the need to soothe a broken heart?" She answered before Beth could. "That's right, you'd go searching for a little comfort elsewhere. Believe me, Madison's not going to find the kind of comfort she needs in a straight bar, now will she?"

"I guess not." Beth squeezed Isabella's hand. "We'll help you find her. Why don't you go home and try to take a nap since you were awake most of the night. Meet us here at nine this evening, and we'll drive."

"In the meantime," Marcy said, "I'll figure out where we should go. I think this could be a lot of fun. You'll find Madison, and Beth and I will be reminded that being in our early forties doesn't mean we're too old to go out and have a good time every now and then."

Chapter 12

Bobbie rested her elbows on the bar at the Camilla Club. "Karen and Jackie will be here soon. I hope that cheers you up. You okay?"

Madison nodded. "Yeah, I'm fine. I can't believe she slept with him and didn't think it would bother me. Then she lied about it." She shifted her position away from the bar and faced the crowd. "I plan on having a good time tonight, no matter what. I refuse to think about Isabella or the Army. Tonight, I don't care about either one."

Madison gave the attractive brunette watching her every move a smoldering glance. "I may even have a great time tonight. Maybe she'll be enough to help me forget everything, at least for one night." She sauntered toward the brunette who grinned at her approach.

Bobbie said under her breath, "You and I both know that it doesn't work that way." She waved to Jackie and Karen when they came in. They made their way through the crowd to Bobbie. She hugged each of them.

"Where's Madison?" Karen asked.

Bobbie motioned to the dance floor. "Trying to ignore her heart."

They watched Madison out on the dance floor with the sexy woman. Their bodies moved sensuously close together despite the fast speed of the song.

Jackie studied Madison for a moment. "What I wouldn't give for a fraction of whatever it is Madison's got that drives women wild. She could have any available woman in here and probably even some of the taken ones, too."

Bobbie sighed. "The problem is that the woman she really wants isn't here."

* * *

Marcy parallel parked her Toyota Prius on a side street in Boston's South End. "All right, girls, here's the plan. There are two bars on the street next to this one about two blocks away from each other. A friend said that the mixed bar sometimes has women's night and is worth a quick look first since it's on our way. Then we'll go over to the Camilla Club, which is considered the women's bar in the city."

Beth looked at Isabella. "Are you sure you want to do this?"

Marcy laid her hand on Beth's arm. "Don't talk her out of it now. Come on, Isabella, it'll be fun. Don't worry. We'll make sure you get home safe and sound. No matter what happens, we promise."

"What exactly is a mixed bar?" Isabella asked.

Marcy got out and opened the car door for Isabella. "It's a bar that's for both gay men and lesbians. Out with you, scaredy cat, let's go."

They walked to the Club Mystic and went inside. Isabella knew immediately they weren't in a place they'd find Madison. The inside of the club was dark, but the strobe light above the dance floor made it intermittently light enough to see that this was a mixed club. Only not the kind they were searching for. The patrons were mostly men, many dressed in drag.

Isabella was transfixed. "These guys are gorgeous."

"Yeah, and they sure can dance," Marcy said. "If straight men moved like that and were half as good looking, straight women wouldn't stand a chance of saying no to them."

Beth took Marcy's hand. "Your research abilities aren't inspiring much confidence, honey. I thought we were looking for lesbians."

"Hey, it's only the first stop. Let's at least get a drink while we're here," Marcy said.

"I agree with Marcy," Isabella said. "I could use a drink. These guys are worth watching for a little while anyway." Isabella motioned to the bare-chested bartender who was wearing tight black jeans and a collar around his neck. His physique was flawless, yet his perfection didn't do a thing for her.

He strolled over. "You girls are barking up the wrong tree if you're here trolling for available men. If you haven't noticed already, this is a gay club."

Marcy leaned against the bar and winked at him. "Oh, we're definitely not here for men. We've only got women on our minds. We thought we'd stop here for a quick drink to watch some great dancing. After that, we'll head up the street to where the real girl-on-girl fun is. You know, the Camilla Club."

"That's what I've heard," he said with a grin.

Beth rolled her eyes at Marcy. "You lawyers are so full of yourselves. All right, Casanova, why don't you order me a Perrier with lime, and I'll be the designated driver. I'm going to have to keep an eye on both you and Isabella tonight."

"You two are such soul mates. The way you bicker and worship each other all at the same time," Isabella said. "I hope I find a soul mate to call my own someday." Her stomach muscles tightened. She thought of Madison. Isabella needed something to calm her nerves. To the bartender she said, "I'll have a sour apple martini, please."

"Coming right up, sweetheart."

When he handed it to her, she took several long swigs until it was gone.

"You drank that awfully fast," Marcy said. "Guess you're ready to hit the road."

Beth finished her drink and paid the bartender. "Let's go, girls."

They said their good-byes to the bartender and headed down the street toward the Camilla Club. Once inside, Isabella took in the room. Marcy said, "Now, this is the place."

The club was packed wall to wall with women. The crowd was diverse, ranging from butch to chic lipstick lesbians. Maybe it was the martini, but Isabella felt at home and drawn to the female energy that emanated from the dance floor. She scanned the place for Madison. She had a feeling Madison was here, somewhere in this crowd of women.

They moved to the bar to get out of the way of the gyrating female bodies on the dance floor.

Marcy raised her voice above the heavy bass of the music. "What's with the furrowed brow, Beth?"

"This music. What the hell is it? Have you ever heard this stuff before? How can they possibly dance to this? It sounds like someone banging pots together."

"Oh, Beth, you sound like you're sixty-two instead of forty-two. That, my love, is P!nk and the song is called 'So What.' I think it's excellent."

"How do you know who that is?" Beth asked.

"One of us has to keep up with modern culture."

When P!nk's "So What" finished, the music changed to Madonna's dance hit, "Music." Isabella teased Beth, "Please tell me you know who this is?"

"Of course I do. Who doesn't know the material girl?"

The bartender with neatly cut salt-and-pepper hair asked, "What kind of music do you like?"

Beth answered, "A little Prince, a little Sheila E, a whole lot of Wendy and Lisa, but when I'm feeling particularly nostalgic, I prefer Joan Jett and the Blackhearts."

"Ah, a woman after my own heart." The bartender appeared to be reminiscing. "Those were good times. Let me get you ladies a drink. After, I'll whisper your pleasure into the DJ's ear." She took their drink requests.

Isabella ordered another martini. Her nerves were so on edge she barely noticed the effects of the first one. The second one went down too easily.

The opening beat of a new song Isabella had never heard before boomed around the room. Beth bobbed her head to the beat. "Oh yeah, now this is more like it. Wendy and Lisa's "Waterfall," something I can dance to." She mouthed a thank-you to the bartender.

"Go dance, you two," Isabella said. She pulled a bar stool over and sat down. "I'll stay here and watch for Madison."

"You sure?" Marcy asked.

"Yes, I'll be fine. Don't worry. I'm not going anywhere."

Isabella leaned against the bar and sipped the final swallow of her drink as she watched Beth and Marcy make their way to the dance floor hand in hand. Entranced by all the women dancing with women, she hardly noticed the tall dark-haired butch woman pull up a stool next to her.

"Hi, I'm Samantha, but everyone calls me Sam. I don't think I've ever seen you here before."

Sam's demeanor suggested she might be interested in something other than conversation. She shamelessly scanned the length of Isabella's body. Sam had a muscular build with short spiky black hair. Tattoos covered her arms. Oddly, Isabella found her attractive in a lustful kind of way. Since meeting Madison, she was discovering that strong, confident women appealed to her.

Sam moved her arm so that it brushed Isabella's. "Can I buy you a drink?"

Appeal aside, Isabella wasn't interested in anyone other than Madison. She didn't want to be rude or hurt her feelings, though. "Sure, a drink would be nice, thanks."

Sam got the bartender's attention and pointed to Isabella's empty martini glass. "Are you here alone, because if you are, I'd really love to dance with you."

Now what? "I'm not here alone, exactly. My friends are here with me. They're out dancing."

Sam scooted her bar stool closer to Isabella's. "Does this mean you don't have a girlfriend?"

Isabella took the martini from the bartender and thought long about the question. *Do I have a girlfriend? Maybe the question should be do I want to have a girlfriend?* Abruptly, Isabella answered, "No, I don't." That probably wasn't the best answer to give to sultry Sam. She imagined what the words she was about to say would sound like coming out of her mouth. "There's a woman I'm interested in, though. I came to see her. I need to know if she feels the same way about me."

"Mm, mm, mm." Sam shook her head. She hopped off the stool to face Isabella. She leaned down and put her hands on the bar so that her arms touched either side of Isabella's body. Only inches away, Sam whispered into her ear, "I hope when she sees you she realizes how lucky she is. If you were my girlfriend, we wouldn't be here. I'd have you some place cozy and warm, just the two of us. You'd be begging me for more of everything I can give you." Sam stepped back, taking all of the oxygen in the air with her. "I'll be around if she doesn't show up."

Isabella forced a deep breath into her oxygen-starved lungs. She blinked back disbelief as Sam strolled away. First, she couldn't believe that a woman would be so bold in trying to pick up another woman. Second, Sam brazenly violated her space. And third, the part most shocking was that, for a split second, she envisioned being someplace cozy and warm and begging Madison for more. She glanced around for Beth and Marcy. Maybe it was time to call this whole thing off before things went too far. They were already getting way too intense.

She picked up the martini and took a long swig of the sweet, potent liquid. Its warmth burned her throat but calmed her frazzled nerves. She finished most of the drink and reached around to put the glass down onto the bar. When she turned back to face the crowd, she saw her. There Madison was, across the room, sitting at a booth with Bobbie and three other women, one of whom had her hands all over Madison. Isabella continued to watch, astonished when the woman kissed Madison's neck. Madison returned the affection by putting her mouth on the woman's lips.

Isabella didn't know whether to laugh or cry. *She was furious with me over a misunderstanding about Ben. But this is okay?* She was definitely going to get the hell out of this bar now, but not before Madison got a piece of her mind.

Bobbie was the first to notice Isabella approach. She yanked hard on the sleeve of Madison's shirt.

"Jeez, what is it?"

"A pissed off Isabella," Bobbie said.

"What?" Madison asked.

Isabella put her hands on her hips. "Hello, Madison."

Madison extricated herself from the brunette's embrace. "What are you doing here?"

"Obviously, I'm not having as good a time as you are. It didn't take you long to get over me. Maybe it's because kissing women you hardly know is something you do on a regular basis." She ignored the brunette next to Madison.

"You have no idea what it meant for me to kiss you."

"Oh really? Then how do you explain kissing her?" Isabella nodded at the brunette.

The brunette stood and said, "Obviously you've got some issues to resolve with your girlfriend here. I've got better things to do with my time than be a part of this scene." She walked away.

"Kissing you mattered," Madison said. "Kissing her didn't. I only wanted to forget about you."

Isabella heard the pained sincerity in Madison's voice. She took a step nearer to the table. The energy between them whenever they were close took over. Madison's dark blue eyes captured her. *She stops my heart every time I look at her.* The third martini had eliminated Isabella's inhibitions. Her anger aside, she wanted to dance with Madison and be the one Madison kissed. Without breaking eye contact, she said, "I needed to find you."

The music, the talking, the laughter, all the sounds of the club faded into the background.

"Why did you come to find me? What about Ben? Shouldn't you be with him right now?"

The sound of the word, *Ben,* coming off Madison's lips, cut like a knife. "I tried to tell you that nothing happened with him and me, but you wouldn't listen."

"That's because it's none of my business who you sleep with. And I don't want to care. Go home to your boyfriend and spare me the heartache."

Madison's blunt words made Isabella want to cry. "There are lots of things I don't understand right now. What I am sure of is that I had to see you again." Desperate and not sure what to do to convince Madison to talk to her, Isabella took a cue from Sam's come-on earlier. What did she know about picking up women? It was a good thing she had the martinis to give her courage. Standing in front of the table where Madison sat, Isabella rested her palms on it, and leaned down until she was only inches above her. She was aware that the low-cut blouse she was wearing would reveal a line of cleavage as she leaned over Madison.

Isabella caught Madison stealing a glance at what Isabella purposely meant for her to see.

"I... I..." Madison stammered.

"*Balla con me*," Isabella purred.

Bobbie poked Madison in the ribs. "It's a good thing for you that I took those Italian language classes in college. I think she asked you to dance."

"I did," Isabella said.

Bobbie nudged Madison. "What are you waiting for?"

Madison stood.

Isabella reached a hand out to her. Her breath went shallow with Madison's warm hand in hers. She took a moment to drink in the sight of her. The top two undone buttons of Madison's shirt revealed enough skin to make Isabella long to see more. "I want to feel your arms around me."

Madison led her to the dance floor without a word. She turned and pulled Isabella close. They moved slowly to music all their own. Madison didn't have to speak for Isabella to understand her thoughts. Her eyes communicated her desire. She put a hand on Isabella's neck and caressed it with her thumb.

Isabella tilted her head back to invite more of Madison's touch. She longed for the contact. Madison traced a line with her index finger from her chin down to the opening of Isabella's blouse. "Madison," Isabella said and exhaled. The drumming music stopped, and a slow sultry ballad filled the room. Isabella was sure she'd melt into the floor when Madison intimately pressed her body into hers.

Isabella wrapped her arms around Madison's neck. Madison slid her hands up along either side of Isabella's torso. Her hands passed close to Isabella's breasts.

Madison's breath warmed her cheek. "I love how you smell." She kissed Isabella's neck.

Isabella struggled to keep upright when the tip of Madison's tongue made contact with her skin. She moved her head to meet Madison's lips with her own. They kissed each other softly. Isabella pulled away to see into Madison's eyes. She brought a hand up and placed it on the side of Madison's face. "Your lips are the softest things I've ever touched."

Madison kissed the palm of Isabella's hand. "I promise you, there are softer things than that."

Her words raced straight to the place that cried out most for Madison's touch. Isabella had no inhibitions at the moment to slow her body's craving. She had to know what it felt like to touch Madison, to be touched by her. "I need to be with you," Isabella whispered. She leaned in and kissed Madison hard. The intimacy of their tongues moving together left her drunk with wanting. A little voice inside Isabella's head reminded her that she had her hands and mouth all over a woman in a public place. The three martinis and loud sultry music worked wonders to drown out that pesky little voice.

Madison slid both hands into Isabella's thick soft curls and grabbed handfuls as she pressed her body harder against Isabella's.

Isabella moaned her pleasure.

Madison was the first to break their impassioned embrace. She took Isabella by the hand and pulled her off the dance floor into a darkened corner of the room. Things were moving at lightning speed, but Isabella couldn't resist Madison, nor did she want to. Madison pushed her up against a wall and ran her hands up Isabella's sides from her waist to her shoulders, this time her thumbs made contact with Isabella's breasts. Then she pushed her leg between Isabella's.

Isabella gasped, "Please, take me home. I want you to touch me, anyplace and everyplace." A hot dizzy wave rushed up the back of her neck. *I'm going to faint.*

"I want to make love to you," Madison whispered. She closed her eyes and savored the feel of Isabella's body grinding against hers. Even though her brain screamed that this would end badly, her need was too great to stop what was happening between them. She rationalized that they were grown women with the free will to sleep with whomever they chose, Isabella included. Madison cupped Isabella's breasts. She put her lips next to Isabella's ear and said, "I came with Bobbie. She can take my car. We'll go to your place."

Isabella didn't answer. Instead, her body relaxed. Madison's desire turned to worry. She pulled away. Isabella was pale and clammy. "What is it?"

Isabella's voice was weak. "I think I drank too much and it's caught up to me. I probably better sit down. I'm feeling a little sick."

Madison's heart sank as she helped Isabella to a nearby bar stool. Growing up with an alcoholic father had taught her that, under the influence, people did a lot of things they wouldn't otherwise do. *None of this was about wanting me.* The realization that Isabella was drunk left her feeling that she'd have made a giant mistake if she'd gone home with her. "Isabella, where are your keys? I'll still take you home, but that's all."

Isabella put an arm around Madison's neck. "No, I want you to stay with me."

Madison removed it. "Not when you're like this."

Isabella sat up straight. "What is it with you? Why do you draw me in, only to push me away?" She rubbed the top of Madison's thigh. "All I want to do is talk about these feelings I have for you. I'm trying to understand them."

Madison grabbed Isabella's hand to keep from breaking her resolve. "I know, but talking might not be what either of us wants right now. I don't trust myself to be alone with you." She kissed Isabella's forehead. "You have to believe that my feelings for you are real. I'm not ready to take the chance that yours are nothing more than a drunken experiment with your sexuality."

Isabella shook her head. "God, you sound like Ben or my father, telling me what I feel and don't feel. I'm so sick and tired of that. I thought you were different."

"I am different, and I shouldn't make assumptions, but you've apparently had a lot to drink tonight. At least part of your actions come from the alcohol. I only want the part that comes from your heart. Right now, I can't tell the difference."

Isabella turned pale as a ghost. "I think I'm going to be sick."

"Do you want me to take you to the ladies' room?"

"No, I just need to rest a minute. Will you stay with me?" She slumped against Madison.

Madison put her arms around Isabella to keep her from sliding off the stool. "Of course. I'm still going to make sure you get home safely." Madison looked up to see two women looming over her.

"I wouldn't be so sure about that," the shorter of the two said. "You probably don't remember me, but I work with Isabella. Whatever it is you're up to, you can get it out of your mind. Isabella's coming home with us."

"I'm sorry for my spouse's rudeness," the other woman said. "I'm Marcy and this is Beth. We're Isabella's friends. She came with us, and we promised we'd get her home."

"Regardless of what you think, my only intention was to make sure she was taken care of. I'd never take advantage of her, if that's what you're implying," Madison said.

"Seriously?" Beth asked. "With the way you had her up against the wall over in the corner? It's one thing to watch our supposedly straight friend fall for a woman and know what she's going to have to go through with that process, but a player on top of it all?"

Madison breathed a sigh of relief when Bobbie appeared at the edge of the group.

"Trust me," Bobbie said. "Madison is definitely not a player. I know you're concerned about your friend, because I feel the same about mine. Why don't we give these two a moment alone to say good-bye? Then, I'll take my friend home and you can take yours."

Madison gave Bobbie a grateful look. "Thanks, Bobbie, for looking out for me. They were just doing the same for Isabella."

Beth took Marcy's hand. "I didn't mean to overreact. I'm only worried about how Isabella is going to get through all of this. You have no idea how powerful a force her family is in her life. Don't hurt her. That's all I ask. We'll be over there when you're ready to leave." She nodded toward the end of the bar.

"Thanks, I'll be just a minute," Madison said. Beth, Marcy, and Bobbie gave them some space.

Madison brushed the hair away from Isabella's face and kissed her forehead.

Isabella's voice slurred. "I'm sorry."

Madison hugged her tighter. "Don't be." She felt Isabella relax even more against her. "You'd be so easy to love," Madison said. "Maybe I already do." She savored the feel of holding Isabella in her arms for a little while longer and then motioned for the others.

As Madison helped Beth and Marcy hoist Isabella to her feet, she said, "I really do care about her. I'm sorry things got so out of hand tonight."

"She cares about you, too. And if you really do care about her, you'll call her soon," Beth said.

Madison didn't know how to respond. *What am I doing?*

Chapter 13

Caught somewhere between sleep and wakefulness, Isabella inhaled an unfamiliar scent. Instinct told her the pillow her head rested on wasn't her own. It didn't smell like hers. It didn't have the same feel. She was lying on her right side. She pushed her palm down into the mattress. It was too soft. A fragmented memory flashed in her mind. She was in a bar. The music was loud but fit the circumstance. It was an integral part of the whole scene being replayed in her mind. Her back was up against a wall. She was kissing someone with reckless abandon. The beat of the music, the beat of her heart, the aching need reverberating through her body, all came together in a wild crescendo. She remembered that she liked it... liked it a lot. More, she wanted more of this person pressed against her.

Isabella's eyes shot wide open. The light coming through the bedroom window penetrated like daggers. She squeezed them closed. *Oh my God, I was kissing Madison. What did I do last night?* A rush of panic brought her completely awake. Where was she? Still, she kept her eyes closed to the awful light. She reached down and realized she was wearing a T-shirt and shorts. They were too baggy on her to be hers. Whose clothes was she wearing?

She rolled onto her stomach and spread both arms out across the bed. No one else was there. At least she was alone. This time, slowly, she opened her eyes and allowed them to adjust to the piercing sunlight that came through the window. She tried to focus on something other than the brightness of the rays. She spotted a photograph sitting on the table next to the bed. It was a picture of Marcy with her college lacrosse team. Isabella breathed a sigh of relief. She was at Beth and Marcy's, thank God.

Her reprieve was short-lived. A wave of nausea crept from her stomach up to her throat. Her head pounded with such ferociousness, she was sure it might explode. She curled into the fetal position, hoping the queasiness would subside. As she lay there with her eyes closed, she tried to remember the rest of the night. But the memory was too foggy, beyond the kissing and touching against the wall. She worried that she'd made a fool of herself. Another wave of nausea bubbled to the surface. This time it wasn't going to stop at her throat. She flew out of bed and into the guest bathroom. She made it in time to be sicker than she could remember being in a long time.

Afterward, she turned on the shower and waited for the water to get warm. She took off her clothes and stood still under the spray while another wave of nausea passed. The shower seemed to help her terrible headache. The threats from her stomach were fewer and farther between as well.

Feeling better, she toweled off and pulled a clean pair of sweatpants and a T-shirt out of the top drawer of the bureau in the bedroom. The thick, clean cotton against her skin eased her discomfort. Still shaky, she made her way gingerly down the stairs to the kitchen to face Beth and Marcy.

When she walked into the room, Beth said, "We were starting to worry about you until we heard the shower."

"How's your head?" Marcy asked.

Isabella eased into a kitchen chair. "Awful, but it's not as bad as my stomach. I don't remember the last time I was that sick. A martini will not be on my list of things to drink any time soon."

"Maybe if you stick with one next time, it wouldn't be that bad," Marcy said.

Isabella pinched the bridge of her nose. "I might never drink anything again. Thank you for bringing me home with you last night. I hope I didn't embarrass you too much."

Beth went to the counter, took a piece of dry toast out of the toaster, and poured a cup of black coffee. "We've all gotten a little crazy after one too many drinks." She placed the toast and coffee in front of Isabella. "You should try to eat something." She sat back down. "What happened between you and Madison last night anyway? Did you talk at all?"

"You have to ask? Wasn't it obvious?" Isabella nibbled the toast.

Marcy gently punched Isabella's arm. "The only communication I saw was your hormones screaming."

Isabella recalled being helped to the bar stool by Madison after she started to feel faint. She remembered being angry because Madison refused to take her home and the reason she said she wouldn't. She'd never forget what happened next. "Madison told me she might be in love with me."

"You're kidding. What did you say?" Beth asked.

"I didn't say anything. If I had, I would've told her I fell in love with her the day we met. I didn't know it for sure until last night. I've never felt this way about anyone."

Marcy rocked back in her chair. "You're sure full of surprises this weekend. I never would've guessed you'd come over to our side. We're glad to have you on the team."

Isabella's head pounded and her stomach churned, but not all of it was from the lingering aftereffects of too much alcohol. "I don't know what I'm supposed to do next. This is all foreign to me. I don't know the rules."

"There are no rules," Beth said. "All you can do is buckle up for the ride. Falling in love with a woman is the easy part. Dealing with the fallout is what's hard. And believe me, there's always fallout. A lot of things, like the bonds with your family that you think are unbreakable, might fracture over this. It doesn't make sense, but that's the way it happens too often. What you need to do next is talk to Madison about how you feel. Get everything out on the table. Go from there."

"I'm sure my family isn't going to like the idea, but they'll come around. They love me. That'll be enough, right?" Isabella asked.

"I don't know," Beth said. "I hope so. For now, figure things out with Madison. That should be your focus. We'll take you home so you can call her."

* * *

Madison helped Bobbie and Jerome put the lunch leftovers away. She was glad Bobbie convinced her to come over. It helped to talk about what had happened with Isabella. The coming week, she was scheduled to be away for training at Fort Bragg in North Carolina. The week after, she'd be on leave at home in Boston.

"Thanks for your advice, Bobbie," Madison said as she closed the refrigerator door. "You're probably right. Isabella and I need to spend some time alone without any distractions or interference." She leaned against the kitchen counter. "Maybe she'll agree to spend some time with me while I'm on leave the week after next when I get back from Fort Bragg."

Madison's cell phone rang. She reached into her bag sitting beside the kitchen table, pulled it out, and checked the caller ID. "It's Isabella."

Bobbie grabbed Jerome's arm. "You better answer it. We'll be in the other room."

"Okay." Madison waited for one more ring, took a deep breath, and flipped her phone open. "Hello."

There was a long silence. "Hi, Madison. It's me, Isabella. Do you have a minute to talk?"

Madison sat on one of the chairs near the table. "I'm glad you called. I was planning to call you later this afternoon anyway."

"If this isn't a good time, we could talk later."

Madison felt her knees go weak. Good thing she was sitting. "No, now is fine."

Isabella hesitated. "I... I don't know where to start. I'm sorry for the way I acted last night. I hope you know it's not a habit for me to get drunk like that. My nerves got the better of me."

Madison closed her eyes in disappointment and rested her head against the wall behind her chair. *Here we go.* It was as she feared. Isabella, the straight woman, was about to apologize for leading her on... for wanting her when she should've been elsewhere, like with her boyfriend. In a minute, she'd hear Isabella say it was the alcohol that made her do those things that had melted Madison's heart at the bar. She couldn't bear to hear it. "Isabella, stop. You don't have to apologize. What happened between us was as much my fault as it was yours. It won't happen again. I hope we can still be friends, because I'm sorry, too."

The silence on the other end of the line was broken by Isabella's sobs.

Madison sat up straighter. A shot of pain punched her in the gut at the thought that Isabella was crying over the guilt she must feel for her lesbian misadventure. "Isabella, it's all right. Please stop crying. You don't ever have to see me again if that will help."

"God, that's not what I want," Isabella said through the sound of her tears.

"Tell me what you do want, and I'll do it." Madison braced for the reality that she was only an experiment.

"Madison, there's so much I want to say to you, but I don't want to say it over the phone. I wanted more than anything to go home with you last night." A thick silence separated them. "But I'm glad you said no. Because if you hadn't, and something happened between us, you'd still be wondering whether my feelings for you were real."

"What about Ben?"

"I told you, nothing happened that night before you saw him at my condo. I really wish you'd believe me. We were out late with my family, and I didn't want him to drive home after all the wine he'd had." Isabella paused. "I did think about sleeping with him, though."

"Why, if you don't love him?"

"I was confused about my feelings for you, and I needed clarity."

"You should've at least called me so I wouldn't have had to see him like I did."

"I would've called you if I'd gotten your message. I figured out later that Ben erased it. He suspects something's going on between us. He obviously wanted you to be upset, and it worked. Don't let him come between us again. I promise that I won't."

"I'm sorry I didn't trust you. Did you find the clarity you were looking for?"

"I did. I couldn't sleep with him because all I could think about was you. He's not who I want to be with. You are."

Madison pushed her fear of getting in too deep aside. "Isabella, I have to leave town tomorrow morning for a week. I'm taking a short leave at home when I come back. Would you like to stay with me for a couple of days over the weekend?" She didn't want Isabella to think the request had to do with anything other than talking. "I have a spare bedroom. It's small, but it's comfortable. We could spend some time just getting to know each other better."

"I'd really like that," Isabella said.

Madison stared up at the ceiling. Isabella was a beautiful blue-green ocean that she was about to jump feet first into. She prayed there wasn't an undertow lurking beneath the surface. "I'll be flying back from North Carolina on Friday night. I could pick you up on my way home from the airport."

"If you can get a ride to the airport tomorrow, I could pick you up instead. That way you wouldn't have to spend any of your vacation time driving me back to the North End."

Madison liked the idea. If, for some reason, Isabella wanted to back out, it would be more difficult if she'd already promised to give her a ride home from the airport. She'd be forced to talk to her in person even if she got cold feet. "Okay, great. Let me give you my flight details." She dug them out of her bag and read them off. "Meet me at the baggage claim area next Friday, okay?"

After hanging up, Madison went into the living room. Bobbie peeked up from the magazine she was pretending to read. "You were on the phone a long time. Is everything all right?"

Madison dropped into the chair next to the couch. Jerome never looked away from the basketball game he was watching on TV. "More than all right. Can you give me a ride to the airport tomorrow morning?" Madison knew she was grinning, but she couldn't help herself.

"Sure, but I thought you were taking your own car. What changed? The Army isn't making you stay longer, is it? I hope this duty thing you have to go to doesn't have anything to do with going back to Iraq."

The grin on Madison's face faded. She didn't want to think about the possibility of returning to Iraq. "No, I'm still coming home on Friday. Isabella's going to pick me up. She's going to stay with me over the weekend."

"Well, well, my dear, it appears as though a little gambling has finally paid off."

"Too soon to tell, but I sure hope so," Madison said.

Chapter 14

Standing in the baggage claim area at Logan International Airport, Isabella checked the monitor that showed when the day's Continental flights would be arriving. Madison's flight, from Raleigh/Durham, North Carolina, had landed. Isabella scanned the baggage claim area, looking for her.

Despite a healthy dose of nerves, Isabella couldn't wait to see the tall, stunning, sandy-blonde soldier who had stolen her heart. There were still a million things to figure out, but for now, all that mattered was spending time with Madison. Isabella's heart was in complete control anyway. Any practical advice that came from her head to reconsider their weekend together was swiftly dismissed.

The excitement generated by the prospects of being in love for the first time outweighed the fears associated with the fact that the person she'd fallen for was a woman. Complicated though it was, it wasn't any less real or exhilarating than if Madison were a man. For so long, something had been missing, but all that changed when Isabella met Madison. She continued to search the crowd for the one person she most wanted to see.

She started to worry. The throng coming down the stairs had thinned, and there was still no sign of Madison. She studied the clusters of people around the baggage carousel, thinking maybe she had somehow missed her. Then she heard a small child off to her right say in an excited voice, "Mommy, there's a lady soldier." She turned and saw the little boy pull his hand from his mother's and run toward the stairs.

Madison was coming down them. Wearing her desert Army combat uniform, she appeared strong, confident, and as always, beautiful.

Isabella restrained her desire to throw her arms around her and hold her tight. There were too many people watching for such a public display of affection. She waved instead, sure that anyone watching closely would have seen the wordless exchange between them that spoke volumes.

The small boy stepped into Madison's path with his arms outstretched. His mother was close on his heels.

Isabella stood captivated. Up until now, her only connection to the war had been nightly news reports. Now a piece of its substance was playing out in front of her.

Talk about a reality check. This woman with whom she'd fallen in love was a soldier in a time of war. She'd served in Iraq. For all Isabella knew, there was a possibility she could be sent back. Madison was, for all intents and purposes, owned by the United States Army. What if she let herself love Madison in the face of so many obstacles only to lose her in the end to a war? Isabella's work with the veterans had taught her there were plenty of ways in which war could steal a person from the people they love.

The dark-haired child with chocolate brown eyes and skin looked to be about five years old. He reached up and tugged at the bottom of Madison's uniform blouse. "Were you in Iraq? Did you know my daddy?" The little boy's lip quivered. "Mommy said he's never coming home again. He stayed there with the angels."

Madison looked away from Isabella, who was now close enough to touch, and down at the boy. She was at a loss for what to do or say. She'd witnessed firsthand enough deaths in Iraq to know what it meant for a soldier to be with the angels instead of coming home to family.

The boy stared at her with pleading eyes that begged to know that everything was okay, that his father was okay, wherever he was. Madison's heart broke again, like it did every time she recalled all the soldiers she'd seen leave this world without the chance to say good-bye to loved ones. Now she was staring into the eyes of one of those left behind, a young boy begging for answers that might somehow help him feel the slightest bit of comfort.

The boy's mother grabbed his shoulders and pulled him away from Madison. The woman seemed angry—not at the boy for slipping away from her, but rather at the world for the unfair fate that had fallen on her. It was a subtle anger that Madison had seen other times.

"I'm sorry my son bothered you. I'm sure you've got other things to do. Of course you didn't know my husband. Iraq is a big place. You probably haven't even been there yourself." The woman's voice cracked as she held back tears. Anguish was written all over her face. "We're both still trying to learn how to cope with the loss. My son misses his father."

She smoothed the boy's hair tenderly. "Come on, Phillip, we need to get going." The mother gazed at Madison with a bottomless depth of sadness. "As I said, I'm sorry we bothered you. We'll be on our way."

Madison couldn't let them leave without doing something that would bring them some comfort. "It's okay. You're not bothering me." She knelt down in front of the boy so that she was eye-level with him. She placed her gear bag on the floor and laid the bouquet of flowers she carried on top of the bag. "What was your dad's name, and what unit did he serve in?"

The little boy squared his shoulders and stood up straighter before answering, "Sgt. Phillip Baxter of the 380th Airborne Field Artillery Unit, 82nd Airborne."

Madison reached down and touched the outside of the deep pocket on the right leg of her trousers. She could feel the ring she always carried inside the pocket of her uniform. Touching it brought back the memory of that soldier—the one she'd never forget for as long as she lived. While she worked hard to keep the memory at bay, in this moment she let it wash over her. It was as vivid as if it happened yesterday.

The sun had set over the outskirts of Fallujah. Even in the dark of night, the temperature and humidity inside the surgical tent were unbearable. The heat exacerbated the putrid smell of blood and sweat. Madison closed her eyes and tried to imagine the smell of fresh spring flowers instead. It didn't work.

She was serving in the multi-service base hospital at Camp Fallujah alongside fellow soldiers and marines. The hospital's key role was to stabilize seriously wounded soldiers before they were moved to hospitals in Baghdad and then onto Germany, or the States, if necessary. In the early days of the insurgency, after the fall of Baghdad, the surgical unit routinely found itself in situations where triage of injured soldiers was a necessity.

The unit was divided into four stations. The two busiest consisted of the one for soldiers with non-life-threatening injuries who could wait for treatment. The other was for those needing immediate care. The third station was for soldiers still alive but with little to no hope for survival. Soldiers who passed away, referred to as angels, were sent to the fourth station where their bodies would be cleaned and prepared for transport back home.

On this particular night, a call came in that a group of soldiers from the Army's Seventh Cavalry Regiment had been tasked with locating a group of insurgents known to be hiding in a cluster of houses within the city. As the soldiers neared the city in the dark of night, an improvised explosive device was detonated by an insurgent hiding in a nearby ditch. The ensuing battle killed the insurgents, but not before the soldiers had taken several casualties of their own.

Seven men were down and needed immediate transport to the base hospital's surgical unit. Two died in transit, three had non-life-threatening injuries, and two were grievously injured. The surgical unit staff kicked into high gear. Maj. Jim Barns, Capt. Madison Brown, and a small staff of medics coalesced around one of the two soldiers in dire need of immediate care.

The soldier, Lt. Scott Stevens, was losing blood faster than they could get it into him. Madison could feel the warm sickening wetness of it fill her boots and saturate her uniform as it fell and pooled on the floor. Amazingly, he was still conscious, despite his injuries and the drugs they administered to him. He grabbed Madison's wrist with a bloody hand and whispered, "I don't want to go. Don't let me die." She could see a fear in his eyes that was indescribable. In defiance of that fear, his tight grip on her wrist revealed that he was determined to fight with every last breath.

A medic pulled the soldier's hand away from Madison so she could continue to work. Dr. Barns ordered that he be given an anesthetic to calm him down and that he be prepared for surgery immediately. Once they had him opened up on the surgical table, it was clear there was too much damage to his vital organs to be able to put him back together before he died. Nevertheless, they tried their best. All they could really do was keep him as comfortable as possible until he passed from the ranks of the living into the army of angels who had gone before him.

After all the soldiers were cared for and the surgical unit was properly cleaned, things fell silent. It was two o'clock in the morning. Exhausted after having been awake for over twenty-one hours, Madison was filled with a despair that would never let her sleep. She went to where Lt. Scott Stevens lay dying and sat down by his bedside. Ever the fighter, he struggled to open his eyes.

The only movement he could muster was to wiggle the fingers on his hand near Madison. She reached out and took it in her own. Scott turned his head slightly to look at her. In a weak, barely audible voice, he said, "I know I'm going to be an angel soon and that you tried your best to save me. Don't be sad. I'm not afraid to go now."

Madison wanted more than anything to cry. But she never would. Here he was, on the verge of dying, something he desperately had not wanted to happen, yet he was trying to comfort her. She squeezed his hand and said, "Is there anything at all I can do?" She stood to release a dose of morphine from the bag of Ringer's solution hanging near his bed.

"Please, don't... as long as I feel pain, I know I'm still alive." He gave a sad smile. "I'm glad the last person I get to see is so kind. I only wish I had known love in this life. It wasn't meant to be for a gay man in the Army, though." He coughed and squeezed his eyes closed from pain. "How sad that I have to lay dying before I can admit that out loud. At least you're here with me. I won't have to die alone."

Madison sat back down on the chair and leaned over to kiss him on the cheek. Then she wiped the sweat from his brow with a damp cloth. "I promise I won't leave you."

"Where's my uniform?" Scott asked.

"Here, folded under the bed."

"Please, my West Point ring should be in one of the pockets. I want you to have it."

"I can't," Madison said.

"It's the only thing in this world I've ever been proud of." His energy was clearly fading. He said to her, "Please, take it. I want you to have it."

Madison shook her head. "No, Scott, I can't. Your family will want it." She found the ring in the left breast pocket of what was left of his uniform blouse. She placed it into his hand and closed his fingers over it.

A single tear ran down his face. "I don't have a family that will care, and since you're the last person I'll ever see, I want you to have it. I'm going to be an angel now. I want you to keep it to remember me and know that I'm somewhere watching out for you." He seemed to struggle to find the energy to speak his last words. "Please, honor a dying man's last request and keep the ring. It's how I'll keep you safe. I accept my fate as an angel." His smile was a little less sad. "That's what angels do, right?" He asked the question as if he were asking it to someone else in the room other than Madison.

"Okay Scott, I will."

Scott closed his eyes and drifted off into a fitful sleep.

Madison put the ring into her pocket and held his hand tightly. She was so tired. The chair she was sitting in couldn't have been more uncomfortable, but she would keep her promise. She would not let Lt. Stevens die alone.

Despite having never met this man before, Madison's grief over his imminent passing was overwhelming. She was heartbroken for him and all the others who had gone before, as well as those left behind. He had paid the ultimate sacrifice for a country that denied him the most basic human need: love. It was denied to him for no reason other than that he was gay. She was also sad for herself and the burdens of her own losses over the years. Was this how life was supposed to be? Surely, there had to be another way. Shortly thereafter, exhaustion claimed her and she fell asleep.

The next thing she remembered was feeling a gentle nudge to her shoulder. "Ma'am, wake up. Capt. Brown." She opened her eyes to see one of the medics standing in front her. "Ma'am, I'm sorry, Lt. Stevens is gone. Are you all right?"

Madison glanced at the lieutenant's lifeless body. She was still clutching his hand. Despite her slumber, she had somehow managed to not let go. Now that he was gone, she finally released his hand. "I'm okay. I'll leave you to tend to him." She stood and placed her hand in her pocket to clutch the ring. "Good-bye, Scott. I promise I'll never forget." Madison walked out of the tent. She breathed in the hot humid morning air of Iraq and tried to shake off the horror of the loss of another precious life.

Madison pulled her thoughts back to the present. No, she hadn't known the boy's father personally and hated to lie. But she did know the story of his father's last days—last moments—all too well. It was a story she'd seen played out so many times during those long, hot, miserable days in Iraq. In this case, a lie would do more good than harm. The boy had to believe that someone was watching out for him and his mom, and that his dad was more than okay... that he was safe with the angels.

Still crouched down in front of him, Madison put a hand on his shoulder. "Yes, I knew your dad. He was a brave man... a hero. He loved you and your mom with all of his heart. He always will."

The boy's eyes welled with tears. "Sometimes, I'm afraid because I miss him so much."

Madison pulled him into her arms. "I know. We all get scared. But you have to remember that your dad is still with you." She put her hand on his heart. "He's right there, forever."

"I wish I could hug him again." Tears ran down his face.

Madison's heart ached. Scott Stevens seemed to urge her on. She reached into her pocket and took out Scott's ring. "Your dad is with the angels now. They want you to have this." She held the ring in the palm of her hand for him to see. "Keep it with you to always remember him."

Madison put the ring into his hand. She struggled for composure. "You're brave, like your dad. Always take care of yourself and your mom, okay?" Madison stood and handed the bouquet of flowers to the boy's mother. "I'm sorry for your loss."

The mother, now quietly crying, hugged Madison. "Thank you for what you've given to my son. Please stay safe." She took the boy's hand and disappeared into the crowd.

As Madison watched them go, someone tugged at her sleeve. She turned to see Isabella. "Oh, Isabella, don't you cry, too." Madison wiped a tear from her cheek. "I'm so happy to see you."

"Me, too. Can I hug you?"

After reliving the memory of Lt. Stevens's death, there wasn't anything she'd rather do than fall into Isabella's arms. "I can't. Too many people are watching. I'm afraid they'll see right through how I feel about you."

"Later then?"

"I hope so. By the way, I owe you some flowers. The bouquet I gave away was for you."

"Thank you for thinking of me. She needed them more than I did. Besides, I have you instead."

Madison picked up her gear bag to thwart her desire to kiss Isabella right then and there. "I'd like to get out of here and out of this uniform."

"Sure. I'll bet you're hungry. Why don't we pick up a pizza along the way? I know a great place not too far from the highway."

* * *

An hour later, they arrived at Madison's house. On a quaint street, it nestled among a line of well-kept cottages on Great Neck, overlooking Plum Island Sound in Ipswich. The house was painted a pleasing pale yellow. Rather than a lawn, the diminutive yard was made up of perennial plants beginning to poke their heads above the surface in the mid-April warmth. Isabella imagined Madison tending to her summer flowers. The vision of the warrior nurturing Mother Nature's fragile bounty added to Madison's enigmatic charm.

"Your place is adorable," Isabella said as she shut off the engine.

Madison opened the car door. "Thank you. Let's get inside before the pizza gets cold." The sun was beginning to set, which meant the chill of the evening would soon replace the warmth of the day. "You grab dinner and I'll get the bags."

Isabella followed her inside. The glimmer off Plum Island Sound through the glass door at the back of the cottage captured her attention. "The view is spectacular. In fact, it's divine."

"I'm glad you like it. Let's leave the pizza in the kitchen, and I'll give you a tour. As you can see, it's small. It won't take too long. We'll make our last stop the deck."

Isabella put their pizza on the counter and followed Madison, who carried their bags to their rooms and showed her the rest of the house.

The place consisted of a small kitchen, living room, two bedrooms, and a bath, so the tour was, indeed, short.

"How long have you lived here?" Isabella asked when they were back in the living room.

"Almost four years now. I bought it at a bank auction. At the time, it needed a lot of work, but it was something I could afford. I did most of the renovations myself with the help of Bobbie's husband, Jerome." Madison walked to the sliding glass doors that opened onto a mahogany deck. "Come. I'll show you the view of the sound from outside."

They stepped out onto the deck and into the cool ocean breeze. Isabella put her hands in her pockets. "It's chilly."

Madison put her arm around her and pulled her close. "Pretty, isn't it?" she asked as they watched the rolling waves.

This new world that Isabella traversed had no signposts. It was a landscape yet to be charted. Even though her brain had no idea which way to go, her heart did. Being in love with a woman seemed the easiest and most natural thing in the world. She turned and embraced Madison. "It is, and so are you."

Madison placed her hands on either side of Isabella's face. She lightly brushed Isabella's lips with her own and then enveloped her in her arms. "You're cold. Let's go inside."

Isabella had always hoped she'd one day have such a profound connection to another person. It wasn't about physical desire, but the heart's deepest desire, the need to find home in the love of a soul mate. Isabella was anything but cold. "Sure."

Madison took her by the hand and led her to the guest bedroom. "I'm going to take a quick shower. Please make yourself comfortable. You're welcome to use the dresser drawers if you'd like to unpack your things. They're empty. First, I'll get a fire going in the wood stove so the house will be warm when we eat." She chuckled. "And we can reheat the pizza."

"I can tell you're tired. Don't worry about the fire. I'll get it started. You go shower while I get dinner ready." Isabella was still holding tight to Madison's hand.

Madison brought Isabella's hand to her face. She turned it over and rested her cheek next to its palm.

That simple act made Isabella long for her more. Her heart filled with such emotion for Madison. She closed the distance between them. They stood motionless, bodies touching, staring into the other's eyes. There was something haunted behind Madison's.

"Are you all right?" Isabella asked.

Madison rested her head on Isabella's shoulder. "I don't know."

"Is it my being here with you?"

"No. You can't imagine how happy I am that you're here."

"What is it then?" Isabella pulled Madison down so they were both sitting on the edge of the bed.

"I can't stop thinking about the little boy at the airport. I shouldn't have told him that his dad is still with him."

"Why?"

"Because I don't believe that love lasts forever. Pretending his dad lives on inside his heart won't bring him back. All I did was set him up for a hard fall when he realizes I lied to him. His father's gone. He died a cruel death and is never coming home again. That ring I gave him was nothing more than a reminder of that. I only prolonged his realization that, one way or another, people always leave you."

Isabella scooted back on the bed and beckoned Madison to come with her. Her work with veterans had taught her that their stories often went untold because they were too painful to tell. Isabella didn't want Madison to hold the memory inside. No good ever came from bottling up one's tragic past. "Do you want to tell me about the ring and what it meant to you?"

"I've never told anyone before."

"It might help to talk about it," Isabella said.

"I'm afraid if do, I'll fall apart."

"If that happens, I'll be here to hold you together. I promise."

Madison nestled into the safety of Isabella's arms and for the second time that day relived the death of Lt. Stevens. "We couldn't save him. He died all alone in this world."

Isabella smoothed Madison's hair. "No, he didn't. You were with him."

"I feel empty without the ring, sort of like I gave him away."

"Maybe you feel empty because the ring symbolized a hope that you're wrong about love? That his wish for himself is yours, too."

"I don't know." Madison buried her head in Isabella's shoulder as tears broke free.

Isabella held her tight while she cried. There was no place in the world she'd rather be than protecting this soldier from all her cares. In the quiet comfort of each other's arms, they fell asleep.

Isabella woke to Madison covering her with blankets. "You don't have to go." She longed to have her in her arms again.

"Yes, I do. I need to put our dinner in the refrigerator since we never ate it. I'm a terrible hostess."

"Talking seemed more important at the time."

"I know it's late, but we could eat now, if you'd like," Madison said.

"I'd rather you get back into bed with me and let me hold you."

Madison sat on the edge of the bed. "I'm sorry, Isabella. Not tonight. Thank you for listening. It meant a lot for me to tell you." She kissed Isabella lightly. "Sweet dreams."

Madison left before Isabella could protest. It would be so easy to follow her into her room and crawl into bed with her. There was no longer any question as to whether Isabella's feelings for a woman were real. The issue was what lay ahead. What if Madison's heart remained too frozen to let her in? Or what if she had to go back to Iraq? How would Isabella come out to her family? Could she come out to them? Too many questions, when all she really wanted in that moment was to fall asleep listening to the sound of Madison breathing. She slipped from underneath the covers and fumbled in the dark for comfortable clothes to sleep in.

Chapter 15

Madison tried to be quiet while Isabella slept. She'd have to remember to thank Bobbie for shopping for her while she was away. She rarely made dinner from scratch. Her cooking skills, if they could even be called that, were a disaster. She specialized in anything from a box that required adding water or thawing in the microwave. But really, how hard could cooking be? She had recipes that were clear enough and all the right ingredients were on hand. Well, mostly. She forgot to put breadcrumbs on the grocery list for Bobbie. Not to worry, she did have bread. If breadcrumbs were good enough to hold meatloaf together, bread might be even better. Madison was determined to show Isabella how special she thought she was by making a feast for her.

"Good morning." Isabella leaned against the frame of the entryway to the kitchen with her arms crossed over her chest. "I heard kitchen sounds and decided to investigate."

Madison fumbled in a drawer and wondered if the vegetables she cut for the salad were too big. "Hi, I hope you slept well. There's coffee in the pot, and cups are in the cabinet behind me. I hope I didn't wake you. I decided to put dinner together now. That way when we get back later, all we'll have to do is warm it in the oven." Isabella came into the room and stood near enough for Madison to smell her perfume. Madison dropped the knife she was holding. *Get it together*. She smiled.

Isabella poured herself a cup of coffee. "Can I do anything to help?"

"No, dinner is my treat this time. I've got some bagels, cream cheese, and fruit. Help yourself and go sit on the porch. The ocean is really beautiful this time of day. Take a blanket, though, it's breezy. I won't be long."

Madison hoped Isabella would leave the kitchen before she had a chance to witness her lack of culinary aptitude. Despite wielding surgical knives with precision as a trauma nurse, kitchen knives were a foreign concept—not to mention that Isabella was a dangerous distraction standing next to her in a T-shirt and sweatpants. It was achingly obvious she wasn't wearing a bra. Madison averted her eyes before running the risk of chopping off one of her own fingers with the damn knife. She plunged it into a carrot with the palm of her hand with more force than necessary. An end shot across the counter and nearly hit Isabella as she spread cream cheese on a bagel. *That ought to inspire confidence.* "Sorry about that."

Isabella laughed. "No worries. Is that a meatloaf you're making? I've never seen it made with whole pieces of bread before. It that a special Midwestern recipe?"

"No, I got it off of the Web." Madison paused. "I know what you're thinking. Who gets a meatloaf recipe from the Internet?"

"A lot of people, I bet. I'm sure it'll be delicious. I fixed a bagel for you. When you're finished, I'd love it if you'd join me."

"Thank you. I will. After we eat, we'll go over to Crane Beach for a walk along the shore, if you're up for it. The Parker River National Wildlife Refuge is there. It's one of my favorite places. The weather's supposed to be cool and unsettled. We'll probably have the whole beach to ourselves."

"That sounds lovely," Isabella said.

* * *

The rhythmic cadence of the lapping waves as they walked the length of Crane Beach helped to clear the cobwebs from Isabella's mind. Madison moved in silence beside her. A group of cormorants caught Isabella's attention. The way they worked together to catch fish and celebrate each successful dive reminded her of her family. Like the flock of sea birds, the Parisi family was at its best when they were all together. She reflected on what her family would think if they knew she'd fallen in love with a woman. She was pretty sure they weren't going to like it. Then again, they always said that it was her happiness that mattered.

They walked a bit farther down the beach. Madison had been right about them having it mostly to themselves. Other than a woman walking a dog in the distance, they were the only ones on the beach. Isabella took her hand. "Why did you leave last night?"

A long silence preceded Madison's answer. "Make sure you really want to know the truth before you ask."

"I want to know everything about you."

"I left because I don't want to fall in love with you."

Isabella stopped and tugged Madison to a halt. "Why?"

"I'm a coward. I don't want to give my heart to anyone." Madison pulled her hand free. "Love hurts too much when it goes away."

"But love doesn't have to go away, does it?"

"Everyone I've ever loved has left me." Madison looked intently at Isabella. "Aren't you afraid of what's happening between us?"

"Of course I am. I have more questions than answers. But one thing I'm sure of is how you make me feel. I've walked on beaches like this one countless times, and I always tried never to take its beauty for granted. This morning, here with you, it's not just beautiful, it's breathtaking. It's like you've lifted a veil that kept me from really seeing what was around me. Now, everything is so vivid, including my feelings for you." She took Madison's hand again. "You said I'd know love when it happened. It has. I don't know what the future has in store, but I know I'm in love with you."

"You've never been with a woman. How can you be so sure?"

"The same way you are." Isabella grabbed a handful of Madison's fleece jacket. "You probably don't realize I remember what you said to me at the bar, but I do. You told me you think you love me. Whether you want to run or not, that can't be undone. You feel it, too."

"I am in love with you, Isabella." Madison dropped Isabella's hand and took two steps away. "But I'm not convinced things could work between us. You deserve someone who isn't carrying around so much baggage. I don't think you understand the price either of us might have to pay if we give in to this."

Isabella closed the gap between them. "I'm willing to take my chances. I can't go back to going through the motions of pretending to love someone. Now that I've met you, I don't think I'll ever love anyone but you."

"That's easy to say when no one is telling you you're throwing your life away." Madison put her arms around Isabella. They held each other with no more words passing between them.

Sporadic drops of rain and dark clouds threatened to become a downpour. "I think the sky's about to open up on us," Madison said. "We'd better head back."

* * *

Isabella put the salad and mashed potatoes on the table next to an open bottle of wine while Madison took the meatloaf out of the oven. Isabella hated the tension surrounding them. She felt like they'd come to the first crossroads of their relationship. She was certain which path she wanted to take… if only Madison would let her. The smell of dinner filled the room. They sat down to eat.

"I forgot something." Madison went to the refrigerator and pulled the ketchup bottle from the shelf on the door. She put it on the table between them as she resumed her seat.

"What's that for?" Isabella asked.

Madison squirted a dollop onto her meatloaf. "Don't tell me you'd have preferred gravy."

"I don't think I've ever had ketchup on anything other than fries." Isabella squirted some on her meatloaf. "I'm willing to try it."

"Is it because you're Italian that you've never had it before?"

"If you'd ever tasted my Grandmother's tomato gravy, you'd understand." Isabella took a bite. It was edible, but not much more. Madison might be the worst cook in all of Massachusetts. "It's good."

Madison swallowed a mouthful and eyed Isabella. "You're being polite."

Isabella took a bite. "I don't know what you're talking about. I've never tasted anything quite like it." She swallowed it down. "I do have a question though. Did you use any salt or other seasonings for the meatloaf?"

Madison grinned. "Was I supposed to?"

Isabella laughed.

"We could warm up the pizza we didn't eat last night if you'd prefer that instead," Madison suggested.

"No, this is good. I want to eat it because you made it for me." Isabella's belly gurgled.

"Was that your stomach protesting?"

"Of course not, silly."

"Either you have the stomach of a junkyard dog, or you're the bravest woman I know. When you finish, I have dessert, too."

Isabella raised an eyebrow. "Did you make it?"

"Lucky for you it's a pound cake Bobbie picked up at the grocery store."

Isabella lifted another forkful. She stopped before putting it into her mouth. "Maybe we should start with dessert first."

"It's really bad, isn't it?"

"I thought I could handle it. It was sweet of you to go to so much trouble." Isabella put her fork down." She held Madison's gaze. "I'm not that hungry now anyway."

"How can that be? We ate lunch hours ago."

"I think you know why," Isabella said.

Madison fixed her eyes on Isabella's empty wineglass. "Do you want more wine?"

"No, I don't."

Madison's hand shook as she stacked their plates. "Why don't I warm up the pizza? You have to eat something." She took their plates to the sink.

"I'm sorry if I upset you," Isabella said.

Madison busied herself with scraping their uneaten dinner into the garbage disposal. "You didn't."

Isabella feared that, even if Madison stayed in the room, she was on the verge of running away emotionally. She summoned her courage and confronted the issue head-on. "What is it then? Why do you keep running from me?"

With her back to Isabella, Madison gripped the edges of the sink. "I tried to tell you before, but you don't seem to want to hear it. Someone will be broken in the wake of us loving each other."

Isabella walked over to Madison. She stopped inches behind her and put her hand on Madison's waist. "And I'll ask you the same question I asked before. How can you be so sure?"

Madison continued to stare into the sink. "If we give in to our feelings, I suspect there's a strong likelihood that your family will make you choose between them and me. Whichever one you pick, the one not chosen will break. You can't win, Isabella. Once you're forced to make a choice like that, you'll break, too." She exhaled loudly. "I'm not trying to be cruel. It's just the reality as I see it." She pushed Isabella's hand away from where it had been resting on her waist and turned to face her. "Plus, I'm in the military. I'm not allowed to love you and keep my job."

"That's not true, Madison. We both know 'don't ask, don't tell' was repealed. They can't throw you out anymore for being a lesbian."

"I know what the law says. I've also seen how the military works. Just because the law has changed, don't think the way gays are treated has changed overnight. I might not get thrown out, but there are still enough people who think gays don't belong that they could make my life miserable if it was common knowledge."

"But you could take legal action against them."

"Yeah, and pay the price every inch of the way." She pressed her back against the edge of the counter. "I'm not interested in being at the forefront of trying to change old attitudes to keep up with the new law. I just want to do my job and be left alone."

Isabella tried to process everything Madison had said. What if she was right about Isabella's family? How could she possibly choose between them and the beautiful woman in front of her? Her brain cautioned her about inevitable heartache. Her heart urged her to heed the siren of love, and the rebellious drumbeat of her body's ache for Madison refused to be silenced.

She slipped her fingers underneath Madison's sweatshirt. She tentatively caressed the warm skin hidden below the heavy cotton. "Maybe you're right. I don't care if you are. Just please stop running from me, at least for one night."

"I'm so afraid," Madison whispered.

Isabella brought her other hand to the other side of Madison's torso. She leaned closer so that their bodies touched. "Don't be, because I'm not." Isabella put both hands on the silky plane of Madison's hard stomach. She let her pinky fingers slip below the waistband of Madison's jeans. Madison's body tensed under her touch. Isabella longed to break down Madison's walls to finally reach the nucleus of her heart.

"Isabella, please be sure this is what you want," Madison said.

"I've never wanted to be with anyone more." Isabella moved her hands higher. "I want to know what it's like to make love to you." Madison wasn't wearing anything underneath her sweatshirt. Isabella's body reacted unambiguously to the sensation of touching Madison's exquisite body. Her fingertips pulsed with the need to touch Madison everywhere. A blend of desire, nerves, and love made her dizzy. Time slowed as she moved closer to the point of no return.

Madison gripped the edge of the countertop. "Convince me you want to make love to me."

Isabella closed her eyes and savored the feel of Madison's skin under her touch. "If I do, will you let me explore all the things that make you a woman?" She moved a palm over the rigid nipple of one of Madison's breasts. Madison's whimper emboldened her. "I'm especially interested in the parts you promised were even softer than your lips." Searing desire doused any inhibition that remained. Loving Madison came as a powerful waterfall. Isabella captured both breasts in greedy hands that no longer cared what her brain had to say. This was the passion she craved. "So soft," she said and sighed.

Madison tilted her head back, inviting Isabella's discovery, "Keep doing what you're doing, and you'll find all of my softest places."

"No more running?"

"I'm yours. You can do whatever you like." Madison put her lips to Isabella's and kissed her. Their tongues mingled, unhurried.

Isabella unzipped the front of Madison's sweatshirt and slipped it off her shoulders. The sight left her breathless with wanting. "Tell me what to do."

Madison took Isabella's hands in her own and guided them back to her breasts. "Make love to me like it's the first time for both of us." She laced her fingers into Isabella's thick hair. "Put your mouth on me."

Isabella kissed Madison's lips, her neck, and the top of her chest down to the soft round flesh of a breast. She tasted Madison with the tip of her tongue.

Madison writhed against her. "You're so incredible."

"I love how your body reacts to me. I want all of it." Isabella fumbled with the button of Madison's jeans.

Madison grabbed her wrist. "Slower."

"No more waiting," Isabella said, breathless. She pulled her hand free and unfastened the button. "There's too much clothing between us. I want my skin on yours." She grasped the bottom of her own T-shirt and pulled it over her head. The hungry expression on Madison's face reminded her of her own starvation. She reached behind her back to unclasp her bra. Again, Madison took hold of her wrists.

"You were one of those kids, weren't you?"

"What kind of kid was that?" Isabella asked.

"The kind that rips their Christmas presents open so fast they never notice the wrapping."

Isabella didn't fight the hold that Madison placed on her. "You weren't?"

Madison used one hand to continue to restrain Isabella. "I never got many presents. So when I did, I savored the process of opening them as much as having what was inside them." She slipped her free hand under Isabella's bra and fondled the treasure it held. "Exactly how I intend to have you."

"Madison," Isabella whispered. It didn't matter that she'd never made love to a woman before. Her body knew the road even though it had never been on it. "Take all the time you need so long as we end up naked in your bed."

Madison let go of Isabella's wrists. "Count on it." She put her fingertips under the straps of Isabella's bra and slid them off her shoulders one at a time. Madison kissed the bare skin of each as she did. Then, she reached around and undid the bra's clasp. It fell to the floor. "God, you're the most beautiful woman I've ever seen." She filled her hands with Isabella's breasts. "Please, don't let this be a dream." She kissed Isabella hard with her mouth wide open.

A puff of air escaped Isabella's throat. No matter where Madison put her hands and mouth, the effect was the same. The intimate places of her body echoed with an urgent plea to be satisfied. "Make love to me."

"I intend to by kissing every inch of your body."

Isabella put her lips next to Madison's ear. "If you're going to kiss every inch of me, wouldn't it be easier without clothing in the way?"

"You're absolutely right. Not a single stitch." Madison unfastened Isabella's jeans and slid her hand into them. She stopped just short of Isabella's wet warmth.

Isabella tried to force Madison's hand lower. "Please."

"Not yet." Madison led her to the bedroom. They stopped at the edge of the bed. She eased Isabella down into a lying position. "Are you sure?"

"Yes, I love you." Isabella reached for her. She kissed Madison deeply. Every cell of her body was alive with the sublime feel of Madison's breasts pressed to hers. "Love me back."

"I do, and I will." Unhurried, Madison pulled off Isabella's jeans. She ran the palms of her hands from Isabella's ankles to the tops of her thighs. Her thumb brushed Isabella's throbbing center.

Isabella groaned, not from the faint touch, but from the lack of full satisfaction.

Madison slipped her fingertips under the waistband of Isabella's underwear and slid it from her body. She stood and removed the last of her own clothing.

Isabella watched in anticipation. A jolt of desire coursed through her at the sight of Madison's nakedness. Isabella opened herself, beckoning Madison to finally take her.

Madison rested between her legs. She moved against Isabella in a tantalizing cadence.

The friction caused Isabella's need to build. She raised her body in yearning. "Please, touch me."

Madison ran her tongue along Isabella's neck. "Where would you like to be touched?"

Isabella clenched the bed sheets. "Everywhere."

"Everywhere and back, I promise." Madison rolled so she was lying beside Isabella. She slowly traced the length of Isabella's body from her neck down to the top of her thigh with a fingertip. She caressed Isabella's need. "Is this what you want?"

Isabella tried to utter words. She arched her back and begged, "Please. Yes." She put her hand over Madison's and pressed it to her.

"You deserve everything I have." Madison's mouth and fingers moved in and over her in exquisite union, satisfying every desire. Isabella's sharp intake of breath drove Madison deeper.

Isabella's sweet release started as a low rumble, shaking gently at first until it exploded into an earthquake of sensation. She roared from the utter pleasure of it.

Madison stayed inside her until her tremors subsided. Then she moved back up the length of Isabella's body coming to rest in the comfort of her arms. She laid her head on Isabella's chest. "I could get used to the sound of your heart beating fast because of me."

After several languid minutes, Isabella spoke. "That was unbelievable. You made my toes curl." She hugged Madison tighter.

"Mm, we'll have to shoot for that every time. For now, all I want to do is lie here wrapped around you."

"Sorry, I can't allow that. You haven't kept your promise to me yet."

Madison rose up on one elbow. "I haven't?"

"You promised to show me something softer than your lips." Isabella kissed them. "I'm still waiting to find out what that is."

Madison shook her head. "You're astonishingly hot for your first time making love to a woman." She took one of Isabella's hands in her own. "I like to keep my promises." She guided the flat of Isabella's hand down the length of her own body to that softest of secret places. "Can you feel how much I want you?"

"Yes." Isabella moaned as her fingers explored Madison. "You're a woman of your word, Capt. Brown. This is by far the softest place on earth. I hope you don't mind if I take my time."

Madison exhaled. "Not at all." She gasped when Isabella entered her.

Isabella marveled at how natural and instinctively she made love to Madison. It was as if the instructions had always been written in her heart, waiting to be discovered. "I love you."

"I love you, too," Madison whispered.

Isabella closed her eyes and let loving a woman consume her. The taste, sound, feel, vulnerability, and power combined to create an otherworldly beauty that humbled her. "I want you to feel me touch your heart." In her quest to master Madison's body, Isabella quickly discovered the path to her ecstasy. She pushed deeper until Madison dug her fingernails into her back and screamed her climax. Isabella relished the moment of freedom she had bestowed on Madison. Tears filled her eyes. It was the most splendid thing she'd ever done.

Madison sighed as she clutched Isabella closely. "I wish that we'll never end."

Chapter 16

"These past two months with you have been the best of my life." Seated across from Madison in the hospital cafeteria at Boston Central, Isabella set her empty coffee cup down. People bustled all around them. She stole a glance at the crowd to make sure no one was watching and put her hand on top of Madison's resting on the table.

Madison turned her hand over and laced her fingers with Isabella's. "That's sweet of you to say that, but we both know it's not a hundred percent true."

"You mean because I still haven't told my family about us, don't you?"

"I know how important they are to you, Isabella. I don't like feeling that I'm some kind of ogre who's turned you into someone you're afraid they won't love anymore."

"It's not that." Isabella caressed Madison's pinkie with her thumb. "I don't like telling them half-truths about what I'm doing any more than you like feeling like I'm hiding you from them. I just need to find the right time to tell them about you and me." She gave Madison her brightest smile. "Once they get to know you, they'll love you as much as I do."

Madison returned the smile. "It's a shame so many people are around. I want to kiss you." She let go of Isabella's hand.

Isabella smiled. "Maybe that's a good thing. A kiss from you is never enough for me, and I've got lots of work to do today."

"There's always later tonight." Madison winked.

"Later is too far away." Isabella reached over her shoulder to retrieve her shoulder bag hanging on the back of the chair. "I should head upstairs before you break my resolve to do work. Besides, the General is probably finished with his tests by now. He'll want me to walk back to the shelter with him."

"I hope he's all right."

"Me, too," Isabella said.

"Has he been cooperating with his doctors?"

"Sort of. For the most part, when he does, it's only to humor me. Since his lung cancer diagnosis, he's become distant and even more stubborn about staying at the shelter. I can't convince him he needs to be someplace else."

"He's probably retreating inside himself. It's a defense mechanism. I've seen it more times than I want to remember."

"I saw someone do that, too." Isabella looked lovingly at Madison. "You, and I'm glad we're moving past that."

"Me, too. You have a way of drawing me out."

"Good, because I want all of you, even the hidden parts."

"You have me completely," Madison said. "We both better get to work. I'll be thinking positive thoughts for the General."

"Thanks. I keep hoping he might rally and beat the odds. He's one of the best people I know."

"Let's hope and pray for the best then." Madison stood. "Come on. I'll walk with you."

*   *   *

The doctor sat down at his desk across from Isabella and the General. His expression gave him away before he spoke a word. "Mr. Cutter, I'm sorry to tell you this, but your cancer has spread. We do have some treatment options available to us. They'll slow the progression of your disease, but it's only fair that I tell you we can't stop it altogether."

"Can you give us a likely prognosis, Doctor?" Isabella asked.

The doctor directed his reply to David. "With treatment, you've probably got six months to a year. Without it, I'd estimate about three months. I'm very sorry."

The General looked straight ahead without speaking.

"David, please say something," Isabella said.

His eyes welled with tears. "There's not a whole lot for me to say. Other than trying to help the men at the shelter, I have no purpose for living." The General looked at Isabella. "Truth be told, I'm tired of fighting all those Vietnam demons—in me and in them."

"Would you like me to call your family?" Isabella asked.

"No, dammit. I don't want you to call them."

Isabella patted his shoulder gently. "I didn't mean to upset you, but maybe they'd like to be here for you now. You must miss them."

"Yeah, I miss them. Always have." He looked away. "Especially now that I'm about to die. The past is the past. Thinking about seeing them only makes my regret and loneliness stronger. I've survived all these years by forcing myself to forget how all alone I've been. Seeing them would make everything worse."

"You can't mean that." Isabella's heart broke for him

"I do mean that. Death will let me stop running away from everything that makes me sad and afraid, and that includes my family." He wiped a tear from his eye. "God damn it, Generals aren't supposed to cry." He cleared his throat. "Doctor, do you have anything more to say to me?"

The doctor leaned forward. "I'd like to discuss treatment options."

The General coughed and swallowed. "Damn this dry throat." He swallowed a second time. "Will any of these so-called treatments make me sick and keep me from taking care of myself?"

"You'd probably have some side effects from the chemotherapy."

"Like what?"

"Nausea is common, and so are headaches. Because of your age, and not having someone to care for you, there's a good chance you'll have to be hospitalized. The sooner we start your treatments, the more effective they're likely to be. Shall I go ahead and schedule your first session?"

"No, I don't want to be in any hospital. I don't want to be an invalid, and I don't want to postpone the inevitable. I'm going back to the shelter. That's that."

"Mr. Cutter, you're a very sick man. Please, let us help you," the doctor said.

"Could we have a minute alone?" Isabella asked.

The doctor rose from his seat. "Of course. When you're finished, let my nurse know. She'll have me paged." He nodded to the General as he left.

Isabella turned to him. "David, please think about having the treatments. Instead of staying at the hospital, I could get you into the veterans' home. You'll be comfortable and well taken care of there. I know how you feel about the men at the shelter, but for once, please consider taking care of yourself instead of them."

"It won't matter whether I'm in a home or the hospital. It's all the same. Someone will always be telling me what to do and when to do it. I can't have people constantly hovering all over me. I need my freedom." He picked up one of Isabella's hands and kissed it.

"Sweet girl, you're like a daughter to me. Of all the people in the world, you're the one I'm saddest to leave behind. But you know I can't be caged up like some animal. I refuse to be locked up in one of those places, even for a day." He coughed again. "I'm ready to meet my Maker. I've been in this world long enough. Please, let it be."

"You have to let me find you a better place to stay for a while. I can't bear the thought of you being on the streets while you're sick. I can be just as stubborn as you. I'm not going to give in. You know that, right?"

"I won't leave my men," the General said.

"Then at least let me call your son. Maybe you can make amends with your family. Will you let me do this one thing for you? Maybe you don't want to see him, but doesn't he have a right to have a choice in whether he gets to say good-bye to his father?"

He glowered at her. "You're pretty brave to ask me that question again after I've told you no a thousand times. I have to give you credit, you're a fearless girl. You would've made an excellent soldier." He shook his head in resignation.

"I can't imagine not having my father in my life, especially if he died without my saying good-bye to him. What if your son feels the same way? He was only a boy when you left. For all you know, he's missed you every day of his life. He's your son, and nothing can change that. Please, give him the chance to see you one last time."

The General shifted in his chair. "Damn, these things are uncomfortable. I ache when I sit in them for too long. It's why I prefer to stay on the move. I'm definitely not going to spend my last days in a hospital bed."

"Okay, fine. No hospital, but what about your son?"

"Look at you trying to wear an old man down in his weakened state." His face took on a faraway expression. "I've often wondered who my son became and whether we even look alike... whether he has children of his own."

"You can find out before it's too late."

"It wouldn't be fair for me to contact him now. I'd only open old wounds. Let them stay scarred over, where they belong. I'm sure my family's moved on. My coming back into their lives would be selfish. I'd only remind them of all the pain they suffered because of me. As much as I'd like to see them again, I won't."

"For the life of me, I can't fathom what you could've ever done that caused you to have to leave your family. Blood is supposed to be thicker than water. No matter what, families survive if they really love each other. I know you love them." She paused, "You never told me what happened. Maybe if you did, I'd be able to understand, because right now, especially under these circumstances, I don't."

Isabella watched countless unidentifiable emotions flicker over the General's face. She waited to see if he'd share his history with her.

"I guess I owe it to you to explain." He breathed in deeply. "When I came back from Vietnam the first time, my wife knew right away that the person she fell in love with didn't exist anymore. I left him out on the battlefield, and he was never going to come back. Strange as it might sound, as happy as I was to be home, all I could think about was going back to the fight. I didn't know who I was except when I was fighting the enemy with my men. Being home terrified me more than the war. At least when I was on the battlefield, I didn't have time to think about all the death and destruction, even though it was going on all around me. I was numb to it until I came home. At home, I couldn't avoid it, and I didn't know how to confront it." His voice grew hoarse. "All this talking is making my throat hurt. Would you mind getting me some water, Isabella?"

"Sure." She filled a paper cup from the water dispenser and handed it to him.

He took several sips. "I'd been home for six months when I got orders to go back. My son was three years old at the time, and my wife couldn't understand why I'd gotten so little time at home before being called to duty again. I think she was suspicious. She could see I was miserable at home, so she asked me outright if it was my decision or the military's for me to go back. I wasn't going to lie. I told her I'd asked to go, because I needed to take care of my men who were still there."

"From things you told me when I asked about this in the past," Isabella said, "I thought you left because your family wanted you to. What you're telling me now says it was more for your sake than for theirs."

David was slow to reply. "I guess it was really for both them and me. Yeah, I was running from my demons, but by leaving, my family didn't have to face them with me. I couldn't put them through that. They deserved to have someone who was whole. No matter how unaffected a person who comes back from war might appear, don't think for a second that there isn't some part of him that's damaged forever." His voice quivered. "It left me empty inside. I couldn't cope with how insecure I felt around my own son."

Isabella took his hand and held it tight. "David, I'm sure they loved you, demons and all. If you'd given them the chance, you probably could've worked things through. It's never too late to try and fix things with the people you love. I've spent enough time around veterans to understand that your hurt can run deep. I'll bet anything they'd have been happy to help you get through it."

"I don't know if I ever could've healed." David used his free hand to gesture toward himself. "Look at me now. Do I really look like a man who's recovered? Besides, when my wife found out that it was my decision to go back, she gave me an ultimatum. She said that if I went, she and my son wouldn't be there when I came home." Tears ran down his cheeks. "I never admitted this to anyone, but... sometimes, I really wish I'd stayed with them. I had a choice, and I made the wrong one. I should've embraced the love of my family instead of the war. I went back to my men, and when I did, I let my future with my family slip through my fingers." He swiped at his tears with the back of his hand. "No matter what happens in your life, Isabella, don't let the people who mean the most slip away from you."

"Oh, David, I'm so sorry."

He removed his hand from Isabella's grasp and clasped his hands together in front of his bowed body. They shook uncontrollably, and he stared them. "I feel so old. I'm just a feeble old man who's come to the end of the road. I guess a lifetime of wear and tear is finally showing through. The fight's all gone out of me." He dropped his head to his hands and sobbed.

Isabella put her arm around him. "Then please, let me call your son."

Chapter 17

A day later, Isabella hung up the phone, closed the General's file on her desk, and exhaled a sigh of relief. Her conversation with the General's son had gone well. Rich Cutter was glad to learn his father was still alive and that he was reaching out to see him after all these years. He didn't remember his father at all, but he hoped it wasn't too late to get to know him. Rich had tried several years ago to find him, but David Cutter's trail went dry shortly after he returned home from his second tour of duty in Vietnam.

As she reflected on the upcoming reunion between father and son, Isabella reminded herself of her belief that family bonds were unbreakable, no matter the circumstance. Too bad she couldn't cling to that notion when it came to telling her own family about Madison.

She placed the General's file back into the cabinet near her desk and locked it. Her sadness over his diagnosis was tempered by his agreement to see his son. Adding to her good feelings, she was going to spend a long weekend with Madison in Provincetown. They'd hide away in a place where they could be themselves completely.

Isabella pulled open the drawer of her office desk. She took out the small box from O'Neil Jewelers, one of the best in the city. She admired the gold watch inside. It could never replace the ring Madison had given to the little boy at the airport, nor was it meant to. She wanted it to signify a new beginning. Isabella took the watch out of the box, turned it over, and ran a fingertip over the engraving: *To Madison, always. Love, Isabella.* She planned to give it to her over the weekend.

As Isabella put the watch in its box, Beth came around the corner. Isabella moved the box so it was partially hidden behind a stack of reference manuals on the back corner of her desk.

"Hey, Isabella, I'm heading out now. Marcy wants me to come home early to help her pack for our trip. We're really looking forward to spending the three-day weekend with you all in P-Town."

"Amy couldn't get out of work on Saturday," Isabella said, "so she and Cheryl will meet us on Sunday at the ferry terminal."

"Sounds like fun." Beth was carrying a cooler and had her briefcase slung over a shoulder. "Thanks for loaning us your cooler. Would you mind giving me a hand taking it to my car? I've got a bunch more stuff in my office that needs to go, too."

The phone on Isabella's desk rang. The caller ID indicated it was the office secretary. "One second, Beth. Let me get this. I'm expecting Madison to stop by." She picked up the phone. "Thanks, tell her I'll be right there."

Beth used her elbow to point toward the phone. "Your gorgeous soldier, I presume? I hope the two of you will be able to keep your paws off of each other long enough for us to go out and play at least a little bit this weekend."

"I never knew what I was missing all this time sleeping with a man. I can't resist her. I promise to make an effort to control myself, though. At least part of the time anyway." Isabella's skin flushed thinking about all the things she intended to do to Madison once she had her alone. The several hours ahead of them before that occurred would be torture if she let such thoughts linger. *Focus on getting ready.* "Madison and I are bringing food to make a picnic lunch for Saturday."

Beth raised an eyebrow.

"Don't worry. I've been working on her cooking skills. She's getting better. You have to give her credit for trying. Come on, let's go find her."

* * *

The clicking of Maria's high heels on the linoleum floor got the attention of the office secretary. "Hello, Sandy, I'm here to see my sister. Is she in today?"

"Hi, Maria. Yes, Isabella's in. I just spoke to her. Go on back, if you'd like."

"Thank you. Could you remind me again where the ladies' room is? I need to make a quick pit stop first."

"Around the corner and to the right. You can't miss it."

"Thanks. Enjoy the rest of the day."

The clicking of Maria's heels resumed. She'd be glad to catch up with Isabella, given that she'd seen so little of her lately. It wasn't like Isabella to be this scarce, especially with John home for the summer. Something or someone was filling her time, and it wasn't Ben. When she ran into Ben downtown a couple of weeks ago, he scowled at the mention of Isabella's name. She suspected her sister might be seeing someone else. She spotted the ladies' room icon on a closed door and went inside.

Once she finished, she headed to Isabella's office. Isabella wasn't there. Maria glanced about. The first thing she noticed was the box from O'Neil's jewelry store. The upscale jeweler sold only high-end products. People didn't shop there unless they either had a lot of money to spend on themselves or were buying a gift for someone special.

Maria couldn't resist the temptation. She opened the box and cocked her head when she saw it contained a woman's watch. On a social worker's salary, Isabella had to be frugal. The only conclusion Maria could draw was that someone had given her sister a very special gift. Maybe it was from Ben. That would make sense if it was his way of apologizing for whatever might have happened between them. Curiosity got the better of her, and she lifted the watch from the box. "Or maybe it's from her new mystery man, if she and Ben have called it quits," she said under her breath.

She examined the watch more closely. "Whoever you are, you certainly have good taste." A Swiss watch, it was made of white gold and had a simple but elegant design that could be worn with either formal or casual clothing. "Very nice." Her forefinger rubbed against an etching on the back. Maria turned it over to read the inscription.

It puzzled her. "*To Madison, always. Love, Isabella.*"

Several times over the past six or eight weeks, Isabella had declined invitations to get together with Maria because she'd already made plans with Madison. Maria vividly recalled the scene in their uncle's store and how Isabella had appeared uncomfortable to admit that she was getting special ingredients to make dinner for Madison. Come to think of it, Madison's name seemed to pop up in ways that suggested she was more than a casual acquaintance. Evidently, they'd developed a special friendship. Nothing wrong with that. Many women only entrust their deepest secrets to their close girlfriends or their sisters. Men aren't good at discussing feelings. Except maybe Anthony.

She shook her head, bewildered. Even if they were close friends, the intimacy of the engraving spoke of something more. Perhaps the inscription explained why Isabella had been so secretive lately. She put the watch back in the box and returned to the lobby. There had to be a logical explanation—other than the one her suspicions led her to.

She stopped at the front desk. "Sandy, Isabella wasn't in her office. Any idea of how I happened to miss her?"

Sandy looked up from her computer. "She must've gotten past when you stopped in the ladies' room. She just left with Beth and a friend of Isabella's. Madison, I think her name is. I thought you'd run into each other in the hall. You could probably catch her. They said they were going to the parking garage around the corner of the building. Check the first floor. That's where our assigned parking spaces are. Beth drives a green Subaru. That might help you spot them." She studied Maria for a moment. "Is everything all right? You look worried."

"Everything's fine. I do need to try and catch her, though. Thanks." Maria rushed out of the building. When she entered the parking garage, she saw Isabella from behind. She and Beth were standing next to a green Subaru with both back doors and the trunk open. Isabella was with Beth and a tall woman with long, sandy-blonde hair. That must be Madison. The tall woman turned so that Maria had a clearer view of her. Maria had to admit she was strikingly attractive. Be that as it may, whatever crush her sister might have on her, Isabella was as straight as a girl could be. Her involvement with Ben had proved that. Worries to the contrary were ridiculous.

None of the three had noticed her. Maria overheard Beth say, "You're really going to like the inn I booked us in. I got you two a suite next to mine and Marcy's. After we pick you up tonight, we should stop for something to eat along the way to wait out the traffic. It's going to be gridlock heading to P-Town at that hour."

P-Town? Imagining her sister in a suite in the gayest town in Massachusetts with this Madison woman galled her. She couldn't believe it. A woman? Maria couldn't care less who other people chose to sleep with. She held no ill-will against gays and lesbians— as long as they were in someone else's family. But a lesbian in the Parisi family? Unimaginable.

She watched in disbelief. The woman said something to Isabella. Her voice was low, so Maria couldn't hear the words. She didn't have to. The glance the woman gave her sister told the story. It was one Maria knew well. Anyone who knew true love would recognize it anywhere. She and Anthony had exchanged that look countless times.

Isabella placed her hand in the small of the woman's back with the intimacy of a lover. The gesture left no doubt in Maria's mind that there was much more than friendship going on between them. She cleared her throat to make her presence known.

Madison did a double take. The dark-haired woman coming toward them had to be a Parisi. Oh, right. She'd seen her countless times in the photographs at Isabella's condo. In person, her resemblance to Isabella was unmistakable, even though she was an older, more cosmopolitan version with her high heels, flawless makeup, expensive jewelry, and a Gucci handbag. *What did Isabella say her name was? Maria, I think.*

They made eye contact. Maria seemed to size her up. She didn't appear angry, but she didn't seem friendly, either. Her posture expressed the kind of message a mother lion might send to a would-be predator walking too close to her cubs. This wasn't how Madison had envisioned her first meeting with a member of Isabella's family.

Isabella turned when Madison stiffened. "Maria? What are you doing here? I mean, hi... I mean, I'm glad to see you." She moved half a pace away from Madison. "I'm surprised to see you."

"You're a bit tongue-tied, little sister," Maria said. "I dropped by your office in hopes we could have lunch together." She smiled at Beth. "Hello, Beth. Good to see you."

"Hey, Maria, good to see you, too."

Maria shifted her gaze to Madison. "We've never met. I'm Maria Greco, Isabella's sister." She held out her hand.

It was a cordial but chilly handshake. Madison made the effort not to be the first to let go. She wanted to be polite but tried to send a subtle message through a firm grip that she wouldn't be intimidated.

Before Madison could respond, Isabella seized the moment. "Maria, this is my... friend Madison. The nurse from the VA clinic, remember? She and I were just on our way to lunch."

Madison tried to ignore the jolt of pain at Isabella's choice of words. Friend. But how else could she expect Isabella to refer to her when she hadn't explained their relationship to her family? Even so, it stung like a betrayal. She hoped she saw regret in Isabella's eyes.

Isabella took Madison's hand and said, "Actually, Madison is much more than a friend."

Madison felt rooted to the spot. She had no idea what to say and suspected it was probably best not to say anything at all.

Isabella had just come out to her sister. Madison stole a quick look at Beth, who appeared to be equally astonished.

Maria shifted from one foot to the other, a risky maneuver in her high heels. "I'm not sure I'm following you, Isabella."

Isabella looked at Madison. "I need to have lunch with my sister so I can explain to her about us. I'm going to tell her everything. It'll be okay. I'm ready to do this. I'll call you later this afternoon." She put her arms around Madison and kissed her cheek.

Madison whispered into Isabella's ear, "You're a brave soldier, sweetheart, and I love you for it."

"I love you, too, Madison."

"What just happened?" Maria asked.

Isabella offered her arm to her sister. "Remember when you said you only want me to be happy? Well, I finally am."

Maria reluctantly accepted Isabella's arm.

Isabella laid her hand atop Maria's as it rested on her forearm. "Let's pick up lunch somewhere and find a nice bench in the Common to sit and talk. There's something I need to tell you."

Chapter 18

The women's section of the beach at Herring Cove in P-town was packed with summer vacationers. Isabella leaned back against Madison's chest. Madison reveled in their time alone in the sun while Beth and Marcy swam. The temperature hovered around ninety degrees under a cloudless sky on a July day. P-town's asylum gave her the rare opportunity to not have to hide her affection for Isabella from the world. The weekend would be their nirvana.

Isabella sat between Madison's legs on a cotton blanket as they faced the shimmering waters of the Atlantic. Madison squeezed her tight and kissed her cheek. It was too hot to wear anything but swim trunks and bikini tops. Madison preferred it that way. She loved the feel of Isabella's skin next to hers.

Isabella leisurely ran the palm of her hand along the outside of Madison's leg, raising goose bumps all along the path of her touch.

Desire stirred in Madison. "Careful, Beth and Marcy will be back soon."

Isabella reached over her shoulder and caressed the side of Madison's face. "I love being with you and the feel of your body next to mine. I could stay like this forever."

Madison put her cheek next to Isabella's. "Me, too." She prayed for forever. She still feared the bottom would drop out eventually. "I'm glad things went so well with Maria at lunch yesterday. Maybe we were wrong about how your family would react." She rested her chin on Isabella's head. I don't want you to feel like you have to tell the rest of them, though, until you're ready. The important thing is that we're together. We have time."

As she spoke the words, Madison's heart sank. During the previous week, the rumor had been circulating that her unit might be sent back to Iraq. She should say something to Isabella about it. She had a right to know, but Madison couldn't bring herself to do it. Maybe after the weekend, but not now when everything was so serene and promising.

Isabella patted Madison's knee. "I know you'd never pressure me. It was the right time to tell Maria. She and I have always been close. I knew she'd understand, or at least try to. Besides, when she saw us in the parking garage, she'd already figured it out. Nothing much gets past my sister." Isabella shifted slightly. "She did suggest that I hold off telling my parents until after Michael's wedding. I think she's right about that. They're not going to take it well at first, but I'm sure they'll come around once they get to know you and see how happy you make me."

Although she'd never say so out loud, Madison thought Isabella straddled the line between optimism and naïveté when it came to her family. "I hope so." Her stomach growled, reminding her of the lunch Isabella had brought for them. "Let's eat when Marcy and Beth get back from their swim. I'm starving."

Isabella twisted her body around and pulled Madison down on top of her. "Hmm, I'm hungry, too, but not for food. Something besides my stomach is clamoring for attention right now."

Madison grinned as she rubbed her thumb over Isabella's bottom lip. "Now isn't the time or place for me to satiate those other hungers. This will have to tide you over." She covered Isabella's mouth with her own. Her tongue hinted at what would come later when they were alone.

Marcy's voice cooled their passion. "If you two aren't careful, you're going to light the beach on fire."

Madison rolled off Isabella. Resting on her elbows, she squinted up into the sun. "You have impeccable timing, Marcy."

"I know. I'm sorry to intrude on you two lovebirds, but I can't stop thinking about lunch." She plopped down on the blanket and opened one of the coolers. It contained cold water, sodas, and a bottle of Pinot Grigio. "You guys keep your eyes peeled for the park rangers while I pour us some wine. They wouldn't go easy on a lawyer with an open bottle of booze on the beach, would they?"

Beth took a spot on the blanket next to Marcy. "Well, it's a good thing we know so many lawyers, in case you get arrested. Sorry we interrupted you two, but we probably should eat soon. Marcy gets cranky on an empty stomach."

Marcy poured wine into each of the four plastic cups. "You know, Madison, I was wondering… do you ever worry that you'll be seen by someone in the military when you're in a place like this, kissing your girlfriend on the beach?"

"Now that 'don't ask, don't tell' has been repealed, I think about it a lot less. Don't get me wrong. It's not like everyone in the military has suddenly figured out that gays are real people, too, and just as much entitled to love anyone we want to. I've heard about some ugly stuff that's gone on for some soldiers who've admitted they're gay. I figure the smartest thing is to keep a low profile and mind my own business."

"But the law says it's okay to be gay and be in the military now," Beth said.

"Unfortunately," Madison replied, "what the law says and what people think are two different things where this issue is concerned. There's still a lot of resentment and plenty of soldiers who aren't happy at all with the law having been repealed."

"You'd think," Marcy observed, "with everything a soldier or sailor has to endure, guarding their sexual identity shouldn't have to be something they need to worry about."

"You're right," Madison said. "It was exhausting always having to look over my shoulder. I did enough of that in Iraq when the bad guys were shooting at us."

Marcy scowled. "That's my point. You're fighting for our country. You ought to be able to kiss your girlfriend on any damn beach in this country if you want to."

Madison stole a glance at Isabella. "Regardless of what's happened with 'don't ask, don't tell,' maybe it's time for me to think about getting out now that I've found Isabella. I've got a lot of other things I want to do with my life."

"Really?" Isabella asked.

"Yeah. Don't get me wrong, the military's been good to me. It gave me opportunities I never would've had otherwise. In some ways, it saved my life. I doubt I'd have met Isabella if I hadn't ended up here because of the Army. I think I've about done my time, though." She smiled at Isabella. They'd have to continue this conversation later when she could tell Isabella that she might have to go back to Iraq before she could think about giving up her commission. Madison gave Isabella a fleeting kiss on the lips. "If you guys don't mind, I need to cool off in the water before I eat. I'm baking in this sun. You start lunch without me." Madison extracted herself from Isabella's arms and legs. "I'll be right back."

"Sure, take your time," Isabella said.

Isabella finished putting their lunches together as Madison came out of the water. The vision caused her heart to skip a beat. Madison pushed the long wet strands of hair away from her face.

Her sculpted arms were a reminder of her muscular feminine body. Isabella craved her.

A group of attractive younger women stopped to gawk as well. One in particular wasn't subtle. She raised her sunglasses and whistled.

Aghast, Isabella asked, "Did you see that girl ogle Madison?"

Marcy swallowed a bite of her sandwich. "If you're going to date a high-performance sports car, Isabella, you better get used to other people enjoying the view."

Beth slapped Marcy's arm. "That sounds like something a guy would say."

Madison sat next to Isabella.

"Oh really?" Marcy said. "Let me ask Madison this question. If you had to describe Isabella as a type of car, what would it be?"

"A Maserati... a very fine Italian sports car," Madison said.

Isabella reddened. "You're right, Beth. That does sound like something a guy would say."

Madison grinned. "There a few things we lesbians have in common with straight men. We love women, and some of us really like cars, too."

"Cars, huh? What other surprises do you have in store for me?" Isabella asked.

"Stay with me long enough, and you'll learn them all. I promise," Madison said.

Marcy put her sandwich down and turned her hands palms up. "I rest my case. You see, the thing is, lesbians come in such a wide, delicious variety. I love cars, too, and I definitely love lesbians. Therefore, the car analogy is my way of describing all the things I like about them both." She gestured out at the beach. "Take, for example, the group of women sitting under the blue beach umbrella. They're definitely your basic Subaru types. Look at how practically they're dressed for the beach. They're sort of utilitarian in their approach, with an eye toward not getting too much sun exposure. I like how sensible that is." She pointed to the long-sleeved T-shirts she and Beth put on over their bathing suits after the swim. "Likewise, Beth and I are definitely your basic Subaru types."

Beth responded, "Okay, Einstein, what about those very butch women playing volleyball over there?"

Madison answered first. "That's easy. Toyota Four Runners, definitely. Tough, rugged, dependable, go anywhere, no-nonsense types."

Marcy nodded in agreement. "Absolutely, but let's not forget the very popular, and ever growing, population of lipstick lesbians." She gave Isabella's expertly manicured toenails painted a feminine shade of lilac an obvious visual inspection.

Isabella laughed. "Really, you think I'm more of a lipstick lesbian?"

Marcy, Beth, and Madison nodded in unanimous agreement.

Isabella glanced at Madison's toenails, which were manicured and painted a dark shade of blue. "If painted toenails make a girl a lipstick lesbian, then Madison must be in that category, right?"

Marcy shook her head. "No, Madison is one of those women you can't easily categorize."

"What do you think, Isabella?" Madison asked.

"I don't want to label you. It would be too much like putting you in a box. I love that you're so many wonderful different things. You're sometimes strong, sometimes fragile, always soft and beautiful. Your mysteries amaze me."

Madison held up her hands. "This is getting too mushy. You're going to embarrass me if you keep saying things like that in front of Beth and Marcy." She picked up one of Isabella's hands and kissed it. "How about one of those sandwiches you made?"

"For you, anything," Isabella answered.

Beth lay back on the blanket next to Marcy. "Ah, young love is such a great thing to witness."

* * *

"I loved our day together." Isabella held tight to Madison's hand as they walked under a warm, humid night sky. The slight breeze off the ocean cooled her skin as they neared their suite.

"Best I've had in a long time—spending the day at the beach with Beth and Marcy, having lobster for dinner, and dancing." Madison followed Isabella up the stairs to the entrance of their suite. "And now I get to have you all to myself."

"I like the sound of that. I wish we could have more days like this where we didn't have to hide our feelings for each other and got to wake up in each other's arms."

"We'll have to plan more weekends here in P-town." Madison took the key to their room out of her pocket and unlocked the door. She reached for Isabella when the door closed behind them.

Isabella's body melted into hers. Madison was the puzzle piece that exactly fit the empty space in her life. "Did you mean it when you said you might get out of the military?"

"I did. My commission's up in a year. I've never considered leaving the Army until now, so it's a lot to think about. What I know for sure is I want to be with you."

"I want to be with you, too. It's a big decision. I don't want to put pressure on you, but it would be a huge relief not to have to worry that you'll be sent back to Iraq."

Madison nuzzled Isabella's neck. "I'd rather talk about anything other than the Army or Iraq." She moved her hands underneath Isabella's T-shirt. "In fact, I don't want to talk at all."

"Maybe we should shower first," Isabella said.

"Good idea. Why don't you start without me? All that dancing made me thirsty. I need to get some water. Would you like a glass, too?"

"No, I'm good." Isabella chose something for each of them to sleep in from the bedroom and went into the bathroom to turn on the water. When she turned around to undress, Madison stood naked in front of her. A tidal wave of heat crashed over her, so hot she was sure it could melt steel. The only thing she could think about was how to remove her clothes as fast as possible, so there was nothing between her skin and Madison's. Before Isabella moved, Madison's hands were on her, frantically pulling off anything and everything that got in her way.

They scrambled naked into the shower. Madison dominated her with need, her touch frenzied. Madison's mouth and hands played Isabella's body faster and faster to a climax of sheer satisfaction.

Wrapped in each other's arms, they stood panting under the cool water. Isabella held on tight to Madison, her legs weak and unsteady, her breathing ragged. "No one has ever done the things you do to me." She took the bar of soap, and in between passionate kisses, they washed each other's bodies.

After they stepped out of the shower, Isabella dried them off. Then she took Madison by the hand and led her to bed. Madison lay down, pulling Isabella on top of her. Isabella fondled Madison's thigh. "Hmm, should I open my present fast or slow?"

Madison arched into her. "Slow."

Isabella brushed her hand between Madison's legs. "That's my plan, one sweet second at a time."

She tasted and felt Madison into the night until their desire was satiated. The emotional and physical power of their lovemaking transcended anything Isabella had imagined possible. Their bodies lay tangled as she listened to their rapid heartbeats slow to a restful rhythm. She caressed Madison's cheek. *"Come sei bella.* How beautiful you are."

"I don't even need to know what you're saying to like it."

"I'll teach you."

"Okay. Tell me how to say 'I love you.'"

"All right. But cover your eyes. I have to turn on the light first."

Madison put her hands over her face. "You can't tell me with the light off?"

Isabella took the silver box from O'Neil's out of the drawer of the nightstand.

"Sometimes things are best said without words." She tugged at one of Madison's arms. "You can open your eyes."

Madison smiled at the box Isabella held out to her. "You don't have to give me a present."

"I know, but I want to." Isabella handed it to Madison.

Madison opened it and took the watch out of its nest of cotton. "Isabella, it's gorgeous. No one's ever given me anything this nice. I love it." She turned the watch over and read the engraving.

"What do you mean by 'always?'"

"At first, I wanted to give you something that might replace the ring you gave to the little boy. When I thought about it, though, I knew the ring could never be replaced. The more time we spent together, the more I realized I wanted my first gift to you to be a symbol of our beginning."

Madison put the watch on. "A beginning with no end?"

"Yeah, always."

"I love it, and I love you." Madison wrapped herself around Isabella. "Thank you."

Isabella laid her head on Madison's chest. The confines of Madison's embrace were her favorite place to rest. Contented, she closed her eyes. "I love you, too." She fell fast asleep in Madison's arms.

Chapter 19

It was a hot, sunny, Sunday morning. Ben rested his elbows on the railing of the Yankee Clipper III, a charter fishing boat out of Provincetown, making its way back into the harbor. He glanced over at Isabella's father, Robert Parisi. The man was an imposing figure with a full head of dark hair, a well-kept physique, and a chiseled jaw line. He could pass for a man half his age. Robert gazed out at the shimmering waves as they steamed full-speed ahead and the Provincetown marina grew closer. "Thank you for inviting me along today," Ben said.

"Glad you could make it," Robert replied.

"I wouldn't have missed the opportunity to spend the morning fishing with you and your sons. How did you manage to pull off this last-minute trip? These boats are usually booked weeks in advance."

"Capt. Roland is an old friend. He used to take the boys and me out every year around this time. We'd go for cod. Isabella's mother would salt the catch so we'd have it to enjoy for months after. There isn't a better place in Massachusetts to cod fish than off of George's Bank out of Provincetown. I bumped into the captain a couple of days ago in the North End. When I told him John was in town, he suggested my sons and I go fishing for old time's sake. The group he had scheduled for today had to cancel due to a family illness. It was an offer I couldn't refuse."

"I'm honored to be included among your sons." Weeks had passed since Ben had last spoken to Isabella. His knew his best hope of winning her back was through her family. They had often said he was destined to become part of the family when he married Isabella. If he had to play the family card, so be it.

Robert cupped the back of Ben's neck with his large hand. "It wouldn't have been the same without you. I'm glad you could find the time to get away from work. Isabella must be keeping you busy otherwise. We haven't seen her around much. You're taking good care of her, I hope."

Ben wasn't sure how to answer. He didn't want Robert to think his problems with Isabella were too serious, but just the same, he needed Robert's intervention. He couldn't comprehend this thing between Isabella and Madison. If anyone could get through to her, it would be her father. "I would if she'd let me. To be honest, I haven't seen her much in the past couple of months. We had an argument. I've been trying to give her some space so she can get over being mad at me. Maybe you could talk to her. You could tell her how sorry I am for being a jerk. She'll listen to you."

Robert grinned. "Get used to this kind of thing, kid. Women are temperamental. Isabella's no exception. She's been headstrong since she was a little girl. I'm sure whatever you did, she'll forgive you. She may have a mind of her own, but she doesn't hold a grudge."

"Thanks." Ben contemplated his next remark. If he could get Robert excited about the prospect of another wedding for one of his children, the greater the likelihood Robert would do his best to turn the tide and get Isabella back into his arms instead of Madison's. "I'd like to ask Isabella to marry me. Do you have any reservations about that?"

"It's about damn time." Robert slapped him hard on the back. "You'd be good for Isabella. Of all my kids, she's the one least settled. She needs someone strong like you to keep her feet planted on the ground. She's a free spirit, which means she'll keep your life interesting. You can count on that. I'm thrilled you've finally decided to ask her." He chuckled. "I'll bet whatever it is she's mad about will disappear with your marriage proposal. Good man!"

Ben detected a pronounced shift in Robert's demeanor. Something was suddenly wrong. His ashen, pained face didn't match the words he'd just spoken. *Oh my God. He's having a heart attack.* The brothers must have noticed, too, because they rushed to his side. "Mr. Parisi, what is it?" Ben asked.

The veins in Robert's hands bulged from the grip he had on the railing of the vessel. Any tighter and he'd crush it with his bare hands. Despite the breeze from the movement of the boat, beads of sweat formed at his hairline. They fell in steady succession.

John grasped his shoulder. "Dad, what's wrong?"

Robert tore his eyes away from the shore and shot daggers at Ben. "How could you let this happen?"

Ben gazed at the point on the shore where Robert had been staring. The meaning of Robert's baffling words became apparent. There on the dock railing sat Isabella with Madison all but

124

swallowing her up. *This cannot be happening.* "I tried to put a stop to it, Mr. Parisi. I swear I did."

Robert ignored Ben and his sons as he stepped off the boat as soon as Capt. Roland tied her to the dock. His deportment made it evident that an angry explosion of atomic proportions was imminent. Even though Ben worried for what was about to befall Isabella, he hoped Madison finally got what was coming to her for messing up their lives.

* * *

"Amy and Cheryl should be here soon," Madison said. "The ferry's due in a few minutes."

"Good," Marcy said. "How about you and Isabella wait here for them? Beth and I will go get the tickets for the Kate Clinton show tonight while you get them checked in. If we don't get tickets now, it might sell out. Let's meet here in about a half hour."

It was nearly eleven o'clock in the morning, and the sun blazed down on the marina, scorching hot. After Marcy and Beth left, Madison lifted Isabella into a sitting position on the railing. She stood between her legs and wrapped her arms around Isabella's waist to keep her from falling back into the water. "I could get used to seeing you walking around in a bikini top like this every day."

"Isn't it a bit risqué to be so scantily clad in public?"

"Not when it's so damn hot out." Madison kissed her neck. "The weather isn't the only thing that sizzles. Your body is amazing. And it's all mine."

Isabella wrapped her legs more tightly around Madison. "Too bad we're in public. Otherwise, I'd have even less clothing on. By the way, I like the butch look you're sporting today. A baseball hat and tank top suit you."

"Do you think our friends would miss us if we disappeared back to the room? I could let you explore my butch side more thoroughly."

Isabella giggled. "An adventure I'm sure to love. Unfortunately, Beth and Marcy would miss us. Not much gets past those two. Not to mention that Cheryl and Amy are expecting us to meet them when the ferry docks."

An angry voice shattered Madison's morning. "Isabella, what in God's name are you doing?"

Isabella pushed Madison away and hopped off the railing. "Daddy, please, I can explain. I was going to tell—"

Robert clenched his fists. "Cover yourself up and get your things. You're coming home with me and your brothers." He bestowed a condescending, hateful look on Madison. "Now, Isabella." His tone left no question as to the authority he believed he held.

Ben, Anthony, and the Parisi brothers stood thunderstruck behind Robert. Madison wished she could melt into the water and disappear. Their scrutiny left her feeling naked and exposed. She put a hand on Isabella's shoulder. "It'll be okay. I'll bring your things back to the city if you want to go home with your family."

Robert turned and stormed away toward the parking lot.

Isabella didn't answer Madison. She grabbed a T-shirt out of her beach bag, put it on, and ran after her father.

Madison watched her go. Her heart ruptured into a thousand shards. Fear and sadness threatened to engulf her. This was worse than anything she ever could have imagined. So much for their hopes that Isabella's parents would accept their lesbian daughter and that the family would welcome Madison as Isabella's partner. A man she recognized from photographs to be Isabella's brother, Michael, approached.

He stopped inches from her. He pointed a finger in her face. "You fucking dyke, don't you ever put your hands on my sister again."

Her anger helped to restore her composure. It was bad enough that Isabella had taken off without a word. Now she had to face Isabella's brothers and Ben by herself. She wasn't in the mood and didn't intend to listen to their judgment of her. "A piece of advice. Get your finger out of my face before you lose it. I'm warning you. Don't underestimate me."

He moved even nearer. Thankful for her long legs, Madison pulled herself to her full height. Instead of having to endure him looking down on her, both literally and figuratively, she looked him square in the eyes.

"Michael, you need to calm down," one of the other brothers said. He stepped between Michael and Madison. He gripped his brother's shoulders. "This isn't how a Parisi conducts himself in public. Isabella's behavior was bad enough without you disgracing us, too."

Madison turned to go. She had to leave before she lost her self-control completely.

Ben blocked her path. "You're the poorest excuse for a woman I've ever known. I'm not even sure I'd call you a woman."

Madison lowered her voice so only he could hear. "If you have a question about whether I'm a woman or not, why don't you ask Isabella? She can shed some light on that for you."

Ben's upper lip twitched. "Maybe so, but you still can't give her what I can. You saw how quickly Isabella went after her father. She practically ran over you to catch up to him. If you ask me, as of that moment, you became invisible to her. Don't kid yourself. She'll never choose you over her family. You're nothing more than one of Isabella's flights of fancy. She isn't a lesbian any more than I am. You'll never have her." His face hardened. "You should be ashamed for trying to destroy her family."

Madison bit her lip. She wouldn't give Ben the satisfaction of making her cry. She stood in silence as he continued his effort to belittle her.

"Maybe you should cut your losses while you can," he said. "I have a feeling she'll be begging me to take her back now that she's had her misguided fun with you."

"Shut up, you bastard. You don't know anything about how we feel about each other." Madison pushed past Ben and walked away as quickly as her legs would carry her. Ben's tirade only made her all the more determined to keep Isabella.

Ben called after her. "Here's what I know. If you push enough buttons, eventually you hit the right one. I think I did."

Madison ignored him as she yanked her cell phone from the pocket of her shorts and dialed Beth's number. When Beth answered, Madison said, "Isabella's father is here. He saw Isabella and me kissing. He was so angry that she ran from me. I'm going back to the inn. Come wait for Amy and Cheryl, will you?"

The walk back to the room she shared with Isabella seemed to take an eternity. She resolved not to cry until she could lock herself away. Tears welled in her eyes as she placed the key in the door. Relief flooded over her when she opened it.

"Isabella." Madison closed the door and ran to her. She put her arms around her, hoping her embrace could hold all the pieces of Isabella's broken heart together. "I'm sorry."

Isabella sobbed. "I never dreamed my family would find out this way."

"I know. I know. Shhh. It'll be all right." Madison rocked Isabella in her arms. Deep inside, she knew Isabella's innocence—and maybe her relationship with her family—was lost forever.

Chapter 20

Ben Jackson was an early riser. Morning, shortly before the sun took its place in the sky, was his favorite part of the day. Since he spent the vast majority of his time trying to solve other people's problems, he preferred daybreak, when most were still fast asleep. Even in the heart of the city, things were peaceful and quiet at that hour—especially on a Sunday morning, which was why the knock at his door annoyed him so. It wasn't like he didn't already have enough to be upset about. Two weeks had passed since the Parisi family collapsed in chaos. Isabella's father still blamed him, but not as much as he blamed Madison.

The knock came a second time. It was tentative, like the person behind it already knew that his presence wasn't welcome. Ben finished lacing his running shoes and went toward the door. "Whoever's there better have a damn good reason."

There was that infuriating knock again, this time, less tentative. He glanced at the clock on the wall. Five-forty a.m. He quickened his pace. Gritting his teeth, he said, "Damn it, I'm coming already."

He swung the door of his Beacon Street apartment open wide. "What the hell?" Except for the homeless man rummaging through a trash can across the street, no one was around. Homeless people near Beacon Street were rare. The police saw to that. Maybe the guy was looking for a change of pace from his usual hangouts. Ben eyed him suspiciously. When he turned to go back inside, a large brown envelope lying on his front step caught his attention. There was no return address. The scribbled letters simply read, "To Benjamin J. Jackson, Attorney at Law." The handwriting was vaguely familiar.

He scanned the street, but saw no one. The homeless guy across the street appeared oblivious to his presence. He looked content to dig for any edible morsel of food somewhere in that trash can. Ben bent down, picked up the envelope, and went back inside.

His morning run would have to wait. He poured himself a cup of coffee and went to his study. Inside the envelope was a two-page handwritten letter on the back pages of a flyer for the veterans shelter. It dawned on him then where he had seen the handwriting before. As part of his pro bono work at the shelter, he'd recently completed a Living Will and Health Care Proxy paperwork for the General. Damn shame the old man was dying of cancer. The General had been adamant that Ben make sure he wouldn't be resuscitated or kept alive by "hospital machines and tubes," as he had put it.

Ben sat in his leather office chair and unfolded the letter.

Dear Attorney Jackson,

By the time you read this letter, I will mercifully be gone from this world. I came into it with nothing and will leave with nothing. Therefore, I cannot pay you in the manner to which you are accustomed. However, after I say what I have to say, I will close with a piece of advice that I hope you will find more valuable than anything money could buy. My dying request is that you act as my attorney to ensure that my last wishes are met. If you do, I promise good karma will follow.

First, please say good-bye to Isabella for me. I have loved her like a daughter. She brought me great happiness and comfort these last few years. When others shunned me, she was my friend. She is a compassionate person. Even at her young age, she has already earned a place in heaven. I hope the events of her life, including my death, will not harden her gentle heart.

I'm afraid she won't accept my choice to leave this world in the way I have. One of my requests is that you don't let her blame herself. I'm a man who understands fate and choice. There are things in this world we have no control over. They are predetermined for us. Quite simply, they are our destiny. It's what we choose to do with fate that matters.

The funny thing about it is that it sometimes comes to us in a subtle whisper, not meant to be heard but rather felt, like a distant rumble of thunder. We could live a lifetime before we recognize it. It took me a long time to understand this. The cancer running through my body determined that I would die soon. Therefore, my choice is not whether to live or die, but rather how to meet my end.

Please let Isabella know that I'm at peace with this choice to go now, before I become a burden to anyone. Thank her for all she has done for me, which is greater than she will ever know.

As for my son, please tell him that, despite what the world may have thought of me, I found happiness and purpose living among the men of the shelter. They loved me unconditionally. There's no greater gift a person can receive than that. Love and happiness are sometimes found in the most unlikely of places, if we only keep our hearts open to the possibility.

I want you to apologize to him on my behalf for breaking our appointment to meet. Perhaps I was too much of a coward after all these years to look him in the eyes. There was so much broken between us that it could never have been repaired in what little time I had left. I couldn't bear the thought of opening old wounds only to leave him again in the end. Maybe someday he'll understand that I did love him with all of my heart, even though I left all those years ago, and that I made the choice to leave again now. Sometimes, it's impossible not to break a heart no matter what our choices are in this life.

The details of my death are as follows. I have taken the entire bottle of pain pills the doctor gave me on Wednesday. You'll find my body in its eternal slumber on the bench near the Zakim bridge monument that overlooks the Charles River.

While I've instructed them not to be seen when the authorities arrive, my men will be in the area to guard my remains until you find me. In the breast pocket of my Army jacket you'll find a picture of Isabella and me. Please see to it that she gets this photograph. It brought joy to my heart every time I looked at it. I hope it will have the same effect on her as it did on me. The people who make us happy are truly priceless. Under the bench will be a box of my Army medals. They are for my son, if he wants them to remember me by. My last wish is to be cremated and set free in the Atlantic Ocean.

I've planned my death so you will find me on a Sunday morning when the death of a homeless man is less likely to be sensationalized in the news. Please tell Isabella in person about my passing before she reads about it in the papers or finds out at work. Then ask her to call my son.

In closing, I leave you with this advice from a dead man, which surely should hold a lot of weight. It is the dead who finally come to understand life's greatest mysteries. I give this advice to you as my most valuable parting counsel before I go. Please share it with Isabella and my son. Never settle for anything less than unbridled happiness and love, even if it comes to you in a form you never could have predicted for yourself. That is the greatest gift of fate. Receive it with open arms, and you will know your true meaning in life. Be warned, however, that fate doesn't always play fair. Sometimes it requires something in exchange—a "quid pro quo," if you will. Don't be afraid to give up what it requires in exchange for your unbridled happiness, so long as you always remain true to yourself in the end. Keep your heart open to it.

I thank you for this kindness that you will do for me.

Sincerely,
David Cutter

David's letter rattled Ben to his very core. Even in death, the eccentric old soldier challenged his beliefs about how the world was supposed to work. Ben always considered "fate" to be overrated. People used it as an excuse for too many troubles of their own making. He never considered the General's point that fate and choice were two distinct things. It made sense that there were certain events in a person's life that happened of their own accord, driven solely by the winds of destiny. Sickness, accidents, meeting the love of one's life... *Yeah, but when it comes, we get to decide how we react to it.*

Until that moment, he had blamed Isabella entirely for wreaking havoc on her family and on her relationship with him. For the first time, he considered the possibility that Isabella didn't choose to fall in love with a woman. He still couldn't understand how that could happen, but for the sake of argument—he was a lawyer, after all—he was willing to acknowledge it as a reality. She still had choices, though. In the end, he wanted her to choose him, regardless of her feelings for Madison.

He made a copy of the letter and put it back into the envelope. If he found the General's body by the bridge, he would give the original to the police. He'd have to retain a copy for his own records so he could carry out the General's last wishes. Nothing in it was required to be kept confidential because of the attorney-client privilege. It was both a suicide note and the General's attempt at a last will and testament. The police would keep the original until they'd completed an investigation into the death.

Ben pulled a pair of sweatpants on over his running shorts and headed toward the bridge. He walked rather than ran. What he expected to find wasn't anything he was in any hurry to get to.

True to his word, the General's body lay motionless on a bench in the quiet of the early morning. He rested peacefully on his back with his eyes closed, hands clasped together on his chest. A hint of a smile on his face suggested that he had been a man satisfied with his time in the world. If Ben didn't know better, he'd think he was some happy drunk sleeping off a bender. The pallor of David's skin and the lack of any movement told a different story. No doubt about it, the General was dead.

Ben stared down at the body. "Shit, he really did do it." He took his cell phone out of his pocket and dialed 911. "Hello, my name is Benjamin Jackson. I'm an attorney at Galliano, Lawton, and Simpson. Please send an officer and ambulance to the Charles River esplanade over by the Zakim monument. It appears a client of mine has committed suicide."

While he waited for an officer to arrive, he surveyed the scene, being careful not to touch anything. He peered under the bench. There was a box, exactly as the General said there would be. How on earth was he going to tell Isabella? This could destroy her—not that what had happened in P-town hadn't already made a good start on that. Perhaps it would shake some sense into her that she needed him and her family now more than ever.

He had to figure out how to find her. The last he knew from Maria, she was still staying with Madison. Ever since Isabella's father made her choose between Madison and her family, she hadn't been seen in the North End. Words from the General's letter flashed in his mind. *A quid pro quo, if you will.* Isabella had choices all right. It wasn't too late. He hoped she'd come around and choose him and her family over Madison.

The General's unfortunate demise might have opened the door to him getting Isabella back. His showing up unannounced on a Sunday morning at the home of a woman who detested him might be palatable, given Isabella's feelings for the General. He considered calling Maria to find out where Madison lived. He might even ask her to have Isabella give him a call to arrange to meet him somewhere. A lot could go wrong with that plan. Maria would insist on knowing what was going on. She couldn't be trusted to keep the information quiet long enough for Ben to tell Isabella himself.

Then again, Isabella might refuse to see him, no matter how important his reasons were for needing to talk to her. The only good option happened to be the most difficult.

Before the police and ambulance sirens got too close for him to make a call, he quickly dialed his cell phone. "Mendez, I'm glad I caught you. Look, I need an address and fast. Get it within the next fifteen minutes, and I'll pay you double."

Ben raised his voice. "I know it's Sunday morning, but you're the best private investigator money can buy. I need you to do this for me." He paused. "That's right, double. The name is Capt. Madison Brown. All I know is that she lives somewhere on the north shore... Good, I'll talk to you shortly." Ben flipped his cell phone closed and greeted the authorities as they arrived on the scene.

Chapter 21

In the warmth of the morning sun, Madison tugged carefully at the tenacious weeds threatening to consume the wildflowers in her tiny garden. Tug too hard, and the weed roots would take her flowers with it. Tug too little, and the tops would break off only to leave the suffocating roots behind.

Tending her garden made her think of Isabella. The strength of her family's roots, like the dogged weeds in the garden, threatened to strangle her relationship with Isabella. Isabella's father was determined to tear them apart. Isabella had been staying at Madison's house since the confrontation in Provincetown. Her father treated Madison as though she were a common criminal. Madison was, after all, the terrible culprit who lured Isabella into a life of crime. He went to great lengths to make Isabella unwelcome in the North End, with or without Madison. For Isabella, the North End had always been home. Mr. Parisi's tactic was simple: if Isabella didn't give up Madison, he'd take away everything else that Isabella loved. Even when she'd dreaded the very worst, Madison couldn't have predicted how brutal his reaction would be.

For selfish reasons, she was glad Isabella had stayed with her in the wake of her family crisis. She'd be happy if she stayed forever. Eventually Isabella would have to confront her father. If she didn't, he'd succeed in taking away the people and places she loved.

Isabella obviously missed her family. They were a part of who she was. Still, the thought of Isabella locking horns with her father terrified Madison. She'd only dealt with him that one time, but there was no doubt he was a man accustomed to having things his way. What if Isabella left her to be with her family? Worse yet, what if she stayed with Madison, but grew to resent her for making her lose her family?

Madison pulled another weed and told herself again to be careful not to pull too hard, or too little, on the love she shared with

Isabella. She'd put her best effort into nurturing it. If this love died, her ability to ever love again might well expire with it.

The sound of a slowing car caught her attention. A black BMW pulled to the curb in front of her house. She didn't recognize the car and couldn't imagine who would be paying her a visit at this hour on a Sunday morning.

Her blood went cold when Ben Jackson stepped from the car and made his way toward her. She reminded herself that she probably wouldn't look good in prison stripes. *Arrogant bastard.* She grabbed the pruning shears lying nearby on the ground. She rose and planted herself between him and the front door. He'd have to go through her to get to Isabella.

Isabella was still asleep inside the house. Madison kept her voice low so as not to wake her. "What do you want? Are you some kind of stalker now?" She stepped closer to him. "You've gone too far by coming here."

Ben raised his hands and backed two steps away. "Madison, please calm down. I'm not here for what you think. I'd also appreciate it if you'd put those pruning shears down. You're scaring me."

"Scaring you is going to be the least of your worries if you don't get out of here. Why shouldn't I call the police and have you arrested for trespassing? Oh wait, I forgot. Big-time fancy lawyers are above the law, right?" She stood only a few inches shorter than he did. She got up even closer to his face. "I'm not afraid of you, and I'm not going to take your bullshit this time."

He eyed the shears in her hand. "I swear I'm not here to cause trouble for you or Isabella." He moistened his lips. "I've got some bad news to deliver."

"It's not her father, is it? Is everything all right with Isabella's family?"

"If you discount having a daughter who won't speak to them, then yes, they're fine."

"It's the other way around, and you know it. They're the ones not speaking to her."

"That's where you're wrong. Her family is dying for her to come home. This whole thing is killing her mother. Isabella is holding all the cards. She's the one choosing not to come home."

"Have you forgotten the strings attached to her so-called choices?" Quarreling with Ben wasn't worth the effort. "Why don't you get to the point of why you're here? I'm in no mood to debate with you. I'd have more success arguing with the lamppost."

"It's the General. He's dead. He killed himself last night using the pain pills the doctor gave him. Someone left his suicide note on my doorstep this morning. He included instructions for what he wanted me to do. He wanted me to tell Isabella before she finds out about it from the news or at work."

"That can't be. He'd never do such a thing. He's supposed to meet his son this week. Isabella told me he's looking forward to seeing him after all these years."

Ben pulled the copy of the letter out of his pocket and handed it to Madison. "Here, read this if you don't believe me."

She scanned the letter and handed it back to him. "This better not be some cheap trick. I'll put these pruning shears to good use if I find out you're scamming me."

"Really, this is on the level. I saw his body myself. He's gone, and I need to let Isabella know what happened."

Madison set the shears aside. "I don't know how much more Isabella can take right now. This is going to devastate her. The General was like family to her. She loved him as much as a blood relative." Madison hung her head as the gravity of the situation hit her. "I don't know what to do."

Ben pocketed the letter. "Convince her to go home. She should be with her family."

"Wouldn't that be a convenient solution for you? I bet you'd be right there, waiting to pick up the pieces while her family talks her out of ever seeing me again. It's not my place to try to convince Isabella of anything. She's a grown woman who can figure out on her own what she needs. Unlike you or her family, I won't stand in her way."

"As long as you're the one she wants," Ben said in an accusing tone.

"This isn't about me, and it's not about you, either. If you cared about her as much as you say you do, you'd try seeing things from her perspective. You're nothing but a patronizing jerk. You took it upon yourself to control whether or not she even talked to me. She's not some child you can order to behave the way you want her to."

"I admit I went too far. But I could see I was losing her to you. Surely you can understand how that would feel. If the situation were reversed, I bet you'd have done the same thing."

Madison heard the front door open.

"No, she wouldn't have," Isabella said as she stepped from the doorway. "The difference between you and Madison is that she understands what it means to love someone. She'd never do the things you did." She reached her hand toward Madison, who grasped it firmly. "You can leave, Ben. I don't have anything more to say to you."

"Fair enough, but there's something I need to tell you before I go." He handed her the photograph of David and Isabella from the General's box.

"Where did you get this?" Isabella asked.

"The General left it for you. I'm sorry to have to tell you this, but he committed suicide last night. The photograph was among the things he left behind. He wanted you to have it."

"No! You're lying to me again. How could you? He wouldn't…" Tears welled in her eyes.

"I think he's telling the truth," Madison said. "I'm so sorry, Isabella."

Isabella slammed her palms into Ben's chest. "I bet you're happy he killed himself. Now you can tell me that you were right about how naïve I've been about him. Go ahead and say it, Ben. David was a broken old man who gave up on living a long time ago." Isabella buried her head in Madison's shoulder and sobbed. "He had no right to leave without saying good-bye to me or his son."

Madison pulled Isabella closer. "I don't understand why the General would do this, but he always had a good reason for everything he did. In his heart, I'm sure he thought it was the right thing to do."

Ben reached out and touched Isabella's shoulder lightly. "I didn't mean to hurt you. Please forgive me. I know you don't believe it, but I do love you. I love you as a special person and a good friend. I only want to help you get through all of this."

Madison was torn between letting Ben try to mend his friendship with Isabella and her desire to keep her from him. Madison strove for objectivity. "Sometimes, things hurt so much that you have to be willing to forgive so you can move on to a better place. The General's son and the guys at the shelter are going to need you to help them accept the General's decision to end his life on his terms." She steeled herself to her feelings and went on. "That means you're going to need your friends, including Ben, to help support you."

Madison studied Ben's face and tried to read his expression. He seemed surprised by her generosity. She hoped she wasn't mistaking it for a look of success at her being stupid for trusting him.

"If you'd like me to," Ben said, "I can help arrange a memorial at the hospital chapel tomorrow. I'm sure the guys from the shelter will want to pay their respects."

Isabella wiped her eyes. "Where is he?"

"They've taken his body to Boston Central. We'll have to move fast on this. I hate to say it, but since he was a homeless man with no family to speak of, they won't keep his body around long."

Madison winced at Ben's bluntness. "Isabella, do you want me to call Beth and ask her to try to reach the General's son?"

Isabella shook her head. "No, I want to call him myself. He'll be as disillusioned and sad as I am." She laughed mirthlessly. "He and I can commiserate over the sham of family ties."

Chapter 22

As she sat in the large conference room at Boston Central, Madison's anxiety mounted. The General's memorial service would start in an hour. She couldn't be late. Isabella was counting on her to be there. *Let's get this over with already.* The prevailing atmosphere in the conference room made it clear that not making it to the service on time was soon to be the least of her worries.

That morning, she'd gotten a call from her commanding officer's secretary telling her to report for an impromptu meeting. That she and her fellow reservists were directed to wear combat uniforms only served to solidify the ominous purpose for their gathering.

She had promised herself that she'd tell Isabella about the rumors floating around regarding the likelihood that her unit was going to be redeployed to Iraq. She'd intended to do so that Sunday in P-town, before the big blow up with Isabella's family at the dock changed her plan. Since then, Isabella had been so upset that Madison decided not saying anything was the wiser course of action. And then, with the General's suicide to deal with, she couldn't bring herself to add another potential stress point to Isabella's load.

Sgt. MacPhee entered the room. Standing straight as the proverbial ramrod, he ordered, "Attention." The soldiers in the room stood in unison.

The Commanding Officer, Colonel Jane Bancroft, strode to the podium and cleared her throat. "At ease. Please be seated."

The back of Madison's neck moistened from trepidation. As much as she didn't want to hear whatever news the colonel was about to deliver, she wanted it said and done with. She had one last year on her current commitment to the Army. If she got sent back to Iraq, how could she hope to hang on to Isabella? She'd be too far away to help her find a way to deal with her family. The General's death added another layer of difficulty. Isabella needed Madison beside her to handle all that life had thrown her way. *Please don't say we're being sent to Iraq.*

Col. Bancroft got right to the point. "Many of you probably assume that I've assembled you to inform you that our medical unit will be deployed to Iraq. This is not what I'm here to tell you."

Madison savored a sense of liberation. It was snatched away in an instant.

The colonel's face betrayed no emotion. "The President of the United States has determined that our unit is needed for a six-month deployment to Afghanistan. We are to report to Fort Bragg two weeks from today."

Everyone in the room sat in shocked silence.

"I realize," the colonel said, "how difficult it is for many of you to have to leave your families a second time to go to war, but this is what we've been trained to do. Our brothers and sisters in arms rely on us to get them home safely and to assist them when they've been injured in battle. It is our duty. We will see our mission through on behalf of this grateful nation."

Madison pinched the bridge of her nose to squeeze back a stress headache that threatened to make her day even worse. The blather about a grateful nation was hypocrisy. Okay, so "don't ask, don't tell" had been repealed, but in most states, gays and lesbians were still denied the right to marry and to live their lives without fear of retaliation if the truth about them came out. It was all noise. The Federal Government and the Army still wouldn't recognize Isabella as her legal partner and take care of her as a veteran's survivor if anything happened to Madison while she was serving her country.

Then the words "two weeks" clanged in Madison's head.

"Stop by my office to pick up your individual orders. Good day, soldiers." Col. Bancroft left the room.

Madison rose to her feet on shaky legs. With all that was swirling in Isabella's life right now, it wasn't fair to tell Isabella that she'd be leaving for Afghanistan in fourteen days. But how could she not? Two weeks might be all the time they had left.

The hallway that led to the hospital chapel where she'd find Isabella felt like a dark, endless tunnel. The sound of her footsteps reverberated off the walls, mocking her, chastising her, telling her that all she'd feared was her new reality. Walking in combat boots on a tile floor was never a quiet endeavor. Now, it was deafening.

In a moment of mad panic, she considered trying to convince Isabella to run away with her—someplace where no one would ever find them. That wouldn't work. The Army always caught up with AWOL soldiers in time of war. She would go to Afghanistan. It was her duty. The walls closed in more tightly around her, and she fought for breath as she reached the chapel doors.

The heavy chapel doors swung open. Isabella hugged each of the somber men who entered. "Hi, guys, I'm glad you could make it. Please, have a seat up front. We'll get started soon." A pang of disappointment pulled at her every time someone other than Madison came into the chapel. The phone call Madison had received that morning had turned her mood pensive. Something was up, but Madison wouldn't talk about it before they left for the hospital.

A familiar voice said her name. "Good morning, Isabella."

She found surprising comfort in the sound of Ben's voice. "Hi, Ben."

The reminder of what she'd lost over the past few weeks made her long for her family but only for a moment. Much as she missed her family, surrendering the real love she felt for Madison was out of the question.

Ben took her by the hand. "Will you sit with me for a minute? I want to talk to you before everyone else gets here."

"Do you mean before Madison arrives?"

"Truthfully, yes. I'm done lying to you. I'll never do it again." He sat down on one of the wooden pews and motioned for her to join him.

Isabella did as requested. "Don't make this anymore difficult for me than it already is."

"I'll try not to." He sat rigidly beside her. "I miss you. Your family misses you. Let me take you to your parents' house after the service. It would be good for you and for them. They'd be so happy to see us."

"Us? There is no us." Isabella stared at him. "I thought you said you were done lying."

"I am. Please believe me. Give me another chance."

"There's nothing to give you a chance for. I've told you before, but apparently I have to say it again. I don't love you."

"You need to be with your family. Let me take you there."

"Ben, you have to let the idea of us—you and me—go. It would be a lie for you and me to show up at my parents'. You and I aren't together anymore. We'll never be together. It would only confuse them and make things worse for me. The only person I'd show up with at my parents' house is Madison. If that were to happen, my father would slam the door in my face. I hardly think he misses me all that much."

"I don't understand what it is she can give you that I can't. Don't you worry that you're taking a huge risk by being with her? What if you never smooth things over with your father? Can you really live the rest of your life without your family? My God, you're a Parisi. Families don't come more tightly knit. You're supposed to be together." Ben kissed the back of her hand. "I'm the one they want you to be with."

Forever? Could her family's rejection of her be forever? Her heart still refused to entertain the notion. The doors to the chapel opened. Again, it wasn't Madison. Isabella examined her reaction to that fact. The most inconceivable prospect she could conjure was a life without Madison. "I'm not in love with you, Ben. You deserve to be with someone who is."

"You loved me before Madison came into the picture. You can love me again."

"I didn't know what it meant to be in love until I met her. I don't want to hurt you anymore than I already have. I've come to understand that I never loved you. I only loved the idea of you. You're a smart, successful, caring man who is going to be a wonderful husband and father someday. You will be because the woman you marry is going to love you as much as you love her. It's not going to be me, though. I'm in love with someone else."

Ben took the note from the General out of the breast pocket of his suit jacket and handed it to Isabella. "You should have this. It's the General's last wishes and musings. I always thought he was a peculiar fellow. He certainly saw the world from a rare perspective. In hindsight, the man was probably right about a lot of things, one of which is the unfairness of fate. You're going to have to give up an awful lot to keep Madison in your life. I hope that the 'quid pro quo,' as the General put it in his letter, is worth it." He kissed her cheek. "And I hope you'll be happy." He looked away briefly. "And I hope we can find a way to be friends again."

Isabella put the letter into her briefcase. "Thank you. I'd like to try."

The doors opened again, and Madison finally stepped into the chapel. "I've got to go," Isabella said. "I'm glad we had a chance to talk." Ben moved to a pew at the rear of the chapel as Isabella got up to greet Madison.

Something was wrong. Madison looked older, and her face was pale. Tiny worry lines spread out from the corners of her eyes. Isabella put her arms around her. With her cheek next to Madison's, she could feel that her skin was flushed. "What's the matter? You don't look so good."

Madison's eyes were moist. "I really need to tell you something. I should've talked to you about it awhile ago. We have to find a place to be alone." She tugged Isabella toward the door. "Now."

"Madison, I can see you're upset, but David's service is starting in less than two minutes. As much as I love you, I'd hate myself for the rest of my life if I missed this chance to pay my respects to him." She swept her hand toward the tattered veterans seated in the chapel. "I owe it to his men, too."

Madison looked as though she were about to insist, but she didn't. "Of course you have to be here." She looked around the chapel. "Just promise me that the minute the service is over, we'll find someplace private so we can talk."

Isabella found the General's memorial service to be very moving. Several of his men offered testimonials about how his compassion and dedication had made a difference in their lives. With Madison right beside her, she felt strong enough to cope with the knowledge that she'd never see her friend David again. In an odd way, wondering what Madison needed to talk to her about helped her keep her sorrow in check. Without that gnawing at the edges of her mind, she might not have been able to bear the poignancy of the moment. At the conclusion of the service, the men rose and saluted the casket as it was wheeled out of the chapel.

Madison took Isabella by the upper arm. "You promised we could talk as soon as this was done."

"Of course. There's a vacant office down the hall that I sometimes use when I'm working cases here. We can go there."

Isabella grabbed her briefcase. They hurried down the hall and into the office. Isabella shut the door. The look of fear in Madison's eyes caused her heart to sink. She put her arms around her. "What is it? Tell me what's wrong."

Madison opened her mouth, but all that came out was a strangled sob.

"Please, just tell me." Isabella's gut knotted.

"I have orders to go to Afghanistan."

Isabella's mouth went dry. The words hit her as if spoken in a foreign language. Slowly, their meaning sank in. "When do you have to go?" She felt herself crumbling. She collapsed on the nearest chair before her legs gave out on her.

Madison knelt in front of her. "I have to report to Fort Bragg two weeks from today."

Isabella fought the bile rising in her throat. "How long have you known about this? If you're supposed to leave in two weeks, you must've had some notice. Why didn't you tell me?"

"I'd heard rumors about a deployment for the past couple of months, but rumors are always floating around when wars are going on. I kept hoping that's all they were." Madison looked down as she continued to speak. "I wanted to tell you, but I was afraid if I did, it would change things between us. Then, when everything fell apart with your family, I didn't have the heart to add one more worry to the stack." She looked up to meet Isabella's gaze. "I know I should've told you sooner."

"You had no right to keep this from me."

"I'm sorry. I was scared. You're so precious to me. I couldn't bear the thought of driving you away. Please try to understand." She rubbed Isabella's arm. "It's only for six months. Then I'll be back, and it's for good this time. I'll resign my commission."

Six months. Madison might as well have said six hundred years. She was falling into an abyss, and there was no one left to hold onto. Her family had disowned her, the General was dead, she'd made it clear to Ben he had no permanent place in her life, and now Madison was leaving and might never come home. Isabella was the starling in the General's story to the judge. She'd dared to trust that she knew how to fly, but all she'd done was smash headfirst into the plate glass window. "No, Madison. No. Please, you can't go. I've lost everyone else. Losing you is more than I can face."

Still kneeling in front of her, Madison pulled Isabella into her arms. "I have to go. I don't have a choice. But I promise, when I get back, I'll never leave again. I want to be with you for the rest of my life. You're everything to me."

Isabella was desperate not to let her go. Too many bad things could happen to Madison. What if she didn't come back at all? What if she came back like the General had—as someone she didn't recognize anymore?

She and Madison wanted the same thing, and that was to be together. Isabella grabbed the collar of Madison's uniform with both hands. "I hate the Army. I hate this war, and I hate that you might never come home again if you go." She shook her hands, still clutching the collar of Madison's uniform, until Madison made her stop. "You know what, Madison? I wish 'don't ask, don't tell' had never been repealed."

"Why? It discriminated against me as a soldier, and it would have kept us from being together."

"Because if it was still the policy, you could tell the Army about us and they'd have to let you out. You wouldn't be sent away."

"It wouldn't have worked out, sweetheart. I'd have been given a dishonorable discharge and lost everything I've worked for." She eased Isabella's hands from the collar of her blouse. "Besides, I'm a soldier, and it's my duty to go where I'm sent."

Isabella put her head down and sobbed into Madison's neck. "I don't want to lose you now that I've found you." She cried harder. "Please, Madison, you're all I have left. Tell the Army you won't go."

Madison understood the agonizing pain of being left behind by someone she loved. She had the scars to prove it. She never could have predicted how excruciating it would be to be the one doing the leaving. The anguish of knowing she had to be away from Isabella paled in comparison to the kind of torment Isabella was inflicting on her. It threatened to break Madison's resolve. She couldn't let it happen. For a million reasons, Madison had to honor her commitment to the Army. "I can't do that, Isabella. I have to go, just like everyone else in my unit has to. They're relying on me. I can't let them down. I made a promise that I have to keep."

"What about your promise to me? Why are you so willing to break your promise to me so you can keep your promise to the Army? Remember, in all but a handful of states, you and I are considered deviants not worthy of being married. Gays and lesbians don't get anything approximating fair treatment in any way you want to name. Yet, I'm the one you're walking away from so you can defend a country that sees you as a second-class citizen, at best. I gave up my family... gave up everything... for you. You didn't even have the decency to tell me, before I gave up everything I ever held dear, that you might be sent back to the war." Isabella balled her hands into fists and pounded on Madison's shoulders.

When Madison squeezed Isabella tighter, she pulled away and out of her arms. "Isabella, I'm not breaking my promise to you. I didn't ask you to give up your family. They chose to throw you out. Please listen to me. Remember, I tried to warn you that loving me might come with a high price tag. I'd rather have been wrong, but it's not my fault that it turns out I was right."

She clenched and unclenched her jaw before saying more. "I didn't have many choices about how I might make something of myself. I had nothing, and no one gave a damn about what happened to me. The Army gave me a way out. I have to repay that debt. Once I've done that, I'm walking away so you and I can be together." She took one of Isabella's hands in her own. She was relieved that Isabella let her make the connection. "I couldn't live with myself if I didn't go. This isn't only about the Army. It's about the soldiers who are counting on me. Units like mine are sometimes all that stands between someone living or dying. I have to go."

Isabella pushed Madison back, and Madison scrambled to gain her footing. Isabella stood. "I get it now. You feel guilty because you couldn't save Scott Stevens. You're just like David. You have this warped sense of duty that you're willing to let destroy you. It destroyed him and his family and left him all alone. He killed himself over it. Iraq already took a piece of you that you'll never get back." She sniffed and swabbed the tears from her face. "Please don't do this," she begged. "Because if you go, I don't know whether I'll be here when you come back. I'm not strong enough to deal with another broken soldier."

A large hand of doom reached into Madison's chest and tried to squeeze the life out of her. No air could get in or out of her lungs. The blood that pumped to and from her heart was stopped cold by that vicious hand. She hated herself for allowing feelings for another person to rip her to shreds again. The pain of loss was too much to bear. She wrestled back her body's desire to cry a thousand tears that had been locked away for so long. This wasn't the time to fall apart. "Don't psychoanalyze me. You don't know how I feel. I thought you did, but you don't. I said I would come back. I promise I will."

Isabella yanked the day's newspaper out of her briefcase and held it in front of Madison. The headline screamed: Five US Soldiers Killed in Afghani Ambush. Through tears she said, "You can't promise me you'll come home. No one who goes there can make that promise." She choked back her tears. "I don't want to do this anymore. I want my old life back. I miss my family. Maybe it's meant to be this way. I didn't know love before you, but at least I knew where I stood in the world. Go fight your stupid war while I try to get my family back."

Madison looked at Isabella as though seeing a person she didn't recognize. "You don't mean any of that. You love me. I know you do." She put her arms around Isabella. "You do still love me, don't you?"

Tears streamed down Isabella's face. "I do love you. But I wish I didn't."

Madison whispered, "I trusted you." She turned and fled out the door. The price for letting Isabella into her heart had come due. She'd be paying the debt for the rest of her life. She resolved then and there to lock her heart so far away that she'd never have to feel anything ever again.

She staggered down the hospital corridor, slowly at first but more quickly with each successive footfall, until she was running. She had to get out of her uniform. The sensation of it touching her skin burned like acid. Being in uniform had always given her a sense of purpose and clarity about who she was. Now, it was a straightjacket, constraining her and keeping her from having all that she wanted in the world. Never losing stride, she unbuttoned her uniform blouse. The T-shirt she wore underneath was already soaked in perspiration. Just before she exited the building, she took off her blouse and threw it in a corner of the hallway.

She bumped into a man out on the sidewalk in front of the hospital. "Are you all right?" he asked.

She hated him for asking. How dare he ask her? He had no right to even speak to her under the circumstances. How could he, in his safe world, ever know the pain of a soldier going to war? He probably went to church every Sunday and prayed that the Defense of Marriage Act be treated like the eleventh commandment. Never mind that Madison loved a woman and that she risked her life time and again for the sake of him and his family. She ignored him and purposely let her shoulder slam into his, knocking him to the ground. She ran faster and faster. Where to? She didn't know for sure, nor did she care. She raced on until her legs cramped and her lungs ached. When she finally collapsed somewhere miles away, she caved onto a park bench and sobbed in anguish.

Chapter 23

Madison gazed out at the Atlantic Ocean and tried to sear the awesome sight of it into her memory. Morning had dawned to an ominous, fiery, orange-red sky over the horizon. As she walked along the beach with Bobbie, the waves that lapped at their bare feet were building. Madison put her hands into the pockets of her shorts and thought about how sailors predicted a coming storm. *Red sky at night, sailor's delight; red sky at morning, sailors take warning.* The remnants of an early hurricane were bearing down on New England. She hoped her flight would make it out of Boston before the storm got too bad for the plane to get off the ground. Never had Madison seen such a crimson sky. It seemed fitting. She couldn't shake the feeling of dread that rested on her like thick clouds.

Bobbie broke the silence. "Are you sure you really want to leave a whole week early?"

Madison looked down at the cool, wet sand and nodded. "Yes, why delay the inevitable? I want to get it over with so I can come home. Besides, now that I've volunteered to go early to help organize supplies for our deployment, I can't get out of it." She breathed the sweet scent of the ocean air deep into her lungs. "I'm going to miss this place." She struggled to speak the next words. "And you and Jerome." No point mentioning Isabella. Better to forget her, Madison reminded herself. Forgetting Isabella was like trying to roll a ten-ton boulder uphill. Still, Madison clung to her delusion of trying to pretend her heart wasn't shattered.

Bobbie put an arm around her as they walked. "I just want you to know I think you're doing the right thing. I'm proud of you for honoring your commitment." She squeezed Madison's shoulder. "I do wish you'd reconsider your decision not to say good-bye to Isabella. She still loves you, Madison."

Deep down, Madison worried that if she didn't see Isabella before she left, she might never see her again. More than anything in the world she wanted to see Isabella one last time. What Madison wanted and what she would do, however, were two entirely different things. She took her time in responding. "Isabella doesn't want to see me. I'm not going to make this any more difficult for either of us by forcing her to do what she doesn't want to do. She wants to forget about us and go back to the way her life was before she met me. Besides, if I did see her, I might change my mind about going, and you know I can't do that."

Bobbie pulled her to a stop. Madison turned to face her. "I know you and Isabella still love each other. Both of you need to get past this before you leave. Otherwise, you might end up regretting the decisions you've made."

Madison wiped away a tear. She hated crying, and she'd done more than enough of it in the past four days. The once impenetrable protective wall around her heart was being rebuilt brick by brick. She would not let it be taken down again. No more tears. "No, I'm not going to give Isabella or anyone else the chance to hurt me. I can't. I'm not going to go through this ever again. It's over between us."

A flock of cackling seagulls swooped down on the beach ahead of them. Bobbie laughed at their antics. "Most birds have already headed for some kind of shelter before the storm comes. Not the gulls. These birds are tough as nails." She kicked at a piece of driftwood. "You're a lot like them. You're stronger and more resilient than most, yet you're completely vulnerable when it comes to matters of the heart. If you have an Achilles heel, Madison, that's it."

"Which is why I intend to tuck my heart away for the rest of my life," Madison said.

Bobbie pulled Madison into a tight embrace. "Jerome and I are going to miss you so much. Please be safe. You come home to us soon." She kissed Madison's cheek. "I love you, and I promise you this, you're never alone. You've always got Jerome and me."

"Thank you, Bobbie. I love you both. You're the only family I've got." Madison wanted to promise she would come home, but an unfamiliar foreboding, deep in the pit of her stomach wouldn't let her. Regardless of her worries, the reality was that, as war jobs went, hers was comparatively safe. Still, something felt different about going this time. Probably being fool enough to fall in love, only to have it end before it really began, was what was making her upcoming deployment seem so ominous.

"You sure you won't reconsider your decision not to see Isabella before you go? You've still got time to put things back on track." Bobbie hastened a step ahead and stood directly in front of Madison. "Listen to me. You told me this was Isabella's first real love. So much happened to her so fast that she can't be thinking rationally about you or her feelings for you. She's afraid, and so are you. Don't shut Isabella out of your heart. You might regret it for the rest of your life."

Again, those damn tears that Madison hated so much threatened to break from their constraints. "As long as I don't let myself love her or anyone else, no one can hurt me. That's how I want things from now on."

"Okay, I guess you're entitled to make that choice, but you'll end up alone and never know the joys of having someone to share your life with. Everyone could see how happy Isabella made you. When you think about that, can you really say you regret loving her?"

Yes, she'd known pure happiness with Isabella, but it came with a devastating pain when she told her she wished she didn't love her anymore. "She made me happier than I'd ever been, but she broke my heart. I don't know whether or not I regret loving her. Maybe I do. I'm not sure it was worth going through what I'm feeling now." Madison cuffed Bobbie lightly. "Bobbie, I know you're trying to do what you think is best for me, but I mean it. Don't try to make me change my mind about seeing her." Madison checked her watch. "We better head back. My flight leaves in a few hours."

"Okay." They turned and walked back in the direction they'd come from. Bobbie paused. "I couldn't help but notice you're still wearing the watch she gave you. Maybe you need to think about what that means."

"It doesn't mean anything at all."

"If you really intended to let her go, you'd have put that watch in the darkest part of a drawer somewhere so you'd never see it again."

Madison put her hand on the watch. "Okay, I admit it. I do still love her. That doesn't matter, though. My only choice is to let her go. She was clear about that. I have to move on." Madison picked up the pace at which she was walking. "I'm going to start by finishing my commitment to the Army. Maybe when I get back, I'll take Jerome up on his offer to help me remodel my kitchen. I'll be ready for a new start."

"He'd be thrilled." Bobbie smiled at Madison. "You could use it to woo Isabella back by making her dinner again."

Madison laughed ruefully. "I hardly think my cooking would do the trick. You're always plotting and scheming, aren't you?"

"When it comes to love, I guess I am."

"Speaking of my house, I really appreciate you and Jerome looking after it while I'm gone."

"We're happy to do it. Don't worry about it for a minute. We'll even make sure your garden is just like you'd keep it." They walked on without speaking for a few moments. "Promise you'll call or send an e-mail as soon as you can so we know you got there okay."

"Of course I will, but it'll probably be tough for you to get hold of me if we miss each other. I've heard our unit will be on the move quite a bit, and we'll be in places where there's not much communication to the outside world. I've been assigned to a forward surgical team—that's FST in Army talk. Our FST will move directly behind the troops on the front line. We have to keep up with them, so I expect that means we'll be in some rugged places."

"That sounds different from what you told me you did in Iraq."

"It is. In Iraq, I was assigned to a semi-permanent location. For this deployment, twenty of us will have all the gear we need for a mobile hospital. We'll go wherever the troops go. Our job will be to stabilize seriously wounded soldiers so they can be evacuated to the next level of care at the combat support hospital in Bagram Air Field north of Kabul or to Germany or back to the States, depending on the nature of the injuries."

"Sounds dangerous. Please be careful, Madison."

"I will. Don't worry if you don't hear from me in a while. If the fighting is heavy, I won't have much free time for sending messages." Madison gripped Bobbie into a tight bear hug. "I love you. Thanks again for taking care of my house for me." She hugged her once more. "Thanks for everything… especially for being such a good friend."

* * *

Isabella stood with a group of David Cutter's friends on a quiet section of beach on Boston's south shore. The cherrywood box she held in her hands contained the General's ashes. She looked at the flame-red sky and thought it was a fitting setting for this final farewell. Her brother John, wearing his priest collar and tunic, gave a short eulogy based on notes Isabella had given him and then said the Lord's Prayer. When he was finished, he motioned toward

Isabella. She lifted the lid on the box. The General's friends and his son, Rich, gathered around to help scatter his ashes out to sea.

Isabella handed the box to Rich and stepped back from the group. One of the men who'd come to pay his last respects was a homeless veteran known as King William. Isabella hadn't seen him for months and feared the harsh winter might have claimed yet another nameless victim. Like so many of the veterans without family or support, King William drifted where the winds took him—wherever the hope of a better circumstance might beckon.

Seeing King William at the General's send-off brought a smile to her face. He was a handsome, burly man, and he believed he was a direct descendant of William the Fifth, France's Duke of Aquitaine. He was an affable fellow, seemingly well liked by his homeless friends and even by the Bostonians who felt obliged to fill his plastic cup with change every morning as King William serenaded them with cheerful selections.

William would claim a street corner as his stage and sing his happy songs to the city. After each song, he'd offer a hearty, genuine laugh that came from somewhere deep inside his soul. Isabella admired him for his spirit, which remained untouched by darkness despite the obvious difficulties of his life. She had once asked King William how he could remain so cheerful. He told her he walked the streets of Boston joyously oblivious to badness.

Isabella reclaimed the wooden box from David's son and tossed the final handful of ashes out to sea just as King William started to sing a melancholy version of Billie Holiday's "I'll Be Seeing You." The sound of the crashing waves juxtaposed with his melodious voice. His rich baritone reverberated low and slow, a thick cloud hovering right above the earth long enough for the General's soul to climb upon. King William's pitch rose, and the notes came higher and faster.

Isabella could almost see the General far above them, rising ever upward on that cloud until he was finally free from all his worldly woes. King William hit the final, pure note. Maybe it was only the tears in her eyes, but she'd have sworn she saw the General salute as the cloud moved out of sight. She looked around at the General's friends. Men not given easily to crying wept openly as they offered their farewells to that special man.

Many of the men ambled off in various directions. Others stood in groups of two or three, talking.

John put his arm around Isabella. "It hurts me to see you so sad. Your grief is written all over your face."

Isabella pressed her forehead into her brother's shoulder and wept. "There'll never be another person like him. I'm so sad he's gone. I loved him. I never knew losing someone would hurt this much."

"I know." He spoke in the voice Isabella had heard him use when he prayed in public. "People are brought into our lives for a reason. I think you know I'm not talking about your friend the General now." He pulled his arm from around Isabella's shoulders. "I suspect your sadness is compounded by your feelings for that woman you're not supposed to have feelings for. You did the right thing to let her go, and now your faith is being tested. You have to remain steadfast in your conviction to live as God requires. We can pray together if you'd like. We can ask God to help you expunge your inappropriate thoughts about her."

Isabella flinched when John said "her." Maria was the only one in Isabella's family who would utter Madison's name. It was their way of relegating Madison to a status of less than a real person.

"John, I thought you came here to bless the General's life. Why are we talking about that? If you really want me to let her go, please stop bringing her up, okay? And by the way, if you feel you must speak about her, she has a name. It's Madison."

"I'm sorry. You're right. I only want you to know that sometimes the right thing to do is the hardest. I'm trying to support you in this difficult time. I can see that you cared deeply about her, but what you and she were doing isn't right in God's eyes. Perhaps it would help if you came to confession this afternoon."

She has a name, damn it! And stop trying to make me feel better. What was she supposed to confess? That she loved another person to the very depths of her soul. That was her sin?

King William approached them. She gave him a hug and kissed his cheek. "Thank you for your singing. It was beautiful." She nodded toward John. "King William, this is my brother John. John, King William, the best singer on the streets of Boston."

King William looked John over from head to toe. "Your sister is an angel who walks among us. She is one of the few who truly does God's work. As smart as she is, she could have done anything, but she chooses a life of service to the poorest of the poor. Her heaven is the one I aspire to." He winked at Isabella and strolled away, whistling the Battle Hymn of the Republic.

John stared at his retreating form. "There's only one heaven and one path to it. God doesn't make exceptions, even for the most generous of heart."

Isabella emotionally recoiled from the man her brother had become. His brand of religion provided little comfort. Who was he to chastise her for loving Madison because it wasn't the right kind of love? At long last, real love had finally come into Isabella's life, but now everyone was trying to extinguish it because it didn't meet some arbitrary set of rules. Maybe Madison had the right idea— build a fortress around her heart so that no feeling could get in or out. Letting in one thought of Madison was a mistake. Hundreds of other memories threatened to overwhelm her. Before she could get lost in them, someone tapped her shoulder. She spun around.

"Excuse me, Isabella. I got here so late that we didn't have time to talk earlier."

She took Rich Cutter's outstretched hand, then threw her arms around him and hugged him tight. "I'm so glad you came. When we talked on Sunday, you told me you couldn't make the memorial service at the chapel, but I hoped you'd be here for the scattering of the ashes. I'm so sorry about your father. He really was one of my very best friends."

John cleared his throat. Isabella gestured toward him. "This is my brother, John Parisi. John, the General's son, Rich Cutter."

"It's nice to meet you, Father. I appreciate your saying the last words for my dad."

"It was my pleasure. I'm sure you and Isabella have things to talk about. If you'll excuse me, I'll speak with some of your dad's associates." He looked meaningfully at Isabella. "I'll hear you at confession this afternoon, little sister."

"Rich, give me just a moment." She took John by the arm and moved a few feet away. "I'm not coming to confession." John gave her a look that she took as a mix of anger and surprise. "I'm not comfortable sharing my deepest secrets about Madison with my brother."

"In this context, I'm not your brother."

"You'll always be my brother, in any context. Besides, you can't help me with what I'm going through."

"Why not?"

"Because your view of the world is black and white. You seem to believe I can turn off what I'm feeling with a flip of the switch. I can't. You're my brother, and even though I love you as family and respect you as a priest, I love Madison. That's too gray a reality for you to accept. Leave me to work this out on my own."

John offered a disdainful look. "Very well, then. I hope you'll remember that God is clear on the subject. You don't get a free pass from me simply because you're my sister. I took my vows, and I expect you to follow God's teaching like everyone else."

"Even if it makes me miserable?"

"Yes, when it violates God's holy law." John stomped away.

Isabella rejoined Rich. The look on his face said he'd heard at least part of her conversation with John.

"I'm sorry if I interrupted something important."

"No, you saved me from having to endure another second of my brother's misdirected concern for my soul."

"It's probably not easy having a brother who's also a priest."

"You can say that again." She looked carefully at Rich. "You resemble your father a lot."

"I always wondered if he and I looked alike. The only pictures I have of him are from when he was in Vietnam. The resolution is so grainy it's almost impossible to make out his features in them."

"He wondered the same thing about you." Isabella took the photograph that the General had left for her out of the pocket of her dress. She handed it to Rich. "I brought this along in case you came. This was taken Thanksgiving before last. The shelter puts on a huge spread for the homeless veterans every year. Your dad always said it was his favorite holiday because it wasn't about anything other than being thankful and sharing a meal with friends."

"Everyone looks so happy, including him." He looked at the photo for a long minute. "That surprises me," Rich said.

"Why?"

"I always figured his life was tragic and that he was a lonely, miserable man. I thought that was why he left my mother and me."

"In some ways, your father's life was tragic. He lost his naïveté about the world when he was very young." She smiled reassuringly. "It seemed to me he was afraid to trust people, even the people who loved him, and that kept him from living life as fully as he might have. Make no mistake, though, your father found sheer joy in the simplest things. He loved his friends—his men, as he called them—unconditionally."

"I wish he could've loved me that way," Rich said. "He didn't even give me the chance to say hello, and now here I am saying good-bye to a man I never met."

"Ever since we talked on Sunday, I've been thinking a lot about you and wondering why he took his life before you could meet him. I know he loved you with all of his heart. He told me so. I think he believed this would spare you more heartache." She pointed at the picture Rich was holding. "I spent a lot of time with your dad. He never let go of Vietnam, and in a way, that's what made him who he was. He couldn't talk about it much, but that was because he didn't want to burden those he loved with the tragedy of what he lived through."

Rich's face clouded over. "Doesn't unconditional love mean being there for someone even when they're not lovable? Otherwise, what's the point? He never gave me an opportunity to take care of him or to even try to love him. When I look back on growing up without him, I know I'd rather have had him in my life with his quirks, warts, and all than not to have had him at all."

"I know, Rich, but your dad couldn't see the world the same way you do."

"I overheard you tell your brother that his view of the world was too black and white. You're right about that. It's our messiness and imperfections that make us real and worthy of love. All the shades of who we are give us our true worth. I'd rather live a life in full color."

Isabella's eyes misted over. "You not only look like your father, but you're a sensitive and thoughtful person like he was. He would've been so proud to know you. I'm certain of that."

"He wasn't brave enough to trust me to love him. By ending his life before he and I could meet, my father snuffed out the spark of hope I'd always carried that he and I could be friends someday. He cheated us both."

"Try not to be too hard on him. Like the rest of us, he sincerely tried to be the best he could." Isabella caught a tear as it tracked down her cheek. "We can't make our lives be something they aren't, Rich. We just have to make the most of whatever circumstance we're in. That's what your dad did. I'm truly sorry you didn't get to know him. I wish this could have ended differently."

"Me, too." Rich hugged her. "Thank you for taking care of my father and for being a friend to him. I'm glad he had you to count on." He studied the picture still in his hand then offered it to Isabella. "Thanks for bringing this."

"You keep it, Rich. I want you to have it."

He tucked the picture into the pocket of his shirt. "Maybe I'm out of line saying this because I don't know what you're going through that makes your brother think you need to go to confession. Whatever it is, don't let fear dictate the path your heart chooses. My father may have been brave in a lot of ways, but he was afraid to let me love him. He and I both lost out." He gave Isabella a quick kiss on the cheek and walked away to join a group of men sharing reminiscences about the General.

Isabella reflected on what Rich had said about living life in full color. *Can I live without the color Madison brought to my life? Who am I really cheating?* She knew the answers to both questions.

Chapter 23

Isabella watched her brother Michael and his new bride dance the first dance of the evening. The wedding had been superb, despite the heavy rain from the dying hurricane. The storms passed quickly with little damage to New England. And even if the weather hadn't fully cooperated, it would take a whole lot more than the remnants of a hurricane to put a damper on a Parisi celebration and party.

Michael and Sarah looked lovely together out on the dance floor. With his dark hair, broad shoulders, and tailored Armani suit, he looked like a modern-day Prince Charming. Sarah was breathtaking in a classic white satin wedding gown. As they moved around the dance floor, Isabella saw her put her mouth next to Michael's ear. She must have whispered something funny because he threw his head back and laughed out loud. He looked into the eyes of the woman he called his soul mate and smiled tenderly. Sarah kissed him on the lips, which prompted him to pull her closer.

Like everything else since their awful fight, it made Isabella think of Madison. She squeezed her eyes shut and willed her mind to change course. Why did every action, every touch, every glance by other couples have to remind her of Madison?

She tried to focus on the fact that she was surrounded by her family again. Wasn't that what she'd told Madison she wanted? The reception hall was filled with Parisi family members—cheerful, boisterous, a hearty living, breathing entity unto itself. Her family was the same as it had always been. But Isabella had changed. Being surrounded by them wasn't like it used to be. The feeling of contentment and belonging that used to exist was gone. Yes, this was what she'd said she wanted. It destroyed her to realize it wasn't where she belonged anymore.

Isabella's mother sat down beside her. "Are you all right, my darling? You look preoccupied by something. Is it Ben? I haven't seen you two together much this evening."

Isabella couldn't tell her mother about her feelings. Anything she said would get right back to her father. Her father was the family's leader, and everyone, especially Isabella's mother, knew when to step in line behind him. No one ever broke the unspoken rule that his was the last word.

No good could come from Isabella confiding her undeniable feelings for Madison to her mother. She did need to set things straight about Ben, though. He was trying to be a friend, but he wore his ulterior motives on his sleeve. Isabella didn't want her family or Ben to hang onto the false hope that they'd be a couple again. Her relationship with him was over, period. "I'm fine, a little tired I guess."

Isabella's mother caressed her shoulder. "Your father and I want you to be happy. What you're going through will pass. It would help if you tried to work things out with Ben."

Do they really care about my happiness? No one minced words when it came to telling her they thought she'd done the right thing by saying good-bye to Madison. Isabella felt like a stranger in an alien country. Her family didn't even seem to notice. They didn't want to know who she really was inside. In fact, as best she could tell from everything they said, she wasn't supposed to have an inside. The void left when Madison walked out of her life was immense and grew bigger with each new day.

Isabella measured the idea of being honest with her mother. Maybe it would be enough to get her to look deeper at who she was. She couldn't continue to hide her grief. The emotion was too powerful. She gazed out at her happy family—the family that couldn't grasp the happiness they'd insisted she needed to give up—and jumped in with both feet. "There isn't anything for Ben and me to work out. This isn't going to pass anytime soon, and if you really want to know how I feel, I'll tell you. I'm destroyed, and I'm pretty sure I'll never be happy like I was, ever again. I loved Madison... I still do and I always will." She exhaled. For the first time in weeks her heart beat a little more freely.

Isabella's mother looked away from her daughter, as if she was somehow a disgusting sight to see. She made eye contact with Isabella's father. It was probably the signal that it was his turn to try to talk some sense into their recalcitrant daughter. Isabella had an idea what her parents were up to. One way or the other, they were going to break whatever this was that was taking her from them.

Robert Parisi walked with purpose up to his daughter and extended a hand to her. "May I have this dance?"

Having the courage to be honest with her father wouldn't be as easy as it had been with her mother. As a youngster, she idolized him and tried to think of ways to make him proud. She had a hard time imagining a life without his approval.

She looked up at him. He smiled sweetly and took her hand. When she was a little girl, she'd always believed he'd keep her safe, that her father was the smartest and strongest among all fathers. She so wanted that feeling about him and her family to return.

She walked with him to the dance floor. The beautiful singing of Rossini's "Bel Canto" by Maria Callas played in the background as Isabella danced with her father. He used to play it for her when she was little to help her fall asleep.

He said to her, "Isabella, I love you with all of my heart. Because of that, I only want what is best for you."

How could he possibly know what was best for her now that she was a grown woman? She wasn't even sure what was best for herself. How could he know? Maybe it wasn't about her after all, but about what was best for him. If that were true, then he didn't really love her with all of his heart. He loved the idea of who he thought she should be. The realization made her feel completely alone, even in a room filled with the entire Parisi family and their friends.

He had told her she would be "dead" to him if she stayed with Madison. When he first said it, she told herself it was only his anger talking. Isabella still wanted to believe in him like she had as a little girl. She rested her head on her father's chest and closed her eyes. If he noticed that she was crying, he didn't acknowledge it.

Regardless of how much she loved her family, her heart didn't belong to them anymore. It belonged to the one person in her life who had truly loved her unconditionally. Guilt rose in her throat like bitter bile. Madison had risked her heart to let Isabella in even though it terrified her to do so. In the end, she loved her enough to step aside so Isabella could have her family, if that's what she wanted.

Madison was right. She hadn't been the one who placed the requirement to choose on her. It was her father. Such a thing didn't come from a place of love.

The horror of a new realization hit her. Isabella had done the same thing to Madison. Now she would have to live with her regret for having done such an awful thing to her. The difference between Isabella and her father was that she regretted what she'd done to

Madison. He didn't regret what he'd done to Isabella. The look in his eyes made that crystal clear.

Isabella raised her head to get her father's attention. "What if the thing that's best for me is to be with Madison?" She readied herself for his terrible response.

"You aren't thinking clearly because of what she's done to you. She is an awful woman who is leading you into a life of hell. It's wrong, Isabella. I won't allow it."

She pulled away from him. "Daddy, I love you. But I'm not a child anymore, and you don't get to decide what's best for me. Madison is a kind, generous person who is willing to put her life on the line to save injured soldiers. How can you say she's an awful woman? She's willing to go to horrific places like Iraq and Afghanistan to fight for people like you who hate her—hate her without even knowing her and for no good reason." Isabella shook her head. "You should be ashamed. You aren't who I always believed you to be. I made a mistake in giving Madison the same ultimatum you gave me. Love should make a person expand the circle of caring people around them, not make it smaller. I'm proud of who she is and that she loves me. I only hope she can forgive me for what I've done to her."

Isabella waited for her father's anger to boil over.

He spoke in a stage whisper. "You will not cause a scene at Michael's wedding. Watch your tone with me. I saw what you two were doing. Not only was it revolting, she broke the rules of military conduct. She doesn't deserve to wear this country's uniform. You will get this nonsense out of your head immediately. Do you understand me?"

"You're wrong about that, Daddy. 'Don't ask, don't tell' isn't in effect anymore. Even if it were, why should the government and people like you think you have the right to decide who someone loves? Love comes of its own free will, and I'm not going to walk away from it to satisfy you." There was so much more she wanted to say, but words were no longer worth the effort. She said enough. She left her father standing on the dance floor.

He yelled after her. "Where do you think you're going? We haven't finished this conversation."

She turned back to face him. "I'm done with this conversation, and I'm going to find Madison to apologize. She's the only person I ever want to be with. I love her. Her service to our country inspires me. You used to be my hero before I knew what that word really meant. Now that I do, I understand just how much of a hero

Madison truly is. Just like David Cutter and all the rest of those veterans at the shelter." She hurried out of the reception hall without looking back. The Parisi family would have to make do without her.

The cool night air was a welcome contrast to the stuffiness of the reception hall. The freshness filled her with a sense of limitless possibility. Light drizzle fell from the sky. The overhang of the building provided enough cover to keep her dry. She felt like a falsely accused prisoner finally released from incarceration. She wasn't afraid of losing her father's love and acceptance anymore. From now on, he would have to work to gain hers.

The doors to the reception hall swung open behind her. Maria grabbed her by the elbow. "What's going on? Daddy is fuming."

"I told him I love Madison and I only want to be with her. I'm going to her. Don't try to stop me. You can't."

"I don't intend to," Maria said.

"You mean they didn't send you out here to try and talk some sense into me?"

"Actually, they did."

Isabella pulled her arm free from Maria. "You can save your breath."

"If you'd quit being so bullheaded and let me say something, you might be surprised by it." Maria raised an eyebrow in her bossy sister kind of way.

"Fine, say what you've got to say. I can't promise I'll listen. I'm done with people trying to change my heart."

Maria smiled, "No one can change someone else's heart." Maria touched Isabella's face with her fingertips. "Here's the thing. It's pretty simple. You were happier than I've ever seen you, when you were with Madison. Now, without her, you're completely depressed. We only get to travel our road once in this life. We ought to be happy while we're at it. I want to see you laugh again. If Madison's the person who makes that happen, you should always keep her. I couldn't imagine life without my Anthony. I don't want you to have to imagine it without Madison if she's the one you're meant to be with. Besides, I've seen how you two look at each other. I know that look. I call it the unmistakable look of love. You go find her, and I'll deal with Mom and Dad."

"Thank you, Maria. That means a lot. I need your support now more than ever." She kissed both of Maria's cheeks. "You came through for me when I needed you most."

"What are sisters for? You know, most people aren't cut out to live outside the box. I'm proud of you for doing it. You always have." She paused. "I'll tell you a secret. Even though I'm the big sister, I've always looked up to you."

"That's so sweet, but why?"

"Because of the person you are."

Isabella hugged Maria with all her might. "I love you."

"I love you, too. Now, go find Madison. And don't forget to call me to let me know you're all right."

* * *

Isabella pulled into Madison's driveway. She was surprised to see all of the lights out. It was late, but not that late. She considered coming back in the morning in case Madison was asleep, but she had to see her now, had to apologize to her and beg her to take her back, to make love to her, to hold her while they slept. Madison had to leave in just a few days, and they'd already wasted too much precious time.

Isabella intended not to waste a single second more. She was going to spend every last moment before Madison left for Fort Bragg convincing her that she loved her more than life itself, and more important, she would be right here waiting for her when she came home.

She grabbed her raincoat out of the backseat of her car and threw it on over her dress. The rain had picked up again, and it soaked her through and through by the time she got to the front doorstep. She pounded on the door. Madison still hadn't answered the door on the fourth series of determined knocks. She was a light sleeper. She had to have heard her.

Isabella went to the garage and peeked in the window. Madison's car was there. What if Madison didn't want to answer the door? She had every right to be angry. Isabella would have to try something else. She dialed Madison's phone number, but it only rang until the answering machine picked up. Isabella left a message.

She went around to the back deck and banged on the sliding glass door near Madison's bedroom. "Madison, it's me, Isabella. Please let me talk to you." She shivered, both from the cold and from panic.

The neighbor's porch light came on. Isabella had met many of Madison's neighbors when she stayed there after the fracas with her family over the P-Town incident. Isabella recognized Mrs. Spooner, the widow from next door, as she stepped out onto her deck and yelled loudly, "Isabella, honey, is that you making the racket?"

Isabella moved into the light so Mrs. Spooner could see her. "Yes, it's me. I'm so sorry I disturbed you. I'm looking for Madison."

Mrs. Spooner pulled her robe tightly around her body and raised her voice above the sound of the increasing rain. "Well, that's not possible. As close as you two are, I'm surprised you didn't already know. She left yesterday afternoon for her deployment. She said something about going early to help get supplies ready."

"Oh my God, I missed her."

"You're drenched to the bone, Isabella. Maybe you should go inside and put some dry clothes on. I have a key if you need one. I'm sure Madison wouldn't mind. It's awfully late for you to be driving back to Boston, especially in those sopping wet clothes."

Isabella couldn't bring herself to invade Madison's space. "No, thank you anyway. I'll be on my way now. Sorry again to bother you." She moved back out of the light and sat down on the porch steps where Mrs. Spooner couldn't see her. She whispered to the night, "Oh, Madison, please come home to me." Isabella would never forgive herself if she didn't get the chance to tell Madison she'd finally come to her senses. *I love you.*

But the night made no reply. All she could do was wait.

Chapter 24

The days turned into weeks and the weeks into months. Isabella dialed Bobbie's number. She picked up on the second ring. "Hi, it's me again. I just called to see if you've heard from Madison."

"Yes, we got another e-mail from her yesterday telling us that her unit was going to be out of contact for a while again. They're deep inside the country somewhere. She said she's fine and that she'd call or e-mail as soon as she could."

"Did she mention me at all?" Isabella asked.

"No, honey. You know her as well as I do. She's keeping herself busy so she doesn't have to think about you. It's the way she is. It doesn't mean she's forgotten you. If she calls, should I tell her you want to talk to her?"

"No. I'm still worried that it might upset her. I'm not convinced she'll trust me enough to let me back into her life. I don't want her stressing over this while she's over there. If avoiding thinking about me helps her get home safely, I'd rather not."

"Why don't you write her a letter or send her an e-mail?" Bobbie asked.

"I could never put what I feel for her into words on paper or a computer. And I'd hate for anything I wrote to be intercepted by someone who might take it the wrong way. I know she can't be thrown out of the Army for being gay, but the last thing she needs is someone giving her a hard time if they find out she is and they're not okay with it. When she comes home, I'll tell her I love her. A face-to-face may be the only chance that I have anyway. I broke her trust, and I want to earn it back the right way. Could you judge from her e-mail if she's telling the truth about being okay?"

"All she really said was that she misses home. How about if I mention to her the next time she calls that you've been asking about her?"

"Bobbie, no. I want to wait."

"You and Madison are two peas in a pod with your stubbornness, but okay. Take care of yourself and try not to worry. I'll call as soon as I hear from her again."

Isabella hung up the phone and crawled into bed. All she could think about was Madison. At least now, after all the time that had passed, she was able to think about her without crying. She drifted off and was startled awake by a dream she couldn't quite remember. Something bad had happened. The weight of it sat on her chest and made it difficult to breathe. Madison wasn't okay. Isabella got out of bed and went to the dresser drawer. She took out Madison's uniform blouse. She'd found it in the hallway of the hospital the day Madison walked out of her life. She breathed in Madison's scent and clutched the blouse as she cried tears of regret. "Where are you, my darling?"

* * *

Madison listened to the wounded soldier as she tended his injuries. "Death in war is indiscriminate," he said. "Make the mistake of being in the wrong place at the wrong time, and your number could be up. Just like that. The problem with this war is that the enemy hides among the innocent. This makes being in the wrong place at the wrong time a pretty easy thing to do."

Madison muttered something noncommittal that she hoped would make the soldier stop talking about death. She wanted nothing more than to be home. Focus on the task at hand, she admonished herself. "Is there anything else I can get for you?" she asked.

"No, ma'am, I think I'll rest for now," he said. "Thank you."

"Sure," she said. "Pleasant dreams." She continued on her rounds to check on patients at the camp in a mountainous region of southern Afghanistan.

The radio that hung on her belt squawked to life. A voice all but drowned out with the noise from background gunfire screamed its message. "We're coming on the Apache. We've got three casualties. The truck they were riding in was blown in half by a roadside bomb. One soldier is dead, another critical, and the third has minor injuries. We're ten minutes out. Over."

Madison raced into the surgical tent. She depressed the radio button and said, "We'll be ready."

"What've we got?" Dr. Jim Barns asked.

"Three incoming. One dead, one critical, one minor." Madison set the radio back on her belt and scrubbed her hands.

When the chopper landed, the medics rushed the litters carrying the dead and injured soldiers into the mobile hospital facility. The experienced members of the team, including Madison, were on autopilot. She had been through this gruesome task before. The first rule for keeping her head under the circumstance was to shut off the parts of her mind and heart vulnerable to the horrors of it.

"Get scrubbed up, now," Madison said. The rookie, Private First Class Eric Anderson, had only been with the unit for two days. She felt bad for the new medic because he was about to learn the hard way how awful the effects of war could be on the human body. She hoped he could handle it. Then again, he didn't really have an option.

The dead soldier was brought in first. His eyes were still open. Their vacant stare was unnerving, even though Madison had seen it more times than she could count.

Jim pointed at PFC Anderson. "Show some respect and cover him with a blanket."

PFC Anderson grabbed a blanket to put over the dead soldier's body. Madison saw the look of revulsion on the medic's face. Brain matter oozed out of the dead soldier's skull. Anderson turned pale, and Madison barked an order at him. "Cover the body immediately and get over here to help cut the uniform off of this soldier we might be able to save."

In different circumstances, she might have helped Anderson learn how to numb his feelings, but there wasn't time. He needed to do his job, or lives could be lost due to his wavering.

Dr. Barns called for two units of blood for the critically injured soldier. He was bleeding out, and fast. Blood was everywhere. His left leg was completely gone below the knee. The fractured bones and vessels hung in a tangle of red and white flesh.

When the team cut away his Kevlar vest, Madison saw the source of most of the blood that saturated his uniform and the floor beneath the table where he lay. These were injuries he wouldn't recover from. He was going to die. A large piece of shrapnel had made its way underneath the vest, ripping his abdomen with wild abandon as it went. Madison didn't falter at the horrible sight of the soldier's insides laid open and exposed. She continued to apply regular chest compressions in a futile effort to keep the young man's heart beating. Dr. Barns ordered that the soldier's wounds be packed and that he be readied for surgery.

Madison glanced up at PFC Anderson. Every bit of color had drained from his face. His lips were indistinguishable from the rest of his skin. He appeared to be disoriented by the mess in front of him. No one in this situation was allowed to fall apart. Too much was at stake. Falling apart was allowed only after the crisis was over. And then, only briefly, until the next one began. Soldier's lives were depending on them to hold themselves together. Anderson needed to find his military bearing, and quick. Madison shouted at him, "PFC Anderson, what the hell is the matter with you? God damn it, get a hold of yourself."

In that instant, the soldier died. The unmistakable feeling of loss sucked the air out of the room. The departure of his soul left a palpable emptiness around them. He was gone, and there was nothing they could do to bring him back.

PFC Anderson's eyes rolled back as his legs telescoped beneath him. His body hit the ground hard. Madison felt no pity, only anger. Her anger wasn't for Anderson. It raged because another young man was dead, and for what? She really couldn't understand why.

What was really being gained by all of this death and destruction? She rarely let herself think about the politics of the war. She never considered it her place as a soldier to do so. But another young man would never again see the places and people he loved.

Ever since she'd lost Isabella, nothing made sense anymore, especially this vicious war. She pulled the latex gloves off her hands. She nudged the medic standing next to her. "Get Anderson the fuck out of here. I need to get some air."

Madison stepped out of the tent and gazed out at the mountains in the distance that formed the border with Pakistan. But for the barren, rubble-covered landscape that clearly showed the effects of years of poverty and war, the sight might have been beautiful. The snow-covered mountains stood silent and majestic under an emerald blue sky. She sat down on one of the metal chairs outside the tent and took the watch from Isabella out of her pocket. She never wore it for fear that it might get damaged, but she always carried it with her. She tried to relax—tried to forget the unspeakable carnage she'd just witnessed.

She ran her thumb over the face of the watch and thought about the time. Somewhere, Isabella was asleep. It was two in the morning at home. The autumn nights were probably getting chilly. She imagined Isabella under a pile of warm blankets in her cozy North End condo. What she wouldn't give to be there with her under those blankets. Breathing in the sweet smell of Isabella's skin, her silky hair loose against the pillows, and their naked bodies entangled without a care in the world as they slept peacefully in each other's arms. Everything Madison would ever need would be right there in that moment.

Her daydream was short-lived. The sound of the helicopter's rotors told of more wounded and dead to contend with. What was the point of indulging herself with thoughts of Isabella anyway? Madison was never going to lie next to her again. To dwell on it was nothing short of torture.

Jim came out of the tent and sat in the chair beside her.

"How's the last soldier?" Madison asked.

"He only has minor injuries. I'm sending him to the hospital in Bagram for an overnight stay just the same. The damage to his psyche could be a problem. The guy witnessed two of his friends die brutal deaths. His uniform's covered in their blood. That alone is a trauma that may take a lifetime to heal." He scuffed at the dirt with the toe of his boot. "I'm not sure it's possible for anyone to heal after seeing something like that."

"We're all going to go home with emotional injuries that we have to live with forever, aren't we?"

"I suppose so." He rubbed the palms of his hands together as though washing away dirt that refused to be removed. "Speaking of which, I'm worried about you. In all the years we've served together, I've never heard you talk to a soldier like you did to PFC Anderson. You were pretty rough on him. If being in the combat zone is getting to you, you need to let me know."

"I'm all right, Jim. Just tired—tired to the bottom of my soul."

"I know what you mean. I need you. You're a vital part of this unit. Plus, you're my friend. I want you to be all right."

Madison slipped the watch back into her pocket. "I'm sorry for blowing up at Anderson. I'll talk to him. It's just that no one should ever have to die that way. I'll never get used to seeing it. Sometimes, I'm not sure whether the sacrifice is worth whatever it is we're gaining by being here."

Jim laced his fingers behind his head and looked up at the sky. "I often wonder the same thing. That's a dangerous place to let one's mind explore for too long, though. It isn't something we should speculate about. Our job is to put these soldiers back together again so they can go home alive to their families. Whether we agree or not, we have to have confidence in the wisdom of our leaders. Otherwise, it'll drive us crazy."

Madison kicked at the dusty ground like Jim had done a moment earlier. "You're right. I know. I'm proud to be here to make sure that if there's a chance for a wounded soldier to go home alive, he gets it. That said, there's such a huge price to pay for the privilege of it." She paused. She seized the moment to ask Jim about something she'd been contemplating. A stint on one of the Army's Medical Civic Action Programs might help her get through the rest of her tour. "I've been thinking. Maybe I need a change of scenery—a chance to see some of the good we're doing here."

"Such as?"

"I'd like to volunteer for the next MEDCAP in Zangabar Village."

"I'm not sure I like the idea of my best trauma nurse going on a MEDCAP." He ran his hand over his face. "Then again, it certainly would be an opportunity for you to see something positive."

"That's my point, Jim. The MEDCAPs provide medical care to the local civilians. Most of them have never seen a doctor in their lives."

"What if the FST gets caught dealing with a lot of casualties all at once and you're not here to help me? I never have to tell you what to do. You always instinctively know. Besides, MEDCAP missions can be dangerous."

"I really think it would help, Jim. I'm only asking for one."

He weighed his answer carefully. "I'll agree to one mission only. But you've got to promise me you'll keep your head in the game. You have to agree to be the first to speak up if you can't handle what's going on there."

She nodded. "Of course, I will. Thanks, Jim." She stood to leave.

He pointed to her empty chair. "Sit back down, Captain. We aren't finished talking. You've got something more than a MEDCAP mission on your mind. When I came out here, you looked like someone who was missing someone else." He patted the seat of the chair. "You want to talk about that, too?"

Getting what she was feeling about Isabella off of her chest could be a good thing. She was no different from any other soldier going through the agonizing emotions of missing someone back home. "If you'd asked me that when we were in Iraq, I'd have told you no, you're not supposed to ask, and I'm not supposed to tell."

He offered a half-laugh. "I understand. We've worked side by side for years under horrible circumstances, but you've never talked about your personal life." She felt him studying her, as if deciding what to say next. "You must be relieved that DADT was repealed."

"Not really."

"You can't mean that, Madison."

"Yeah, I do. When the policy was in place, there was no question about where I stood with the military. It was simple. I kept my mouth shut and toed the line. If they found out who I really was, I'd be thrown out without a second thought. Now, even though I'm supposedly not at risk for that happening, any number of homophobic jackasses could make my life a living hell if they wanted to." She used the sleeve of her shirt to wipe the sweat from her forehead. "Things haven't changed all that much. The people who hated me before still hate me. Unfortunately, a lot of them are in charge, and I'm still hiding both here and at home."

"I hadn't thought about it from that angle."

"What's worse is that the repeal could have a very short shelf life, depending on the outcome of the next election. There are plenty of politicians clamoring to undo it while I sit here in this godforsaken place in the name of freedom, having lost the woman I love because she couldn't bear the thought of my being here."

Jim waited a moment before replying. "If you ever need to talk about absolutely anything, you have my word you can talk to me in the strictest of confidence. I hope you know that." He adjusted the cap on his head. "You want to talk about her? Maybe it would help."

"You've always been a good friend to me. I'd trust you with my very life." She shook her head sadly. "I'm sorry to say there's nothing to talk about. It's over between us." Madison gestured toward the mountains in front of them. "Isabella was the brightest star that ever shone in my sky."

"What happened?"

"Like I said, she couldn't handle the fact that I needed to honor my commitment to the Army. On top of that, her family pretty much told her they'd never speak to her again if she and I stayed together. There's nothing more to it than that. I really don't want to talk about it, but thanks for asking."

"It might help to get some of it off your chest."

"I don't think so." Madison made a move to rise from her chair. "Am I dismissed, now? I think I'll check to see if I'm needed with any of the cleanup."

"You're dismissed. Let me know if you change your mind about talking."

"I will. And thanks for agreeing to let me go on a MEDCAP."

"You're welcome. I hope it helps you find something good in all this garbage."

Madison stood and briefly rested her hand on Jim's shoulder. "You're a good friend and a great doctor. Thanks for the conversation."

"Try to get some sleep tonight. I want you back at the top of your game tomorrow. By the way, did you mean Isabella from the veterans' shelter? I met her, remember?"

"Yes."

"She's beautiful, and everyone at the shelter spoke so highly of her. You should try to win her back. I would, if I were you."

"Much as I might want to steer clear of her, I may not be able to keep myself from trying."

Chapter 25

Two armored Humvees idled outside Madison's tent. "Capt. Brown, we're ready to head out, ma'am."

"I'm on my way." She secured her Kevlar vest and other body armor. The 9-millimeter pistol in the holster felt heavy. She prayed she wouldn't have to use it. She grabbed several wrapped candies and crammed them in her pockets to use as bribes and rewards for good behavior for the children she anticipated treating that day.

The officer leading the MEDCAP had conducted a briefing for the team members the evening before. He stressed repeatedly that, although the mission was to provide medical care to villagers, they needed to remember that this was still a war. "The enemy could be anywhere and in any form. Don't take anything for granted."

Madison exited her tent and hopped into a seat in the second Humvee. A security vehicle equipped with a .50-caliber automatic machine gun escorted them.

The three-hour drive on the desolate dirt road to the village of Zangabar was mercifully uneventful, except for being jostled around to the point of nausea on the barely passable rock-strewn road. Everyone in the vehicle was on full alert for the entire trip, carefully scanning the road for any sign of bombs, snipers, ambushes, or other deadly obstacles.

When they arrived at the village, the inhabitants swarmed out of their mud and stone huts toward the MEDCAP team. The security patrol tried to institute order as an interpreter relayed their commands to the villagers. "Please, everyone, stop and line up in a single line. You must be searched before you can receive treatment."

Madison had underestimated the extreme poverty of the Afghani natives. She suspected that simply getting through each day with enough food to eat was a major accomplishment for them. Basic medical care was obviously a luxury none of them could afford. She was grateful for an opportunity to do good for some of the people caught in the middle of a war they very likely knew next to nothing about.

She made her way toward the line of eager villagers. Madison noticed a small dark-haired girl with piercing green eyes. She was wearing a frayed, dirty-white, cotton dress. Her eyes reminded her of Isabella's. The little girl was standing in front of a woman covered head to toe in long flowing garments and a burka. It made Madison sad to think that the girl's beautiful eyes would someday be the only part of her that the world would see because she would be hidden under the same kind of coverings once she was a woman.

The little girl made eye contact with Madison. When she did, Madison felt as though the girl had reached out and physically touched her with her earnest curiosity. Unlike many of the other villagers, her eyes held no fear. To Madison, it looked as though hers were filled with wonder and desire to know a different world and life. Madison imagined that these strange soldiers represented something exciting and exotic to her. Madison smiled at her. She took some of the candy out of the pocket of her vest and approached the child.

As Madison moved toward her, she noticed an angry looking boy out of the corner of her eye. He took something out of the pocket of his clothing. He looked to be about twelve years old. The soldiers conducting the searches of the villagers noticed him, too— too late to do anything about it.

The boy dropped the object, and it rolled in Madison's direction. Instinctively, she grabbed the girl. Madison twisted her body around so she was the only thing between the hand grenade and the child she held in her arms.

A flash of light pierced Madison's eyes. A deafening blast knocked her flat. Everything went quiet and black.

She struggled to open her eyes. She couldn't remember where she was. Her ears ached. The anguished wails of women and children brought her back. People bellowed in a language she didn't understand. Soldiers shouting in English added to the cacophony. A hot, sulfuric smell lingered in the air.

Madison's face pressed down into warm, wet dirt. She smelled blood. Its metallic taste was in her mouth. She rolled over and screamed out in excruciating pain. She blacked out. When she came to, she struggled to lift her head. The blood on the ground was hers. It was everywhere and quickly pooling at her waist and legs. Her face burned. She reached up to touch it. Blood covered her hand.

Her fingers slipped into a large gash in the right side of her jaw. Tears mixed with dirt and blood. *Oh God, help me.*

Her right pant leg was shredded and completely soaked through. It was a hideous dark red. Panic threatened to overtake her when she saw the grisly tangle of her leg. *No.* If someone didn't get to her quickly, she'd bleed to death. She tried to sit up without moving her leg, so she could administer self care. When she moved, a piercing pain cut through her lower back. Another bloodcurdling scream boiled out of her. Her body went limp. This time, she lay still and tried to stay calm. She was already thoroughly spent from the pain. Her fellow soldiers would come to her aid soon. She reached down to feel for the watch in her pocket. It was still there. *Isabella.* She blacked out again.

Madison woke to the feel of a tiny hand on her forehead. The little girl wiped blood off her brow. They stared at each other for a moment. Madison had saved the child's life. At least that was something. She drew some measure of contentment knowing that her death wouldn't be in vain.

Abruptly, someone pulled the little girl out of the way. A soldier with a familiar face knelt over her. It was Sgt. Phillip Keyser, one of the medics in the Humvee she'd ridden in to the village. "Stay with us, Captain. We're going to get you out of here. The chopper's on its way." He jabbed her uninjured thigh with a dose of morphine, and with the assistance of one of the MEDCAP doctors, he applied a tourniquet to Madison's right leg, which still gushed blood. Sgt. Keyser packed an open wound to her lower back below where her Kevlar vest reached.

Madison thought she heard the distant sounds of an approaching helicopter, but she couldn't concentrate through states of intermittent consciousness. A force tugged at her like she was being pulled away. She struggled to keep hold. *There isn't enough time. I'm going to die.* She fought to stay focused. The light around her narrowed like someone was turning down a dimmer switch until there was no more light. The last thing she heard before she blacked out for the third time was Sgt. Keyser yell, "Her pulse is tacking. Where the fuck is that chopper?"

The helicopter touched down, and Capt. Madison Brown was loaded on board. Dr. Barns saw how much blood she'd lost from the stain on the ground where she'd lain. The crew on the helicopter started an infusion of plasma, but they weren't able to slow the blood loss.

The chopper arrived back at camp. Madison's breathing was shallow and her pulse was barely detectable. The medics rushed her limp body into the examination tent and cut away the lower portion of her uniform. The upper part of her right leg was grotesquely discolored and swollen from the pooling of blood caused by the tourniquet. The bottom half was nothing but splintered bone and mangled tissue. The rest of her body was white and cold. "She's going into shock," Dr. Barns yelled. "We're losing her."

The medics, including a stoic Eric Anderson, finished cutting the uniform away from her body so the doctor could assess the extent of her injuries before getting her into surgery. Repairing the femoral artery was the first priority. If they didn't get the bleeding stopped, she'd certainly die. The medics gently rolled her on her side to let Dr. Barns assess the wound to her lower back. A piece of shrapnel was wedged into the upper part of her hip bone. They'd have to do surgery to get it out and to stabilize any injuries to internal organs. The deep cut in the side of her face would require several stitches to close.

Medics attached heart-monitoring equipment to her chest, and they infused her with two more units of blood plasma. She was barely clinging to life when they rushed her into the surgical tent.

Dr. Barns examined the shattered bone in her damaged leg. The blast had ripped into it with devastating consequence. "This is bad," he said.

Col. Tom Jenkins, a fellow surgeon, agreed. "We don't have a choice. We've got to take her leg. Otherwise, she's not going home alive."

"We've got to try to send her home in one piece if we can." One of the monitors attached to Madison's chest blared the warning that her blood pressure had dropped precipitously. Dr. Barns was desperate not to lose Capt. Brown—and Jim was equally as desperate not to lose his friend, Madison. "Come on guys, get moving. We've got to get her stabilized, now!"

Madison was aware of her heart faltering. She couldn't hang on much longer.

Jim yelled at her. "Capt. Brown... Madison... don't you dare let go. Hang in there. You don't get to check out on us today, God damn it. Not on my watch."

Madison tried to reach out to him... to anyone... in the room. Maybe making contact with a human being would be enough to keep her from being pulled away from the living. But she couldn't move. Her limbs refused to respond to demands that they do something, anything to show she was still alive. She felt her grip on the world give way. In her mind, she scrambled to hang on, desperately trying to cling to life. She strained to hear the voices around her, but they receded into barely audible murmurs.

The old saying was true.

One's life really does pass before her eyes the moment she's perilously close to the end. Memories flashed in sequence through Madison's mind. She saw herself as a little girl, watching her father boxing in the gym. She laughed as he carried her on his back. Then she relived the grief and shock at his death. Next came anger because her mother couldn't love her for who she was. She felt the sorrow of Jennifer's leaving without saying good-bye. Her Army days replayed, highlight by highlight. There were the good days with Bobbie and Jerome. All the memories came one after another until she got to the sweetest ones of all. *Isabella.*

Her mind slowed down to take them all in. As she watched them unfold again, she finally knew the answer to Bobbie's question. "Do you regret letting yourself love Isabella?" *No, never. I'd die a thousand more deaths like this one for the chance to love her.* Finally, Madison's mind quieted. There were no more thoughts or lights or voices in the background, only a hushed, dark, silence. *I don't want to go, especially not like this, but thank you for letting me know love in this life.* In that moment, Madison's heart stopped beating. She gasped for one more breath that didn't come. *I'm going to walk with the angels now. I love you, Isabella. Please remember me always.*

Chapter 26

Isabella forced down another spoonful of broth filled with miniature meatballs, chicken, and greens. Maria had brought over a pot of their Nana's Italian wedding soup earlier in the day in an effort to get her to eat. Not enough sleep and too much worry had worn down Isabella's immune system. The cold she'd caught weeks ago continued to linger. At least that's what her sister thought. When Isabella told herself the truth, she knew she was buried in deep clinical depression and that the virus was far more a symptom of her true illness rather than its cause.

Every day, Isabella checked with Bobbie, but she hadn't heard from Madison in weeks. Isabella frequently had foggy nightmares about Madison calling out for her, and that only made both her physical and emotional states even worse.

The doorbell rang. Isabella hoped it wasn't Maria coming to coax her out of the doldrums with more of their grandmother's cooking. She pressed her fingers to her thinning waist. Then again, more food was probably in her best interest. From the way her clothes hung off her body, she guessed she'd lost about ten pounds. Without looking through the door's peephole, she swung it open. Only Maria would knock at this hour. But it wasn't Maria.

"Bobbie?"

"Can I come in?"

Nerves soured the soup in Isabella's stomach. The look on Bobbie's face screamed volumes. "Noooo!" Isabella wailed the word as she began to swoon.

Bobbie caught her before she tumbled to the floor. She helped her to the sofa. "It's bad, Isabella, but Madison's still alive."

Isabella clutched Bobbie to her and sobbed. "What happened?"

"She was on a special mission to provide medical care to villagers. A boy threw a grenade at her and the soldiers she was with. Madison was a hero. She put herself in front of it to save a child."

177

"How badly is she hurt?"

"They had to… she lost half her leg."

Isabella closed her eyes, but the image of a disfigured Madison still taunted her. She felt her emotions shutting down, blunting her despair. "Where is she? I have to see her."

"They flew her home this morning. She's at Walter Reed. Jerome booked all three of us on a late flight to DC tonight. The officer who called me said we should get there as soon as we can."

"Is she going to be all right?"

"I don't know."

* * *

Isabella tried for what felt like the hundredth time to doze off. She'd feel so much better if her mind would quiet down long enough to let her rest, even for a few minutes. The strange lighting of the hospital and the uncomfortable waiting room chair made sleep impossible. Who was she kidding? If the circumstances were ideal, worry for Madison would still keep sleep only a distant dream. She, Bobbie, and Jerome had arrived at the hospital around two in the morning. All they'd been told so far was that Madison was still in surgery.

Jerome stood and stretched his arms. "The sun's coming up. I'll get us some coffee."

"Thanks, honey. I think we're going to need it. See if you can find a sandwich or something, too." Bobbie patted Isabella's knee as Jerome left in search of breakfast. "You okay?"

"No, I'm not. I'm tired of waiting. If someone doesn't come soon to tell us how Madison is doing, I'm going to start ripping down walls to get to her." Isabella tried to rub the fatigue from her eyes. "I'm sick from worry."

"I know, sweetie. Me, too, but all we can do is wait."

A soldier in scrubs, carrying a clipboard, came into the room. Isabella and Bobbie stood in anticipation.

"Mrs. Bixby?" he asked.

"That's me," Bobbie answered.

"I'm Sgt. Mayfield. Dr. Gant wanted me to let you know that Capt. Brown is in recovery and doing well. After the doctor checks on another patient, she'll be out to speak to you."

"When can we see Madison?" Bobbie asked.

"It shouldn't be much longer. As soon as she's taken to her room, you'll be able to pay her a brief visit." Sgt. Mayfield lifted the top page on the clipboard. "I have you and your husband listed as Capt. Brown's health care proxies. Since she'll be in intensive care, only you and her next of kin will be allowed in to see her." He said to Isabella, "Are you an immediate family member?"

"I…" Telling him that Madison was the person with whom she intended to spend the rest of her life didn't seem a good idea at the moment. "No. I'm a friend."

"I'm sorry. You'll have to wait until Capt. Brown is out of intensive care before you can see her."

Bobbie rushed to Isabella's defense. "Isabella and Madison aren't just casual friends. They're best friends. You have to make an exception."

He shook his head. "If I made an exception for you, I'd have to make it for everyone. Then, what would be the point of the policy? We do this to protect our patients." Sgt. Mayfield tucked the clipboard under his arm.

Bobbie put her hands on her hips. "You can't tell me you've never broken the rules in a critical situation. I'll bet plenty of boyfriends, girlfriends, fiancés, and fiancées who weren't technically listed as next of kin were given a pass."

Sgt. Mayfield stood his ground. "That's not what we're talking about here."

How would you know? "You have to let me see her. Please!" Isabella said.

"It's beyond my pay-grade to break the rules for you. I'm sorry, but you'll have to wait."

"Hasn't the Army done enough to her already?" Isabella asked. *"Vaffanculo burocrate."* The look on his face told Isabella that, even if he didn't speak Italian, he got the message.

Sgt. Mayfield assumed an authoritative stance. "I understand that you're upset, but if you insist on making trouble, I can have you escorted from the building."

"I doubt that will be necessary," an unfamiliar voice said. Isabella and Bobbie turned to see a woman wearing a surgical hat and scrubs approaching them. "What's going on, Sergeant?"

"Dr. Gant, I'm trying to explain that hospital policy only allows next of kin in the intensive care wing." He gestured to Bobbie. "Capt. Brown only listed Mrs. Bixby and her husband on her official paperwork."

"You wouldn't happen to be Isabella, would you?" Dr. Gant asked.

"Yes, I am. How could you possibly know that?"

Dr. Gant addressed the sergeant. "I'll take things from here. Go take care of your rounds."

"Yes, ma'am." Sgt. Mayfield saluted the doctor and left the room.

Dr. Gant eyed Isabella's still clenched fists. "Don't be angry with him. He's doing his job. This is a military installation, and you know we think very highly of our rules." Before Isabella could offer a retort, Dr. Gant continued. "Assuming your presence doesn't cause Capt. Brown any distress, I'll sign an order that permits you to visit her in intensive care."

"You still haven't told me how you knew my name," Isabella said.

"She's been calling that name anytime she's near consciousness. That you're here in this waiting room tells me you and she are close to one another." She smiled warmly at Isabella. "Patients often reveal what's really important to them when their uncensored subconscious is doing the talking." Dr. Gant removed her surgical hat. "As you know, we had to make a difficult decision in hopes of saving her life. Capt. Brown hasn't been told yet that we had to amputate her right leg just below the knee. She'll need the people she loves to help her recover from that, and not just physically. From the way she called your name, I suspect she loves you very much."

Tears formed in the corners of Isabella's eyes. "I hope she does, because I love her." She choked back a sob. "Thank you so much for understanding. It would have killed me if I couldn't see her."

"Capt. Brown has a steep climb ahead of her. My goal is to get her well enough to go home as soon as possible." Dr. Gant's pager beeped. She checked it. "Capt. Brown is in her room now and coming to. Wait for me here. I'll let you visit briefly after I've spoken with her."

Chapter 27

Madison tried to claw her way back into the light of reality. Every time she got close, pain enveloped her body and dragged her back to a dark, unfathomable hole. The pain made her want to cry out and run away from the brightness of the light, but she could neither cry out nor run. The pain told her she was still alive. How that could be and where she was were mysteries to her, but she was still among the living.

She sensed someone nearby. Her fingers moved a fraction of an inch. She thought she heard Isabella's voice. Was she dreaming? She willed herself to wake up. If Isabella was there, she had to know. Being conscious meant feeling agonizing pain, but she forced her eyes open.

She attempted to focus; her vision was hopelessly blurred. "Where am I?"

A shadowy figure stood over her. "Capt. Brown? Can you hear me? I'm Dr. Gant."

Disappointment. Devastation. The voice didn't belong to Isabella. Madison ignored the woman and gazed up at the ceiling without moving her head. Any movement was piercing, unbearable. Dr. Gant? She must be in a hospital.

Snippets from the events of her life over the past several days crept into her brain. She had grabbed a little girl, and she recalled an explosion. Blood had poured from the bottom half of her body. Then came the memory of the awful sight of her battered leg and the look of concern on Jim's face. She'd never forget that look. She closed her eyes and concentrated on the primary source of pain— her leg.

The incessant throbbing from her right leg threatened to drive her insane. She lifted her head and gasped at the exponential uptick in utter agony the movement brought. She blinked her eyes in an effort to clear her clouded vision. She couldn't see her leg. She could feel her toes, even wiggle them, but her leg ended at her knee. She looked again. And again. "My leg is gone!" She tried to sit up.

Strong arms pinned her down. "Capt. Brown, you have to stay calm."

Madison lay still as a corpse. "You should've let me die."

Dr. Gant released her arms. "We had to take your leg to save your life. I'm sorry for the shock of what you just saw, but you're too young to die, my friend." Dr. Gant adjusted one of the lines on Madison's IV stand. "You still have a whole world of living to do. You might not believe it right this minute, but you're one of the lucky ones. You got to come home."

"Lucky? That's a load of shit. You don't know me." Madison turned her gaze away. She was a mutilated has-been like her father and the General, destined for a life of lonely misery. "I want to die."

"You're not going to."

Madison made eye contact with the doctor. "You can't make me live if I don't want to."

"Maybe I can't, but the people waiting to see you might want a chance to show you how much you're loved and needed."

"Bobbie and Jerome are here?"

"They are. So is Isabella. They're all anxious to see you."

"I don't want anybody to see me like this."

"Trust me, Capt. Brown, they'll think you're the most welcome sight they've had in a long time."

"I'm ugly. I'm disgusting."

"You're a soldier in the United States Army who was wounded in service to her country. That makes you the best of the best."

A nurse came into the room. "Here's the sedative you ordered for Capt. Brown, Doctor."

Dr. Gant took the needle from the nurse and administered the injection. "I'm giving you something to help you sleep and to give you a break from the pain. You need your rest. Your friends will be allowed in briefly as soon as I've gone. I'll be back to see you this afternoon."

Madison wanted to tell the doctor to take her drugs and go directly to hell. Isabella couldn't see her like this. They'd agreed to move on with their lives. Worse yet, Isabella's prediction had come true. Madison had come home damaged beyond repair. She wasn't the same person she used to be, and she'd never be able to reclaim her old life. The drugs swimming in her system blotted out any further thought, and she faded into sleep.

Isabella waited outside of Madison's room for Bobbie and Jerome. It was only a few moments since they'd gone in, but it felt like an eternity. The door opened, and Bobbie came out. She hugged Isabella. "She's not awake yet."

"I don't care. I need to see her." Isabella moved toward the door.

Bobbie stepped in front of her. "I know you're eager, but I need to warn you, she's in rough shape."

"Okay, you've warned me. Now let me go."

Jerome exited Madison's room. "I'm going outside for a while." He gave Bobbie a pat on the arm as he hurried past them.

Isabella leaned her head against the door. Her soldier was on the other side. Somehow, they'd find their way through this, together.

She turned the handle and went inside. Except for the hum of the machines that monitored Madison's heart and supplied nutrients to her body, the room was silent. The lights were dimmed, and Madison lay sleeping. Isabella had dreamed for months of the day when she would see Madison again. The sight of Madison's shattered body reminded her how close she'd come to never getting that opportunity. She took a couple of steps forward but stopped halfway.

She swallowed hard and tried not to cry. What if part of Madison's soul had been lost with the bottom half of her leg? No matter. She vowed not to let Madison shut her out like the General did to his family.

Isabella schooled herself to look objectively at Madison. What remained of her leg was grotesquely swollen. Bandages covered much of her jaw. Where her face wasn't bruised black and blue, it was pale. Her once strong body now seemed fragile as she labored to breathe. Even in Madison's slumber, Isabella saw pain etched on every part of her face. Tears splashed from Isabella's eyes.

She restrained herself from running to the bed and covering Madison's body with her own. Madison had been through so much, but an arduous recovery still awaited her.

Isabella took the final steps forward. She reached out to gently touch Madison's face but pulled her hand back. What if it hurt to be touched? What if Madison never wanted to feel Isabella's touch again? She wrapped her arms around herself and tried to stifle her tears. Her resolve faltered. She had to have physical contact with her Madison, her soldier. Isabella leaned down and kissed Madison's forehead. "I love you so much."

She pulled the only chair in the room close to Madison's bed. She and Bobbie had been told they'd only be permitted brief visits. Fine. Let someone come and tell her she had to leave. She wasn't moving until forced to. Isabella wrapped her fingers around Madison's and squeezed gently. *You'll never be alone again, Madison.*

Madison battled to open her eyes. She thought she heard Isabella's voice again. "Isabella?"

"Yes, it's me—Isabella." She held tightly to Madison's hand. "I'm here."

Madison turned her head slowly in the direction of the voice and opened her eyes. The blurred vision had disappeared.

Isabella took her breath away, just like she had the first day she laid eyes on her and every time since. Madison saw the tearstains on Isabella's face. All the anger and hurt Isabella had caused evaporated in that instant. Madison didn't have the strength—or the need—to hang onto it anymore. "You came," she whispered.

Isabella clutched her hand. "Yes, and I'm not leaving. I'm so sorry for everything. Please forgive me."

Madison's joy at having Isabella here vanished in a heartbeat. Her missing leg, and all it symbolized, said they could never regain what they'd had. "I forgive you, but you can't stay."

"Don't shut me out. Not again. You're entitled to be angry with me. I made a terrible mistake. I want to spend the rest of my life making up for it. I'll never be happy again if you don't let me."

Madison moved slightly to point to her mutilated body. "Look at me. I don't have anything left to give you."

Isabella touched Madison's cheek. "Yes, you do. You can give me the only thing I'll ever want again. You can give me you, my darling."

Madison brought Isabella's hand to her parched, bruised lips. Despite the pain in her jaw, she kissed Isabella's fingers.

Isabella caressed Madison's cheek again. "Let it be my name you call in the night when you're frightened or in pain or need to feel the warmth of a body next to yours. Let me love you."

Madison had two choices: continue to die inside or let go of everything she feared. Emotions she'd buried deep inside flowed out of her on a wave of tears. "Don't ever leave me, Isabella."

"I won't let you give up on us," Isabella said. "I'll stay by your side, forever." She pressed her head next to Madison's. "I love you with all I have in me. We'll get through this. I'm not leaving here without you."

Madison clung to Isabella as best her IV-encumbered arms would allow. "I love you."

Isabella whispered softly into Madison's ear, "You're my world. I'll never let anything or anyone come between us again." Someday, Isabella hoped, her family and the rest of the world would eventually catch up to the simple notion that love is a gift to be treasured no matter its source. "Your love came to me on a whisper of fate when I least expected it. From now on, I'm holding it close and I'll never let it go. Sleep, my darling. I'll be here when you wake up."

Chapter 28

Dr. Gant knelt in front of the wheelchair and secured the prosthesis to Madison's knee. "The adjustment the lab made to the suction valve should help. Would you like to try to stand?"

The graphite and plastic substitute for a leg served as a stark reminder of Madison's loss; not that she was likely to forget. She couldn't stomach the outlandish spectacle, so she looked to Isabella for comfort. Isabella caressed the back of Madison's head. Her constant support for ten long months had helped Madison cope with the damage done to her body.

"I guess I've got to stand before I can walk," Madison said in an attempt at humor.

Dr. Gant came around to one side and slipped an arm underneath Madison's. "Let's get you up out of that chair, then. Isabella, you get on the other side of her. Hold her under the arm the way I showed you. On the count of three, we'll help her stand."

Madison prepared herself for the inevitable jolt of searing pain that would come as soon as she put the slightest weight on her limb. She bit her bottom lip. "I'm ready."

"One, two, three, lift." Dr. Gant and Isabella helped her to her feet.

The pain wasn't nearly as bad as Madison had anticipated. "That is better. It hurts, but it's manageable." The freedom of standing buoyed her spirits. "I want to try a couple of steps."

"Okay, but go slowly," Dr. Gant warned. "We don't want you having any setbacks now that you've come this far."

Isabella tightened her grip on Madison's waist. It gave Madison the reassurance she needed. Tentatively, she took a first step with her prosthetic leg. When she lifted the other, the entire weight of her body was transferred onto the prosthesis. The nauseating explosion of pain where it connected to what was left of her knee caused her to crumble in agony.

Dr. Gant helped catch her before she hit the floor.

"Fuck, that hurt." Exhausted, Madison let Isabella and Dr. Gant guide her back into her wheelchair. Tears of frustration and pain spilled over. "I fucking hate this."

Isabella leaned down and put her arm around her. "I know, but don't give up. It's going to take time. You can do it."

"It's not just for me that I hate this, Isabella. You've put your life on hold for me. I know you miss home. I want to go back to Massachusetts so we can put our lives back together again." Madison clenched her fists. "I want to box and run, not sit here in this goddamn chair."

Isabella kissed her cheek. "For me, home is wherever you are. I promised I'd stay here for as long as it takes. We'll get there when we get there."

Dr. Gant gave Madison's shoulder a reassuring pat. "I'm not going to lie to you. Things are likely to get tougher before they get easier. Each soldier has his or her own timeline for recovery. I know you're sick of all this, but you've quite literally got to do it one step at a time."

"I'm never going to walk again, am I, Doctor?"

"My answer is the same as it's always been, Madison. As shitty a deal as you got when you lost part of your leg, you're one of the fortunate ones. It could've been a lot worse. You've still got your knee. Amputees fitted with a transtibial prosthesis like we're working on for you are very likely to regain normal movement and do all of the things they used to. Not only are you going to box and run again, you'll be dancing with Isabella before you know it."

Madison smiled in spite of the ache in her leg. "Dancing with Isabella again is worth all the effort. Thank you for understanding why I needed her to be here with me every day. I don't think I'd have survived all of this without her."

"Just like any other soldier, you deserve to have your family with you while you recover. I'm happy to have been able to help." Dr. Gant squeezed Madison's shoulder. "That reminds me of something I want to alert you to."

"Have you found something else wrong with my leg?"

"No, nothing like that. You've probably heard of Col. Yarr…"

"Sure, he's one of the bigoted jerks who makes no secret of the fact that he thinks it was a mistake to repeal DADT. What about him?"

"He's going to be in the hospital today with Senator McCaffee. You know McCaffee is considering running for president."

"Yeah, I saw that on the news. The hypocrite—after being injured in service to this country, he more than anyone shouldn't be waving the flag in the name of reinstituting DADT to discriminate against me."

"Let's hope it doesn't come to that, Madison," Dr. Gant said. "But I've been told part of why they're coming here today is to ask wounded soldiers if they'd like to see DADT put back as the official policy."

"Why in heaven's name would they do that?" Isabella asked.

"Right or wrong, politicians have a history of using the sympathy elicited by injured veterans to advance their own agendas."

"I'm so sick and tired of this bullshit." The words fairly exploded from Madison's lips. "I get my leg blown off for my country, and I still have to worry that some emotionally backward stuffed shirt is going to make an issue out of the fact that Isabella and I love each other." A string of swear words fell from her lips. "I suppose I should be glad I got an automatic extension of my commission while I'm recovering, but I have to say, being an officer in the Army isn't all that appealing right now."

The door to the therapy room opened, and a throng of people crowded in.

"Hello, Dr. Gant," Col. Yarr said. He checked Madison's name tag. "Capt. Brown, thank you for your service. I'd like you to meet Senator James McCaffee."

The senator held out his hand to shake Madison's. "Capt. Brown, on behalf of a grateful nation, it's my pleasure to inform you that you've been awarded the Silver Star for putting your life in harm's way to save an innocent child. You are an American hero, and it's my pleasure to meet you."

Although taken aback by the news from the senator, Madison reached for his outstretched hand. Her grip was still weak. She despised having a flimsy handshake. "Thank you. It was my duty."

"We've planned a medal ceremony here in DC for you and other outstanding soldiers, sailors, marines, and airmen," Yarr said. "Several dignitaries, including Senator McCaffee, will be there. I plan to be there myself." Yarr's jaw jutted out proudly. "We want to make sure you'll be able to attend. The major news networks will be covering the ceremony, and we've already given them the list of recipients. America deserves to see heroic soldiers like you. With all the cockamamie talk of getting out of Afghanistan, your story will show them the important work we're doing over there, like saving that innocent Afghani girl." Col. Yarr eyed Isabella before returning his gaze to Madison. "We'll have special seating for your parents and husband, Capt. Brown."

Madison took Isabella's hand. "My father is dead. I don't have a husband. And I can't stand being in the same room with my mother for more than two seconds. So, unless you're willing to let my partner be there, you can count me out."

The colonel's upper lip twitched. "I'm choosing to ignore that comment, Captain, but let me remind you about conduct unbecoming an officer." He took a quick glance at McCaffee. "The ceremony is in three weeks. You're expected to be there. I hope you will not bring dishonor on yourself and on the Army by having this woman sitting where your family should be."

"You're entitled to your opinions, Colonel, but with all due respect, if you think I'm going to that ceremony to listen to a bunch of hollow accolades while Isabella's locked away in a closet, you're out of your mind. As for conduct unbecoming an officer, I might suggest you take a good look in the mirror. Your opinions notwithstanding, the old way of dealing with gays in the military doesn't exist anymore. You need to keep up with the times."

Yarr's face was beet red. "Capt. Brown, you're still a member of the Armed Forces. Your language borders on insubordination. I think you owe Senator McCaffee and me an apology."

Dr. Gant stepped in between the colonel and Madison. "Sir, this is my patient. She's been under incredible emotional and physical strain, and your presence is upsetting her. In the interest of her health, I think it would be best if you left now."

Flustered, Yarr escorted McCaffee from the room.

"Thanks, Dr. Gant. I was just about to lose control," Madison said. "Nothing good could have come from that."

"I know, which is why I asked them to leave. Congratulations on your Silver Star, Captain." Dr. Gant offered a snappy salute.

"Thanks, but I think the Army will have to mail it to me. I'm not going to their stupid ceremony."

"But you've earned the recognition, Madison," Isabella said. "You should go."

"Given the way those two double-dealing bastards feel about us?" Madison looked into Isabella's eyes. "Never."

"Isabella might be right," Dr. Gant said.

"You've been sniffing nitrous oxide, Doctor," Madison said with a chuckle.

"No, hear me out. What better way to beat them at their own game?" Dr. Gant gestured back and forth between Madison and Isabella. "The two of you on stage at that ceremony—living proof that love comes in lots of flavors and that heroes do, too. The media already know who the honorees are supposed to be. Yarr and McCaffee can't un-invite you."

"She's right, Madison," Isabella said earnestly. "It's your chance to have all that you've been through make a difference for gays and lesbians all over the country."

"I'll think about it," Madison said in a reluctant tone. "For now, though, you two need to help me get out of this chair again."

Chapter 29

Isabella helped Madison don her dress uniform. "Are you nervous?" Isabella asked. "I caught some early coverage on TV. There are already a lot of people in the audience, and television cameras are everywhere."

"A little," Madison admitted. "I still think the whole thing is hypocrisy. I can't believe I let you and Dr. Gant talk me into this."

"Yarr and McCaffee were right about one thing. You're a hero, and America hasn't had enough of those lately." She kissed Madison's earlobe. "Besides, the more people who hear your story and see that the love between you and me is as real as any other love, the quicker we can hope this country stops discriminating against us." Isabella used a soft cloth to polish the buttons on the epaulets of Madison's jacket. "You're so beautiful. I never could resist you in this uniform."

Madison stared at herself in the mirror. It felt good to wear the uniform one last time. Except for the bagginess of her right pant leg, her prosthesis was barely noticeable. The thin scar on her jaw was nearly invisible under the makeup Isabella had applied. The last thing Madison wanted at the ceremony was to have people pity her. She summoned her military bearing. "You ready to go, my love?"

"Not just yet," Isabella said. "I want to have you to myself for another minute or two before everyone in America falls in love with Capt. Madison Brown." She put her arms around Madison's waist.

Madison pulled her close. "Thank you for helping me through all of this. It's meant the world to me. Come to think of it, I do have one last thing to ask you before we go."

"What's that?"

"Will you marry me?"

Isabella took her arms from around Madison's waist and placed one hand on either side of Madison's face. She smiled her biggest smile. "Yes. There's nothing in this world I'd rather do. What took you so long to ask me?"

Madison smiled back. "I wanted to know that we'd be okay—well, that I'd be okay. I'm not there yet. But I will be, and I can't imagine spending the rest of my life without you. I love you with all my heart."

Isabella kissed Madison deeply. When the kiss ended, she said, "I fell in love with you the day we met. When you go out there today in front of all those people, they'll feel like you belong to them—that you're their soldier. What they need to know is that you're my soldier, too, and I'll love you always." She took Madison's arm. "Let's go show them that."

Author Bev Prescott   Photo Credit: Joel S. Jaffe

About the Author

Bev Prescott grew up in the Midwest. Shortly after high school, she enlisted in the U.S. Air Force. She considers it one of the best decisions she ever made because it exposed her to a world of possibilities and experiences that, otherwise, a blue-collar kid from Indiana could only dream of. The only decision she considers even wiser was marrying her partner of 20 years.

Bev is an environmental attorney. She and K.C. and their clever calico cat, Lilliput, share a home in New England. Bev writes stories about everyday lesbian heroines who make a difference.

Coming soon from Blue Feather Books:

On the Altar of Justice, by Lauren Darling

Tessa Nolan is a cocktail waitress working towards a degree in Art History. By pure chance, she is the only witness to a brutal double homicide. FBI Agent Aidan Vance is assigned to interview Tessa and protect her until more permanent arrangements for her safety can be made. Tessa possesses special abilities that make her an ideal witness, but the bad guys have a private army and inside information. Even the best laid plans may not be enough to prevent them from getting to her.

The situation is further complicated by Tessa and Aidan's growing attraction to one another, blurring the boundaries between them. Aidan's biggest fear is that her ability to protect Tessa will be compromised if she lets her heart have its way.

Tessa exemplifies what comes to pass when bad things happen to good people. Put yourself in her shoes. If you knew that doing the right thing would rob you of everything you hold dear, would you still do it? Would you sacrifice your own hopes and dreams on the altar of someone else's justice? How much can you lose and still be yourself? Is it foolish to hope when everything has been taken from you?

Life isn't always fair and sometimes, it is the human heart that must be sacrificed *On the Altar of Justice*.

Cresswell Falls, by Kerry Belchambers

Alicia Sanders has been the victim of malicious gossip in the small town of Cresswell Falls and has suffered constant humiliation at the hands of her unfaithful husband.

Christina Brewster, believing she's incapable of falling in love after a painful upbringing, retires from her high-fashion runway modeling and returns home to Cresswell Falls.

These two different women meet and are instantly drawn to each other. Alicia is confused by the strange attraction she feels towards Christina because she's never been with anyone else except her-ex husband. Christina believes that the only thing she'll do is hurt Alicia and her beautiful little boy, so she pushes Alicia into the arms of Tony Simmons.

When professional circumstances force them to tread along the same path, their mutual attraction grows wildly out of control. A deeply-rooted history ties them closer, making it impossible for them to stay apart, while at the same time awakening buried secrets from the past, leading to a shocking suicide that tears both their worlds apart.

Cresswell Falls is a small town that helps these women find forgiveness, redemption, and in the face of tumultuous endurance, love and happiness

Coming soon, only from

Make sure to check out these other exciting
Blue Feather Books titles:

In the Works	Val Brown	978-0-9822858-4-8
Playing for First	Chris Paynter	978-0-9822858-3-1
Two for the Show	Chris Paynter	978-1-9356278-0-7
30 Days Hath September	Jamie Scarratt	978-1-935627-94-4
Detours	Jane Vollbrecht	978-0-9822858-1-7
Possessing Morgan	Erica Lawson	978-0-9822858-2-4
Lesser Prophets	Kelly Sinclair	978-0-9822858-8-6
Come Back to Me	Chris Paynter	978-0-9822858-5-5
If the Wind Were a Woman	Kelly Sinclair	978-1-9356279-7-5
Confined Spaces	Renee MacKenzie	978-1-9356279-7-5
Staying in the Game	Nann Dunne	978-1-9356279-0-6
Unfinished Business	I. Christie	978-1-935627-91-3
The Chronicles of Ratha	Erica Lawson	978-1-935627-93-7

www.bluefeatherbooks.com

CPSIA information can be obtained at www.ICGtesting.com
Printed in the USA
269214BV00001B/88/P